D0292107

LIARS AND LOSERS LIKE US

LIARS AND LOSERS LIKE US

Ami Allen-Vath

Sky Pony Press

NEW YORK

Sky Pony Press books may be purchased in bulk at special discounts for sales promotion, corporate gifts, fund-raising, or educational purposes. Special editions can also be created to specifications. For details, contact the Special Sales Department, Sky Pony Press, 307 West 36th Street, 11th Floor, New York, NY 10018 or info@skyhorsepublishing.com.

Sky Pony® is a registered trademark of Skyhorse Publishing, Inc.®, a Delaware corporation.

Visit our website at www.skyponypress.com.

10 9 8 7 6 5 4 3 2 1

Library of Congress Cataloging-in-Publication Data is available on file.

Cover design by Sarah Brody
Cover photo credit Thinkstock

Print ISBN: 978-1-63450-184-2
Ebook ISBN: 978-1-5107-0027-7

Printed in the United States of America

To the BFFs of my YA years. You got me through the worst of times by showing me the best of times. Anne, Laura, Steph, Heidi, Tera, Beth, Donna, and Holly, for literally saving my life.

ONE

If I wasn't dreading the lame-ass Prom nomination drama about to go down, I'd be staring at the back of Sean Mills's short, sexy, brown hair in peace. To be fair to Mr. Norderick's Language Arts class, the hair's not really the main distraction, it's everything about Sean. He's tall, plays football *and* the guitar, which pretty much makes him a triple threat in my book. He's got these swimming pool blue eyes—the kind you shouldn't look at for more than a few milliseconds because, if he looks back and there's eye contact, you'll drown. Which is obviously the reason I'm sitting in the desk right behind him.

Unfortunately, across the aisle, my best friend Kallie's eyes are practically waving a neon "get ready get set" flag in my peripheral. A tiny piece of folded paper flies from her hand and lands on my notebook. The note practically unfolds itself:

You're gonna do it—right?

Instead of stressing my role in Kallie's Prom Queen scheme, I give her a two-second "chill the hell out" look and go back to not taking notes and Sean. There's even something about his ears that get me. They stick out a little—not too much—just enough to give him character. They make him more accessible, not so perfect. I shove the note into my pocket because I'd rather daydream about hanging out with Sean. Not as a girl sitting behind him getting high off his pheromones either. But on a date, somewhere like the movies as opposed to last period Language Arts.

Tap tap tap. Mr. Norderick's highlighter jolts me to reality.

"All right ladies and fellas. I suppose it's time to deal with these Prom Court nominations. You'll need to nominate five queens and five kings. All senior class votes will be tallied up and your court will be announced on Friday."

Here we go. My armpits sear and my knee bounces like a bobblehead.

The class roars and debates the must-haves and the maybes. As if we all really need another way and day for all the jerks of Belmont Senior High to get off on themselves.

Kallie taps her midnight blue fingernails together in front of her lips, and in spite of her hard-ass exterior, she's dying to get on that court.

"All right, all right guys, calm down," says Mr. N. "Let's get on with it. We need five of each."

Shandy "Kissass" Silvers raises her hand and asks if she can nominate two.

"Brian Wang and Molly Chapman." Shandy, head of the Prom Committee, Yearbook Committee, and everything else boring committee, nods as Mr. Norderick copies the names on the board.

Brian and Molly. Our Senior Class's Homecoming King and Queen and Class President and VP. *Yes, let's honor them with this incredibly humbling surprise, shall we?*

Kallie gives me a sharp head nod. I'm pretty sure her thought is something like *Please nominate me please please please prettyfreakingplease?*

We had a whole conversation about this on the phone last night. My nose crinkles as I think right back at her, *Dignity is not overrated. Don't make me do it.* I told her Prom Court was bullshit and did she really want to be forced into meetings and stage time with Belmont's biggest jerks? Did she really want to be lumped into a category with those guys? Yep.

I get myself ready with a "you can do it" pep talk.

C'mon Bree, it's not that serious. Or maybe it is. Referring to oneself in first person is never a good sign. But I'm just not the best candidate for public speaking or raising my hand to nominate my best friend as a Prom Queen when I think it's an obnoxious idea. My face is getting warm already.

Kallie's hand shoots up right before I'm almost about to raise mine. I'm totally embarrassed for her. *She's seriously going to vote for herself.*

I try to send a telepathic text message: *"OMG, Kallie DON'T DO IT!"*

She blurts out, "Bree Hughes."

Oh. Shit. My face goes from ninety-eight degrees to super freaking hot as my heartbeat picks up. That's me. That's my name. We did not discuss this last night.

My hand shoots up. Without breathing I say, "Kallie Vate" before Mr. N. can call anyone else.

"Well, okay, now we're getting somewhere." He writes our names across the board.

I stare straight ahead, slowing down my breath and wishing I could settle back into my movie daydream.

Shandy turns around sucking her teeth. She looks down her nose as if an unspoken Prom nomination sin has just been committed. Some girls on the other side of the room giggle. My heart's ticking so hard and I want to dissolve into my desk. Pretty sure this is what it feels like for a loser. I shake my head and sigh as Kallie beams at me.

Justin, the guy who never has a problem laughing at his own jokes if someone else won't, says, "Wow, what a crazy coincidence. The two best friends that anyone could have, voted for each other."

I sink farther down into my seat, wondering what it'd be like to actually disappear into the hard brown plastic.

While Justin laughs and breaks into a song about two best friends, the girls name another girl, three more popular guys, and then Sean. Oh wow. His name is practically across from mine. A notion creeps into my head like a tiny spider. Maybe being on Prom Court wouldn't be *that* bad. Seeing Sean in a tux and being on stage with him could be—

A snort erupts from the girl behind Justin. Mr. N. has written "Maisey Morgan" right under my name on the board. Sean laughs under his breath as I look over to check out Maisey's reaction. She's pulling and

3

twisting her hair into her fist and I can only see the side of her face but it's probably the same shade as mine. Like me, no way was she expecting someone to shout out her name.

Maisey Morgan is the biggest nerd in our class. She's pretty much owned that title since elementary school. Maisey's the homely doll at the bottom of your old toy box. Stringy red hair, gangly arms, wobbly legs; eyes beady and vacant. Our class has been singing the Maisey Mouse song to her ever since someone left a dead mouse in her desk in sixth grade. I've never sung the song to her personally, but I'm not going to lie. It's almost a habit to hum it in my head when I see her scurrying down the hallway. Just because I haven't walked up to her and called her "Maisey Mouse" to her face, or thrown wadded up worksheets at her, doesn't mean she hasn't been involved in the punch lines of a few of my jokes throughout the years.

"Oh, to be Maisey's King!" Justin says in a high-pitched squeal. Then he sings in a cartoony voice, "I just caaaaan't waaait to be king!"

Maisey turns, face flushed and her stare is blank. As she turns back, I smile at Kallie, raising my hand again.

"Justin Conner." That shuts Justin up and everyone laughs. Sean Mills turns around and looks at me. (At *me*!)

"Good one, Bree." And he winks. Wait. Maybe it was just a blink. I try super hard not to smile but the rest of my face smiles for me. I feel myself floating out of my chair. I also catch a breeze of his scent. It reminds me of hot apple cider and driftwood. To be real, I'm not even sure what driftwood smells like—but it's for sure a woodsy tone. It feels like I'm immersed in whatever feeling people are talking about when they say someone is "boy crazy." Which could be a good name for his cologne. Or soap. Hell, maybe it's just his natural scent.

Kallie raises her right then left eyebrow and mouths something that looks like "I told you so."

I smirk, pretending to write something important in my notebook while Mr. Norderick copies the names from the board onto his notepad.

"Good work, kids. Hopefully your choices will prevail on Friday and all will be right with BHS and the USA."

4

I give him a courtesy laugh over Justin's groan. Mr. Norderick's not so bad for a teacher. He knows about my parents getting divorced and didn't make a big deal about it.

My dad moved out this summer and I haven't really made a big deal about telling everyone. Or anyone. I didn't feel like talking about it, plus I'm not sure how something like that gets announced. And because it's been like eight months, it feels more awkward to say something now. For some reason, my mom felt a need to call the school counselor to let her know that she and dad were in the middle of a divorce. Maybe she forgot that I'm seventeen. Ms. Selinski, the counselor for all students with last names A–L, must've passed our little family drama on to all my teachers. About half of them mentioned something first semester. But on the first day of second semester none of my teachers said anything except Mr. N. who asked me to stay after. He said he figured I'm still dealing with a lot right now and if his assignments got to be too much or I needed help with anything, to let him know. That's all he said. He didn't pry or give off any kind of creeper vibe, so I appreciated that.

****

That night at dinner Mom asks the usual, "How was school?"

I smile, contemplating how much to tell her. She's tried to have more "sit down" dinners since Dad moved out. Since she's a lot happier these days, it's actually kind of nice. Also, I'm not the best person at putting myself out there to hang with other friends when Kallie's not available. So, "Post-divorce Mom" is kind of like a live-in friend these days.

"Something more than 'fine' I'm guessing?"

I push the mozzarella and baby tomatoes around my plate, sliding them back and forth through Mom's homemade balsamic dressing. The Sean story rests on the tip of my tongue. At the last second, I keep it to myself. "Kind of. Maybe. Prom Court nominations were today and everyone was going crazy about it. But Kallie nominated me, so, yeah, that's that."

"What? Prom Queen? Oh my God, that's great! Congratulations honey, this is going to be so much fun." She does this little squeal thing that instantly has me spearing a tomato and pointing my fork at her.

"Mom. Don't even. It's not like that. They're just nominations, not even the actual court members yet. Every class nominates and then those votes are added up and then there are five girls and five guys to vote for on Prom Night. It's only a nomination and there's no way I got votes in other classes too."

Her smile gets all beamy and she says, "I don't care what you say, it's still fun that there's a chance."

"A fat snowball's chance," I say, popping the tomato into my mouth.

That night in bed, I replay the Sean Mills "maybe a wink maybe a blink" scene over in my head, reminiscing how perfect our names looked together on the whiteboard. Maybe the whole court thing wouldn't be so awful. Standing up there on stage in front of everyone looking like you matter more than you feel like you do. It feels shallow even thinking this way after I'd gone on a million tangents last night trying to convince Kallie she was making a big mistake.

I tally up any other nominations I could have gotten in the other classes today. I do have other friends, but not like really close friends. I'm not sure I'm important enough for anyone else to have raised their hand for me. In our class, the only people that got nominated were the coolest kids, me because of Kallie, and the joke vote for Maisey. I'm an in-betweener. Not cool enough for the popular girls to ask me to hang out, but not uncool enough to be hanging out with Maisey Morgan and her crew. Well, it's not so much of a crew as it's just two other girls she hangs with in the halls between classes and the library after school. Tera Welmore, the girl who wears a uniform to school even though we have no dress code, and Anne Violet, the class brain, who's GPA is probably a four point ninety trillion. They're all equal in nerd stature, but somehow, Maisey's always managed to get the brunt of the teasing. But at least she has friends to hang with.

Now that Kallie is Todd White's girlfriend, things are different. If she's not at work, she's with him at some party everyone'll be talking about on Monday. She used to invite me, and I went to two or three, but every time I'd end up sitting there, by myself, pretending to drink a warm pissy-tasting beer while waiting for someone to ask me what I was doing at such a cool party. After a couple awkward Friday and Saturday nights, I stopped accepting the invites.

I grab my phone and dial Kallie to confront her about the nomination, since Todd, in one of his signature boy-bander impersonator outfits—blazer, jeans, and sneakers—was waiting for her right after class. As usual, he swooped Kallie up to rush her home so they could "hang out" before her parents got back from work.

"Kallie, do you know how embarrassing that was today? Why the hell would you nominate me?"

"Because, why not?" Kallie asks. "You deserve it just as much as anyone else—don't be so modest."

"Modest? Good one. I tried talking you out of it, so why would I want to be on court? Not like I'd get on there anyways. I'm the Libertarian candidate. You wasted your vote."

"Actually, someone else told me they were nominating you and I thought if I did too, it might better your chances."

"What do you mean someone else?"

"Hey, wouldn't it be so awesome if we both get on the court? And even better if Molly Chapman doesn't?"

"You and I both know there's no way Molly's name won't be on that list. Just because she's Todd's ex doesn't mean that everyone else hates her now."

"I'm just tired of being nice. Wherever me and Todd go, there she is with her side bitch, Jane. Molly's the ex-girlfriend that won't go away. I mean, hello? Are you forgetting about the email she wrote when Todd and I first started dating?"

I laugh. "You stole her boyfriend. You're lucky it was just an email. Even Jane was more pissed than Molly."

"First off, I wouldn't call an email with attached Bible verses, *just an email*. Second, I didn't steal him. Todd got bored and started hanging with someone fun. As for Jane Hulmes, barf. She's Molly's best friend, so I get it. But she's a bitch even without a cause. You should've seen her at lunch the other day. She cut in front of Maisey Morgan. Then, Maisey's friend Tera—in her maroon sweater and khakis—was like, 'Hey, that's not cool.' And Jane goes, 'Who cares, it's not like Maisey eats anyway.' "

"That sounds like Jane. I don't even know why Molly hangs out with her."

"When it comes down to it, they're both bitches. Molly just tries to keep it on the down low. She kept telling Todd she wasn't having sex until marriage, but you and I both know she gave it up at summer camp two years ago."

"So everyone says. Who even goes to summer camp anymore?"

Kallie laughs. "Who cares, it's still hilarious."

"Well," I say, "like you said, you're fun, she's not. Let's stop worrying about her."

"You're right. I'm like Beyoncé and she's Be-yawn-cé."

I cough into the phone. "Ahem. Can we get back to me for a second? Who are you talking about? Who said they'd vote for me?" As soon as the words come out, I get a pit in my stomach. "It's not a joke, is it? No one's trying to Maisey Mouse me are they?" I laugh, but in all seriousness, I need her confirmation.

"Oh Christ, Bree, get real. Who else? Chip said he was voting for you too. But don't say anything. It's not a secret that he's still psycho over you, but he made me swear not to say anything. I promised on my grandmother's grave."

"So basically, Nana's going to die now because you have more allegiance to me than to Chip? I'm honored, but damn, I'm gonna miss your Nana."

We laugh, and Kallie says, "Oh hell no, I was swearing on my dad's mom. She died when I was two."

Laughing with Kallie sends a wave of guilt into my stomach. These are the times I wish I had her to talk to about my parents' divorce. Instead, I tell her I'll talk to her tomorrow.

TWO

It's Friday morning—the day we're supposed to find out who's on Prom Court. Kallie's called me every night stressing about it. She's worried that Todd will be nominated and not her. And the angelically evil Molly will sink her fake nail tips back into him. I tell her in a hundred different ways that Molly sucks, but she's still sweating it.

I meet Kallie at the locker we share on the west end first thing in the morning. She's dressed in her Friday best. Her tall military-style boots look shined, like her jet-black hair, waving like a waterfall onto a drop-dead maybe-a-little-too-hot-for-school black and red striped dress.

"Me-*yow*. You didn't tell me we were going all out today," I say.

"Dressed to impress, girl! I've got to be ready in case I'm not in. Todd needs to know that I'm hot—Prom Queen or not."

"Well, I'm dressed for my special occasion too. School."

"You look cute no matter what you wear. Besides, you did get dressed up. You matched your shoes to your shirt and they're not mismatched today."

I squint, looking down at my tight yellow Elvis T-shirt, black jeans, and two yellow sneakers. "You're right. I don't know what I was thinking."

"Maybe you were thinking that since you're almost a legal adult, you should stop wearing two different shoe colors on Fridays?"

"Nope, that's not it. It was definitely a mistake. Too much of your Baby Promma Drama on my mind."

9

"Yeah right. I think you're trying to sex it up since you-know-who was practically all over you in class yesterday."

The warning bell rings, leaving me just enough time to squeeze Kallie's hand and beg her not to make a big deal out of it in class.

"Of course not, I'm cool. I got your back."

We jog down the hall together and I tell her if I don't catch her in-between classes, I'll see her in last period where we'll await her fate and my demise.

During Business Math, I chastise myself for getting so wrapped up in things that shouldn't matter. Like how Dad used to get all worked up over a hall light being left on. I feel like an idiot for worrying about these nominations when I want to be the kind of girl who's above all this stuff. But here I am worried about Kallie getting in, who she would or wouldn't be in with, and of course I'm worried about myself. Sure, I've daydreamed about the high I'd be on if by some apocalyptic miracle I'm nominated, but I know it's highly unlikely. The other stupid thought churning through my head is how to act when my name is *not* announced. It's like the MTV or Academy Awards when the camera cuts to the losers. All those awkward stretched smiles accompanied by courtesy hand clapping. I'll have to pretend my ass off that it doesn't matter and I forgot I was a contender anyway. All day I imagine different scenarios and practice my nonchalant look.

As the bell rings to start Language Arts, Mr. Norderick almost closes the door on my sneaker. "Just in time Ms. Hughes, just in time."

I do a quick sweep of the class to check for Kallie and Sean. Score. I walk over to the seat with Kallie's notebook on it. She whisper mumbles something to me about thanking God and moral support.

"Seat's taken," says Justin in a southern drawl. I can't place it but I know it's another cheesy movie line. I roll my eyes and face forward.

Justin flicks my hair with a pencil. "Your hair smells so good today Jennaaay, like a box of chocolates." Oh. *Forrest Gump*. He really needs to start watching some movies from this century.

Kallie leans into the aisle. "Dude, if you can smell her hair from your desk, I'm filing a restraining order."

"Another thing, Justin, I forgot to give you the memo. My name's Bree and Jenny's dead. Your horrible old movie quotes have pushed her into an early grave."

"Actually," says Justin, "she died of AIDS, which is still a serious problem facing the youth of today."

"You," says Kallie, "are the serious problem facing the youth of today."

Kallie and I stifle our laughs as Mr. N. clears his throat and starts talking about a new series on poetry, with weekly assignments.

Kallie's foot taps her desk leg. I know she isn't listening to any of this. She's probably wondering when Nord's going to hurry and announce the court names.

Looking ahead, I stare at Sean's ears, which offer me the perfect distraction. The sun peeks in through the window shades, a ray hitting his shoulder. I take a deep breath in, and get a whiff of Sean's foresty cologne and wonder if he'll be at any of the parties by the docks at Lake Crystal this summer. Maybe he'd be leaning against a tree jamming on the same guitar he played during the Homecoming Pep Rally. My teeth gnaw the inside of my bottom lip as I copy poetry notes and conjure up my image of Sean outside of school. With his shirt off. I wonder if it's weird for him to be playing the guitar with no shirt, and if I should ditch the half-nudity for a white T-shirt or his football jersey, but realize it's my daydream. So no-shirt Sean stays. With the image of him in blue trunks, hanging low on his hips, his muscles suntanned and sweaty, I make a vow. If there are parties at the lake this summer, I, Bree Hughes, solemnly swear—

"Excuse me?" Shandy Kissass's screechy voice pulls me back into class. I straighten my back against my chair. Shandy waves as if Mr. N. can't see her right there in the front row.

"Mr. Norderick? Are you announcing Prom Court today?"

"Yes, Ms. Silvers, I'll be announcing the names for your little Prom contest, after I finish the lesson and assignments for today."

Shandy slouches back in her seat. Staring at Sean's neck, I want to dive back into my daydream, or reach out, run my hand straight up the back of his neck, and feel his hair in-between my fingers. Instead, I quietly tap my pencil's eraser against the desk, trying to drum a beat slower than my heart, which has picked up the pace. I'm not sure if it's because the nominations will be announced soon or that I still have a vision of swim-trunks Sean in my head.

After a half hour and a couple pages of poetry terms and recommended reading, Mr. N. tells us to watch ourselves and that he'll be right back with our court list. He then gives Shandy a wink and tells her if anyone gets out of line she has permission to use her cell phone to call the police.

Sean turns and faces me. "Did you understand any of that poetry stuff? I have to ace these next assignments to get my grade back up. I bombed the last few essays."

Our eyes meet for a second and I have to look away because I am gone. Laser beams just shot through my body. Well, not actual lasers but *close*. It's a wave of heat that knocks me slightly off-kilter. I look down at my desk, searching my notes for the answer to his question, mainly so he can't see my face getting hot.

"Umm, well, alliteration is actually, um, it says that . . . or maybe if you start right here with the free-writing stuff you can . . ." I stop, realizing I can't even hear myself. My heart is on a treadmill right now.

Sean squints and cocks his head to the side.

"I'm sorry," I crinkle my lips together. "Um. I'm not making any sense. Sorry. Do you want my notes?"

"Sure. You mind if I copy?"

"No problem." I tear out two pages, push them into his hands and he turns back in his seat. My chest caves with the pressure of a highly anxious swoon and I'm grateful for the break from his piercing eyes.

Nord walks back into class, waving a piece of paper as if it's a winning lottery ticket. He says to make sure we bring our first poem in on Monday—no rules except it has to mention or be inspired by an animal.

"Is a chupacabra considered an animal?" Justin asks without raising his hand.

"You bet," answers Nord as Shandy turns and casts Justin the kind of look I usually save for the d-baggy guys who catcall girls in the hallway.

"Without further ado," Mr. N. continues, "here are the results you've all been waiting for, with bated breath and wild anticipation, please do not fall off the edge of your seats. In no particular order, Brian Wang, Todd White, Justin Conner, Sean Mills, Chris Monroe, Molly Chapman, Kallie Vate, Laura Rose, Jane Hulmes, and Maisey Morgan."

Even though the names came out fast, a lot happens. Shandy scribbles the names into her notebook just as fast as they fly out of Nord's mouth. Justin gives himself a high five and does one of those chicken neck, arm flapping, booty shaking football-end-zone victory dances. He ends it on bended knee, head down into his elbow and says, "Thank you little eight-pound six-ounce newborn baby Jesus."

Kallie's got the biggest smile anyone could have while trying to keep their mouth shut. If she was any happier, she'd be wiping away tears. She slides her hands into her bag and starts rummaging around rhythmically. Definitely texting Todd the news.

Maisey barely responds to her name. Slinking lower into her chair, her head hangs over her desk, as she scribbles indifferently into her notebook while the class half-asses an attempt at subtlety. Over half the class fake coughs, giggles, and snorts into their hands and the crooks of their elbows.

Over the roar, Justin says, "You were robbed—Mouse stole your spot!"

I roll my eyes, lean over, and squeeze Kallie's hand. "I'm so excited for you." The little pit that sinks to the bottom of my stomach surprises me. I'm not sure if it's because I don't want anyone to think I care or because I actually do.

Sean spins around with a grin and fist pounds Justin. His eyes hit mine, cranking the heat in my face but dissipating the pit in my stomach. "Too bad you're not on the court," he says. "It would've been fun."

"It's gonna be rough, but I think I'll make it," I say, sounding way cooler than I feel.

Sean shakes his head and laughs. "Well, hey, I didn't finish copying these notes so maybe I could keep them and give them back to you this weekend? Here's my number." Sean doesn't really let me answer before he starts writing his phone number on my black and white comp book.

"Okay, yeah, no problem." I can barely pull my eyes away from his number as the bell rings.

Everyone rushes into the hall to join everyone else in a feast of gossip, disbelief, and high fives over underclassmen regarding the nominations. Todd, in a pink bow tie, cuts between Kallie and me belting his arm around her waist.

"Babe, this dress should be illegal. If I don't get locked up for being your accomplice, we're going to rock the Prom as King and Queen."

I smile, letting them walk off into their own world, as if I have a choice. My eyes skim the crowd for Sean but he's lost in the sea of everyone rushing to get their weekend started.

When I turn the corner, a loud voice bellows toward me, "Mousey Morgan, will you go to Prom with me?"

I turn and Maisey slams into me and my armful of books.

"Sorry," she mumbles to my forearm, then tucks a clump of copper hair behind her ear, lowers her gaze even farther and rushes past me. Her shoulders hunch beneath her backpack as she ducks beneath the laughs and through the bodies mazed before her.

I frown as she disappears into the crowd until I catch a glimpse of Chip Ryan, my ex-boyfriend pushing his way toward me from the left. His shaggy hair swings over one eye while the other meets my eyes for barely a millisecond. I do the same thing I've been doing all year. Look away and try to stop my breath from catching in my throat. I push through the same path Maisey blazed. The Maisey Mouse song rings out at least twice among the Prom gossip and Friday night plan snippets before I'm hitting the double doors to the parking lot.

At home in my bedroom, I jump into sweatpants and peel off my wet-pitted Elvis shirt. Talking to Sean and dodging Chip can have that effect. My whole drive home from school was me pep-talking myself into longer breaths and a million repetitions of "just relax."

Bummer of the day had to have been Sean Mills saying "*too bad*." I don't want him feeling sorry for me. He almost made it sound like if we got on court together, we'd have been hanging out, eating pizza, and engaging in secret Prom activities. But being around Jane and Molly and their clique would've been awkward. And I'd have to fake like hell that it wasn't. It's probably for the best that my name wasn't called.

I once read or heard Oprah talking about being nominated for an award years ago. She was so stressed about how she looked that she didn't want to get up in front of everyone. I can't remember if she won and she was embarrassed about winning or if she lost and was relieved she didn't have to be on stage in the end. Either way, I know what she meant. I'm fairly confident this year about my looks, but sometimes I still feel like my best isn't good enough. Girls on Prom Court like Molly and Jane look like they stepped off the set of the latest teen movie. Getting my braces pried off last year and accepting that my hip bones will never shrink did cut down on mirror critiquing time, but it didn't do much to bump up my social rank at school.

Sean's face flashes in my head so I grab my backpack and fish out my notebook to make sure his phone number is still there. It's slightly smudged but still legible: *Sean 612–555-8000.*

I snap a picture of it and message it to Kallie.

This actually overrides the whole "sorry you weren't nominated" bit. Sean giving me his number means something. Guys don't go around giving their numbers to girls they want to be friends with. Not guys like him. Nope. A voice and smile like his are not hard up for a study partner with no credentials other than "seat behind you" stalking. If only I was cool enough to wait until Monday to see if he says anything about me not calling him, but I don't have that type of willpower.

To text or not to text. Texting in a situation like this is usually something I'd avoid since there's always the chance my words will come off the wrong way and I'll be in a mess until I construct forty more lines to explain myself. It can be a time suck. Sometimes it's the chicken shit way to go. So that's why I might text. I'm worried about my voice quavering on the phone and don't want Sean to hear my nerves.

I pull the phone to my ear and pretend to call: *"Hey Sean, it's Bree. From class. Hughes, Bree Hughes."* Then I get carried away. *"Yes, Bree with dark brown hair and blue-gray eyes. Five foot five and a quarter. I like shows and movies about zombies but serial killer movies freak me out. And you've never seen it, but I have a Massachusetts-shaped birthmark on my stomach and some cellulite on my thighs. Language Arts is my favorite class but your neck is very distracting. Sorry, but it's true. And now you know that, you might as well know that I've been passive aggressively stalking you this whole semester . . ."*

Buzzzz. My text alert goes off and I jump, hoping it's Sean. *Oh, wait. He's the one who gave me his number.* I check the screen.

KALLIE VATE.

Call him now! That's WAY better than Prom Court. But still SORRY u didn't get in!!!! : (Thx for nominating me tho LUV U. I'll call u tmrw!

An out-of-nowhere rock drop feeling assaults me, from the top to the bottom of my gut. My best friend feels sorry for me, too. Ugh. And, as usual, she's hanging with Todd tonight. Weekends are so much easier when your best friend is single or you have your own boyfriend. Chip was the last guy I dated. And since that turned out so shitty, I haven't been actively searching for a replacement. Just dreaming of one. If I can step it up a notch, maybe Sean could be the next guy.

It's probably time to follow Kallie's advice and call him before I overthink myself right into Monday. Sean's number stares back at me as I suck in a deep breath while reciting his digits in my head. I tap them into my phone and then do a half-dancy jumping jack to get myself into "operation call hot guy" mode. It rings twice and I hope for voicemail while my nerves kick harder. Fourth ring and yes. Voicemail.

"It's Sean—say something important or funny." *BEEEEEP.*

His deep drawl followed by a superfast beep throws me off and I almost hang up. But I can't. I have to leave a message or he might wait for me to call back. Or he won't see my missed call. Or he might not know it was me and think I'm some salesperson trying to sell printer ink or pet insurance.

"Hi Sean, this is Bree. From Language Arts and um, Bree Hughes, so I was calling since my notes, um, because you have my—" And then I do something beyond stupid. I'm so nervous that I decide to re-do my message and hope to God his phone has that option like most voicemails do. So, I tap the star button key but nothing happens. Just air. I hit the pound sign. Still nothing. Oh Shit. I can't hang up because that would be totally lame, so out of desperation I drop the phone then pick it back up. The cat clock on my wall grins at me like I'm a total idiot. "Omigod I'm so sorry, my cat just jumped in my lap and knocked the phone out of my hand. Sorry! Anyways, as I was saying it's Bree from Language Arts and you have my notes so if—"

BEEEEEP. An automated robot lady says "Thank you" and hangs up on me.

I press pound and star again, but nothing. My heart punches my chest. I am horrified.

I throw my iPhone. "Screw you robot lady." It lands with a thud on my shaggy blue carpet. For crap sake, I can't call back. Two messages would sound pathetic. Defeated, I pick the phone back up and send a text.

Hey Sean its Bree Hughes from Lang Arts If u need to, u can have my notes til Mon or I can get whenever

I press Send right away so I don't overthink and mess this one up too. Before I can conjure up a story of how I became the proud owner of a nonexistent cat, my mom breezes through my door, asking if I want to go out for dinner instead of pizza, the usual end of the week meal. My face contorts as I worry about looking uncool hanging with my mom on a Friday night.

"C'mon hon, it's been a long week. Let's get outta here."

"Okay. Fine. Can we go to Azumi?" She agrees and tells me to be ready in about an hour. I pick Azumi because yes, I like Japanese but mainly because it's not a typical hangout for anyone in our school. On Fridays most everyone goes to a movie or just hangs out in the parking lot at the strip mall and eventually ends up at 24/7, Belmont's only diner. The funny thing about 24/7 is that it closes at three a.m. Since I'm not a morning person, I don't know what time they open. I make a mental note to check the opening hours next time I go.

A few minutes after Mom leaves my room, my phone rings.

"Hello?"

"Is Bree there?"

"Yep, it's me."

"Hey, it's Sean from class, but I know you know that since you just called and texted me . . . Um . . ."

"Oh hey, how's it going? Crazy day right?"

"Yeah, all the Prom stuff, blehhhh."

"Really? I thought you were into that," I say. "Aren't you the one who said it was going to be fun?"

"Oh, right. I did say that, huh? I guess in a way it's fun and dumb. Does that makes sense?"

"Yeah, actually that does make sense."

"It's crazy that they actually nominated Maisey. I bet she wins too. Molly Chapman would probably—"

I interrupt to say she'd probably shit her pants and then have Jane jump Maisey for the crown. "Yeah she'd probably—probably be pretty bummed out. That's kind of her scene."

"I was going to say she'd wrestle Maisey to the ground for that crown and weird bathrobe they wear. But yeah, she'd be bummed," Sean says.

I laugh, wishing I'd said what I was thinking. After pacing the length of my room a few times, I start rearranging the books in my bookcase by color as a way to calm the butterflies moshing in my stomach.

18

"So . . . thanks for letting me swipe those notes. I didn't even take any in class. All those labels and rules for writing go over my head. It's confusing."

"Yeah, it can. But you don't have to worry, really, since the first assignment is to write whatever you want."

"As long as it's about an animal, right? Maybe I should write about your crazy cat that jumped on your lap and made you drop your phone while you were all alone."

I laugh and cringe, because a) Unless the black cat clock on my wall counts, I don't have a cat, and b) His voice is so handsomely hot and flirty. Or maybe he's just being nice. I frown at a book cover with a guy and girl almost kissing in the rain.

"So when can I get these notes back to you. We could meet up."

Meet up? The inside of my stomach is swishing around like crazy so I offer my stupid Monday idea. "You don't have to do that. I can just get them back Monday if it's a big deal."

"Um, well I was . . ." He leaves the sentence hanging mid-air.

Instantly I regret trying to act indifferent. I'm glad he can't see me right now. Wide-eyed, hot-faced, and pacing, wondering where to shelve a bluish-greenish book with a girl tiptoeing underwater. "Or yeah, we could meet up this weekend."

"Okay, let's do that. Can you meet up tonight? Like later though? I have a . . . a thing. But I could probably meet you at 24/7 or Java Joint around 9:30?"

I hesitate. Meeting up somewhere almost sounds like a date. Unless he's already going on a real date and meeting me afterward. Or hanging out with his friends first and then me second. Not that it matters. *Sean Mills!*

"Okay, that works," I say. "I have a thing too, so that's perfect. How about Java Joint?" My second request tonight in order to avoid a busy social scene.

"Sure, and if you want, maybe you could help me a little with this poetry stuff? Only if you wanted. If you have time or if it's not too late?"

19

He *does* sound nervous. He needs to look in the mirror more. And take more selfies. And send them to me.

"Okay, yeah," I say. "I'm such a party animal anyways. My day pretty much starts at 9:30 at night so it works."

"Great. See you then."

Click. "Good-bye?" I say to the air. I hate when people don't say good-bye when they hang up. But it's Sean, the hottest cutest everything on the planet, so he gets a pass. For now.

THREE

When Mom and I step into Azumi, I'm surprised there's a five to ten minute wait. Along with not having a very adventurous palate, Belmont is one of the smallest towns in Northern Minnesota, especially in the off-season. There are a lot of lake houses and cabins around here so most businesses do better in the summertime—especially places that aren't all cheeseburgers and hot dogs.

We wait on a bench while I give my mom a double take. She's wearing a shimmery black shirt I've never seen before and has heels on with jeans. Guess she really was dying to get out. She does need to get out more, not that I'm sure she's ready to date yet or if *I'm* even ready for that. Seeing her with someone else would be weird. It doesn't feel that long ago when she told me her and Dad were finally calling it quits.

It was the Fourth of July. Mom woke me up with a box of donuts. I knew something was up since she'd been on an anti-processed sugar kick for a while.

"Honey, we have to talk."

My stomach went into instant knots as I prepared for her to tell me she had some incurable disease. My breath started getting away from me, which is something I've started getting used to the past couple years. If my parents were fighting, or sometimes even out of the blue, my throat feels like it closes up and my heart starts beating harder and faster.

Mom laid her hand on my knee. "Your dad and I are getting a divorce."

I let out a sigh and said, "Finally." Immediately I wanted to snatch the word back and even the sigh. It'd come out so sharp that my mom actually jerked back, as if I'd slapped her.

Before I could explain, she was making excuses for all her and Dad's fighting so I tuned her out. I'd been getting pretty good at that. Her and Dad were constantly arguing over stupid shit for at least the last three years. My dad works nights as a police officer for the county and Mom works at Melbrook Elementary with special needs kids. On Dad's off days, he was always hanging out with my uncle Mike. Uncle Mike's a mess and a few years younger than Dad so he says he has to watch out for him. I'm not sure how sitting around an apartment, drinking beers, and watching sports really helps someone get a job or find happiness, and neither did Mom. Usually, while Mom was yelling about having a part-time husband, I'd be in my room with my music cranked up. A lot of times, Dad would just leave in the middle of her yelling and take off in his truck.

I checked back into my mom's long-winded explanation to hear her say, "I'm sorry. I can't believe we've been putting you through all of this for the last year."

I wanted to say it'd been at least three years, but I stayed quiet. I was fixated on my now tasteless donut, taking tiny, clean bites to avoid a powdery red goopy mess on my flowered down comforter.

"I've been waiting on something to change or something to give, but it hasn't. I love your dad, honey, I really do, but we'll be better off apart. And most importantly, it'll be better for you. You're going to be a senior. You'll have so much going on and the last thing you need is two parents fighting all the time."

I imagined throwing the jelly donut across the room and watching it splatter, stick, and slide down the wall. I wanted to scream, "Geez Mom, thanks for finally thinking of me. Thanks for giving me the gift of a 'fight-free' senior year. Now I can sleep in peace or maybe hang out in our living room instead of holing up in my room with Maroon 5 trying to drown out your crying screaming bullshit." But I didn't say any of that.

"I just want you to be happy, Mom. I gotta take a shower, though. I'm meeting Chip for a breakfast date." I walked into my bathroom, leaving her sitting on my bed with the donuts and then spent the rest of the day at the library avoiding calls from everyone.

As I'm picking up my Azumi menu, one of my worst-case scenarios walks into the restaurant. Chip and his whole family. His dad, stepmom, and little brother.

"Quick Mom, trade places with me. I want to be closer to the exit just in case there's a fire."

She laughs, trades seats, and then leans in. "In case of a fire started by your ex-boyfriend Chip and his gang of arsonists?"

"Pretty much."

"If you want to leave, just say the word. We can always grab a pizza and head back home."

"It's fine, Mom." I only say this because she got dressed up for dinner and if I can stay in my seat, with my back to Chip's table, I can avoid any sort of scene. We'll have to wait until they leave first, though, so I don't have to walk past them. I skim the menu, volleying between sushi rolls or chicken teriyaki. Or their Pad Thai. It'd be easier to decide if I didn't have my ex-boyfriend seconds away from noticing me.

Mom says, "Oh cool, Bree. Look! They're going to have music. Some guy's getting ready to play an acoustic guitar. Looks about your age. Look hon, he's a cutie."

"Who says cutie, Mom?" I laugh and think *wouldn't it be just my luck if Sean was at Azumi too?*

I turn my head and the second-worst scenario happens. Sean Mills *is* at Azumi. I freeze. There's no way he's *not* going to notice me, he's sitting three o'clock from me, on a tall stool to the left of the hostess and cashier stand. He tunes his guitar as I wonder how this could get any worse. Then Chip notices me because my head is turned. The good thing is that he looks surprised, which means he wasn't legit stalking me. Which is good since stalking someone with your family in tow would be over the edge. I've seen Chip *at* the edge, but I for sure don't need to see him go over it.

"Bree!" Chip yells across three tables.

Sean glances up from his guitar, meets my eyes, looks away and then right back again. He waves and smiles, as if he sees me in here all the time.

If only I could be so cool. My face is on fire, my heart is pulsating through my shirt, and my mom looks like her head's going to explode as she plots to save me.

Chip gets up from his table and walks my way. I like to think I'm pretty good at eye-talking and what happens next is an example: I give Chip a hard, piercing look as I think, *You crazy mixed-up bastard, for the love of Adam Levine, DO NOT even come over here 'cause you don't want to know what kind of scene I'd cause in front of your family.*

He stops in his tracks, looking torn, then veers right and strolls toward the bathroom instead.

"Are you going to be okay, hon?"

"Really Mom, I'm fine. Boys. Can't live with 'em, can't file a restraining order."

We both laugh. Then to change the subject from anything Chip related, I tell her about Sean. But first I make her promise not to look his way so he doesn't know we're talking about him. We talk in hushed voices behind our menus—me trying to downplay my excitement about tonight and Mom getting all keyed up asking if I should change into something cuter.

Chip stops to talk to Sean who's now strumming "American Pie." I didn't even think they knew each other. The waitress steps up to our table and distracts me from trying to lip read. As she walks away with our order, I try to chill out. I just need to act like it's not a big deal to be with my mom eating Japanese, that I'm comfortable enough with who I am, and Sean isn't the kind of guy who would hate on me for that.

My Aunt Jen uses the phrase "Fake it 'til you make it," and I just might need to adopt it as my new mantra. If I keep acting confident and cool, maybe it'll start to stick. I flip my hair behind my shoulder and sit taller.

Then, in honor of worst-case scenarios, Sean taps his mic and says, "This next song is for Bree from Chip."

"Is this really happening?" I ask my mom.

"Yes, it sounds like it." She smiles and pats my arm. "Did I ever tell you about the time when I was eighteen and was serenaded at a New Kids on the Block concert in the late eighties?"

"Yes, at least a hundred times by you and Aunt Jen. But it was pretty embarrassing, so go ahead and tell me again." Her eyes light up as she tries to assuage me with a story of her falling off a stool on stage at a sold-out concert while her favorite boy-bander sang "Please Don't Go Girl."

While Mom's reliving the most exciting and mortifying moment of her teendom, Sean's voice fills the room and I recognize the song right away. It's the old Maroon 5 song, "She Will Be Loved."

Well played, Chip. He knows I love this song. No way he doesn't remember that it was the song playing the last time we spoke.

Chip and I were supposed to go to the State Capitol the day I found out about Mom and Dad. Up until the divorce bomb dropped, I thought the Fourth might be the night I'd lose my virginity. It wasn't. I avoided Chip's calls all day, crawled into bed around six, and fell asleep with Pippa, my stuffed dog.

The next morning Chip showed up at my house all pissed. We went for a drive and I didn't want to cry if I started talking about my parents, so I said nothing.

The whole convo with Mom had me pushing a big mess of emotion deep into the corner pocket of my stomach, the place where stuff goes when it starts to feel like too much. I let it tangle into a wiry ball. And just as soon as it starts to feel heavy or like it's scraping the walls of my stomach with its spindly claws, I ball it back up, like aluminum foil.

As I sifted through different excuses for standing him up, Chip jerked the wheel right, pulled over, and turned the music down. "She Will Be Loved," the soundtrack to our first kiss back in May, was on.

Chip put the car in park and said, "So?"

I didn't answer.

"Bree? You're going to sit there like nothing's wrong?"

I stared ahead as if the answers would appear through the dirty mist on his windshield.

"You don't have anything to say to me?" His hands gripped the wheel so tight that purple-blue veins bulged from his skin.

When I finally opened my mouth it came out in a whisper. "I guess I was sick." Which was kind of true because I'd been trying to talk myself into getting the whole sex thing over with and it was giving me a stomach-ache. And with Mom telling me about the divorce, it got worse. I must've used the library bathroom at least three times.

Chip said, "Bullshit. If you were sick, you would've texted or called." He went into a rant about me being a liar who'd obviously been hanging out with someone else.

Then I got mad right back at him. For calling me a liar, for trying to fight with me. For not being able to read my mind.

"You're such a jerk. You have NO IDEA what I'm going through. What I *went* through last night. I said I was sick, so that means I was sick. Do you hear me? Sick!"

Chip reached across my seat and I flinched. He opened the glove box and threw a box of condoms onto my lap.

"We might as well throw these away."

It was like one of Mom and Dad's arguments. The hot anger, blaring and choking, filled the car, and it was rising over my head. At that point, I was probably as mad as he was. And it scared me.

"Are you crazy?" I asked. "You're a pig. And who'd sleep with a *little pig*? I'm sick of this *shit*. We're done."

His fist swung through the air and met the driver's side window. The glass crunched and shattered onto the gravel as I grabbed my purse, jumped out of the car, and ran. The thought of what could've happened if I'd stayed in the car propelled my legs to run harder. Pretty soon his car was pulling up beside me. He begged me to get back in the car, but I just kept going.

Not listening not listening not listening. The chorus to the Maroon 5 song played on repeat in my head until he gave up and I eventually reached a Super America gas station.

When Mom picked me up I kept it simple, "He has jerk and jealousy issues."

She hugged me and said she was proud of me for not putting up with a guy like that. I hugged her back as she smoothed my hair. Right then I got a twinge of what it must've felt like for Mom. Being stuck somewhere and letting yourself get pushed to the edge.

"Guys like that, honey," she said, "only get worse with time."

Although it's a C plus for effort, Chip fails with the song request. It doesn't make me swoon and it doesn't make me sad. I'm not even embarrassed anymore. My jaw tightens as I turn and throw another eye dagger at Chip's table. I don't know if Sean is bored with the song or he notices my reaction, but he starts doing a beat-boxy sound into the mic and flows into a fast version of Maroon 5's newest song.

My scowl turns into a big embarrassed smile, and Mom and I laugh. Whether he really is or not, Sean *is* singing to *me*. I'm too unsettled to look right at him but his deep, mellow tone is making me a little dizzy.

The rest of dinner is incident-free even though I can feel Chip burning eyeholes into my back. We get up to leave before Chip and his family are even done with their food. I chant my new mantra in my head and walk past him like I never saw him in the first place.

As we pass the hostess stand and Sean, I lean over and mouth to him, "See ya at 9:30."

He nods, smiles, and strums a new song. Since I don't feel a morbid need to wait around for something else embarrassing to happen, I grab Mom's keys and head to the car while she hands the cashier her bank card.

FOUR

Sipping my chai latte, I click back and forth between screens on my phone, time checking every one to three minutes. It's been fifteen minutes since I sat down at Java Joint, but that's my fault. I got here twenty minutes early. I thought it'd be nice to get here first, just for the satisfaction of watching Sean walk in and make his way over to sit *by me* for once. I clink the ice in my cup and smile over my straw as Mom's words ring in my head: "Don't overthink everything, just be yourself, but maybe a little more chill."

Since it was kind of new for her to give me boy advice, it felt nice. I also followed her suggestion and took a quick shower and changed. Nothing crazy though. Mascara, lip gloss, and a ponytail. I didn't dress up but the Belmont Bengals T-shirt I'm wearing is pretty tight. I take another drink and click to check for any non-ringing phantom phone call or messages. Nope. 9:26 p.m., and nothing.

It's possible Sean might not even show up. Maybe something better came up, like a party or call from one of the Prom Court girls, like Molly Chapman or Jane Hulmes. I pucker my upper lip at the thought of Jane. Just thinking about her tastes like lemons. If Maisey Morgan's considered our class's biggest dork, Jane would be considered the biggest diva. And by diva, I mean her yearbook superlative should read "Class Bitch." For some reason, half our class buys into her bullshit and she's as close to a reality TV star as Belmont High could get. She's got this flawless olive skin, dark eyes, and her teeth are so perfect it's been rumored that she wears a flipper. Jane struts and sails through the hallways as if she's fresh off a pageant stage, which makes sense, because she pretty much is. Obnoxious but true: she actually wears some of her pageant crowns to school.

Last year she walked around for at least a month slapping red DON'T stickers on people's backs. Maisey was definitely included. I'm proud to say that I never got one—only because it's an unspoken rule: you never walk or stand with your back to Jane. Aside from being one of Maisey's loudest tormentors, she actually got in Kallie's face a few times after Todd and Molly broke up in October. Kallie's not the kind of girl to back down to anyone, so she basically told Jane she has nothing to lose and any type of school detention would be worth the personal pleasure she'd get from breaking her nose and pageant circuit dreams. Jane hasn't done more than glare or mutter snide comments since—which, in Jane's world, is as close as you'll get to a truce.

Sean finally walks in. He's changed—into a Bengals tee too. He makes his way over to the table as I cover my shy smile with another quick sip of my drink.

"Hey," he greets me with a crooked grin, waving his hand over his T-shirt. "I'm not late for our school spirit meeting am I?"

"Nope. You're just in time. Go Bengals." I raise my hand and throw up the "Bengal Claw" sign. As soon as I do it, I internally cringe. The bengal claw? Pretty cool, Bree. I don't tell Sean that even though I've been waiting less than a half hour, it feels like three. I smooth my hair and reapply my mega minty lip balm as he walks to the counter and returns with an iced coffee.

"So, looks like we both had big plans tonight, me playing guitar for twelve crumpled dollars and you hanging with your mom. That was your mom, right?"

"Yeah, well, when I said party animal, I wasn't kidding. My mom was begging me to go, so, you know how it is. So, it's cool you have a job playing music. Do you play there a lot?"

"A few times a month, on nights Ace or Mary and Jerry the married violinists aren't available."

I'm not sure if he's kidding or not but I laugh anyway. Neither of us says anything for what feels like two minutes. He pulls my notes and a notebook out of his backpack.

"So do you think you could help me with the poetry stuff for Monday, maybe just help me get started?"

"Yeah, of course," I answer.

We go over a few terms and different types of poetry, and then I help him construct some practice lines. We make up a poem about my *fake* cat. I don't say anything about it being fake though. I use terms like *wild ball of fur blazing through the air* and *snow white poof*. It almost gets me wishing that I had someone like "Fluffy" to cuddle with at night. We work together to make some lines funny, some serious, some rhyming and some not. Once the poem starts to resemble an epic, we stop.

"Thanks for your help. I'm hoping to get my grade up this semester, I was a slacker at the beginning of the year with football going on."

"No problem. Really." As he slides his papers back into his bag, his leg brushes mine.

A bolt of lightning shoots up my thigh.

"Oh, sorry," he says as I lean down and fumble with my own bag and notes so he can't see how flushed I am.

While I'm wondering if this is the part where we say good-bye and I go home, get in bed and bask in my Sean moment, he asks, "So, do you want another coffee or something or do you have to be home for a 10:30 curfew?"

I laugh. "No, I can stay. My mom won't put out an Amber Alert for another couple hours."

He asks what kind of coffee I'm having and heads over to the counter.

This is crazy. I'm really hanging out with Sean Mills and he just went to buy me a drink. Or maybe he went to order it and I'm supposed to pay him back. I offer him a five-dollar bill when he returns with my latte.

He frowns. "Oh c'mon, it's the least I can do since you let me borrow your notes and took time to help me out."

"Well, thanks."

There's another awkward silence and while I try to think of something interesting or topical to fill it with, Sean asks what I was hoping he wouldn't.

"Soooo, what's the deal with you and Chip Ryan?"

FIVE

Telling Kallie about my parents on Saturday afternoon is unavoidable since I'm the one who invited her over. Aside from it being my first invite in over a year, it's the dad-free redecorating of our house that ultimately gives it away. As we walk through the living room, Kallie notices that Dad's burgundy La-Z-Boy chair is gone—the one we used to take turns spinning each other on in elementary school.

"What the . . ." Her eyes move over to the giant new painting of a poppy floating in a sea of blue. It's practically yelling at us from above the fireplace where our family picture used to hang. Kallie's eyes widen. "Bree?"

"Hang on, let's just go upstairs," I say.

Leading her up the stairs answers her questions easier than I can. Almost all the black-and-white framed photos that Kallie always stopped to comment on are gone. Now it's mostly empty spaces on the wall; slightly darker gray squares outlining where they used to hang. Wedding pictures gone. Dad holding Mom with her fat round pregnancy stomach, gone. Dad in his uniform. Gone. The pictures left hanging are shots of Mom, me, and a few pictures of Aunt Jen and my grandparents.

As Kallie closes my door behind her, she says, "I guess you've got something to tell me?" She leans against the door as I sit on the edge of my bed.

I don't want to say it because the words seem smaller than the stupid feeling I have building in my chest.

"Your dad moved out?"

"Yeah," I whisper.

"Are they getting a divorce?"

"Uh-huh. I mean, yes, they already did. It was final a few months ago."

Kallie folds her arms across her chest. "Shit, B. Why didn't you say anything? When did he move out?"

"This summer."

Kallie sits down, her eyes brimming with tears, and hugs me.

I push the loud ball of everything in my gut far down but my shoulders quake with one sob that I turn into a cough. I squeeze her for a few seconds more, then pull away.

"That's like a million months ago," Kallie says. "Why didn't you tell me? It's kind of a big deal. Not a big shock, but still a big deal. Remember the last time I was over? That was forever ago, and it was like a cage match."

"Yes, I remember." It was last year when Kallie and I walked into the kitchen after school only to have to walk right back out when we heard my parents fighting from all the way upstairs. Mom was screaming something about Dad's priorities, then we heard a crash against the wall and Dad yelled for her to stop breaking shit. We didn't wait around to hear the rest. That's when Kallie's house became the only place to hang out at.

"You should've told me. That's really huge, Bree."

"I didn't want to talk about it and now that it's been so long it's not really a big deal anymore, okay?"

"Okay, I guess. I'm just mad you didn't—"

"Mad I didn't give you all the details about hanging out with Sean last night? I didn't even tell you yet that he asked about Chip."

"Okay. Fine, we'll change the subject." She wipes a tear from the corner of her eye. "Wow. Asking about your ex? That's big. What'd you say?" Kallie asks, hopping off the bed onto my yellow beanbag chair.

"I told him we were dating like, forever ago, and that some guys just can't take 'get off my ass' for an answer."

This inspires Kallie to launch into a story about her and Todd's first date, and I sigh a breath of relief. I nod my head, happy to finally spill about the whole Sean thing—and maybe get some advice. I'm also happy to ditch the subject of my parents' divorce.

Although I feel lighter having it off my chest with her, I can still sense it hovering over me. I push the feeling aside again and just decide to roll with the relief that the secret's out.

"But boys can be crazy like that. Are you going to see him again or what? Wait, more importantly, how can we speed this up so he can ask you to Prom?"

"What? Oh, um, Prom Shmom. I'm probably not even going. Chip actually had the nerve to ask me in a voicemail last week if we could go as friends."

"God, Bree, you might *have to* go with Chip if you don't get to work. You can't *not* go. This is our Senior Prom. Even Maisey Morgan is going now. I can ask Todd if any of his friends need a date. I'm sure we could find someone to take you."

"Gee, thanks, but as much fun as it sounds to be a charity case for one of Todd's friends, I'll pass." I roll my eyes so hard that it hurts my head.

Kallie's lips tighten into a tiny scowl. "Don't take this the wrong way but what if you started being a little more friendly and social at school? Or maybe if you just chill out a little—"

"Really, Kal? I talk to more than enough people at school. It's not like I'm walking around the hallways like a loser getting string cheese and paper thrown at me."

"Don't get so defensive, that's not what I'm saying. I meant extending yourself even further." She stretches her arm toward the window. "Outside of school especially. You should be hanging out with us on weekends. You need to go out of your way to be nicer, and a lot more approachable."

"I'm not sure how telling you my parents got divorced and how I hung out with Sean turned into a lecture on how to make friends and influence people. It's not the trade-off I was looking for."

"I was just trying to tell you why no one's asked you yet."

"So, what you're saying is that no one's asked me because I don't have enough friends. Maybe if I start smiling more and stealing boyfriends, I could have a date and maybe even a few friends that call me on a regular basis?"

Kallie frowns. "What the hell, Bree? Are you seriously saying that? I didn't steal anyone's boyfriend."

"I'm just saying that—"

"No," she says. "I heard you. And now I get why you've been such a crappy friend lately."

"Me?" I fold my arms across my chest. "That's hilarious. Where have *you* been? Where have you been this whole year while I've been avoiding my shit-head ex-boyfriend who punched a freakin' car window because I ruined his plans to screw me on the Fourth—the day I found out about my parents?"

Her eyes widen, like an owl's. "I'm not a *mind*-reader! How the hell am I supposed to know what's going on if you never say anything? What kind of best friend are you? You can't expect to make or keep friends if you always have them at arm's length." She grabs her gray hoodie off my floor and huffs out the door. The edges of my Adam Levine poster flap as my door slams. Her voice rings out from the hallway. "And you sure as hell won't get a Prom date that way either."

As her black boots stomp down the stairs, I yell, "Well I guess if I used *your* methods on keeping guys around, I could have twenty dates lined up."

The anger I've been shoving into the little corner of my gut shoves me right back. Tears pool in the corners of my eyes. *Nope. Not doing it. Not worth it.* I hate crying. Last time was in December after Mom made a point of getting rid of every last "her and Dad" item in the house. He came by after Christmas to get the things Mom said were a day away from being Craigslisted. He did it while I was at school and left a card with a sparkly purple Christmas tree on the front. Inside was a stack of twenty-dollar bills. He'd written:

"Just in case you didn't get everything on your list.
Con amor, Dad"

I wished I had the guts to send the card and money back. I'd have crossed out what he wrote and written my own message:

"Sure wish I could buy a live-in dad for $200.
Your biological daughter, Bree Hughes"

But I didn't. I spent the money on a bunch of downloaded music and new purple sneakers.

SIX

Monday inches by like I figured it would. Kallie and I pass each other in the halls and take turns getting things out of our locker without a word. She breathes all heavy and dragon-like through her nose at the locker. The tension is so thick I'm practically peeling through billowy layers of it just to get my Bio book and an extra pencil.

Fifth period Biology drags as I stress about Norderick's class. Is it going to be the same or different with Sean? Is Kallie going to keep ignoring me and will she make it obvious with more heavy nose breathing and teeth sucking?

My teacher rambles about plants reproducing as I try to come up with different ways to hang out with Sean again. Maybe I could offer to help him with the next assignment or ask if he needs help with the next assignment. Or I could use my "fake it 'til you make it" attitude and just ask him out. Just as I'm running through potential conversation starters, Mrs. Young gets buzzed on her intercom.

"Mrs. Young, please send Bree Hughes down to the office."

Everyone's bodies and eyes shift my way as my stomach and head spin with anxiety. I sling my bag over my shoulder, shove my book and notebook under my armpit, and speed walk my way out the door.

It's a long walk to the office as potential reasons for an office visit multiply. I'm not good with surprises. Kallie might've gone to the counselor about our fight, wanting to do that peer mediation thing. Or more likely, they're checking in again to see how I'm doing with my parents' divorce. Hopefully it's not an issue with any of my grades or graduation.

The hallway with classes in session feels library-esque, lonely, cool, and stark. My footsteps on the floor echo against the quiet walls. I'm barely one foot into the office as Maisey Morgan pushes past me. Our shoulders brush and we turn and make eye contact, then look away. Her eyes are red and puffy behind her glasses. If she was in the office for the same reason as me, it can't be good.

I give the secretary my name and she says to go back to Ms. Selinski's office. My stomach spins like a tilt-a-whirl.

Ms. Selinski waves me in with a smile. "Hi Bree. Have a seat."

After I shift my butt around on the hard plastic chair, I do my best to take a deep breath without looking like a freak. My breaths are super short and I'm sure she can physically see the tightness I'm feeling in my chest and shoulders.

Her smile is small but polite as she clicks a few keys on her computer. "Your grades have gone up a little bit since last semester. Does it feel like a little time has helped make things here and at home a bit easier?"

"Yeah, I think so."

"How are you feeling about things at home now?"

I say "Good," and wait to see if a one-word answer is going to fly.

"Good to hear," she says. "It seems like you're doing well enough in your classes, so you should be proud of yourself. Keeping on top of school after a major family transition is never easy. Just remember if you ever need to talk about it or anything else, I'm right here in the corner office." She gives me a wink and I wonder if this is all she has to say.

She says "Hmmmm" and leans in. "So, Miss Hughes, how would you feel about being on Prom Court?"

"Really? Are you serious? There's already a court and I'm not . . ." Maisey's face flashes in my head. "I don't get it, why?"

"One of the nominees has declined and I won't get into the specifics but we need another person to step in."

A string of guilt ties itself into a harsh knot in my gut. I try to untie it by remembering that I'm not one of the kids who raised my hand to nominate her.

I twist my mouth and crinkle my nose. "Well, um, so, why's my name here? I don't think I really had any votes."

Ms. Selinski shakes her head, "Bree, you had a few nominations, you're a good kid, people like you, so don't overthink it. Consider it an honor. You've earned it and you know what, you deserve it."

"Thank you. So, um, okay."

She slides a maroon sheet of paper across her desk that reads PROM COURT SCHEDULE & GUIDELINES. Then she hands me a late pass for Mr. Norderick's class.

As I walk down the hall, there's the slightest bounce in my step and I'm barely bothered that I'm a Prom Queen nominee by default. I'll have more time with Sean and more reasons to talk to him. Kallie's going to freak when she hears. She'll be so excited that—

Shit. My buzz is immediately killed by the sinking feeling I get as I remember our fight. Kallie probably thinks I'm skipping class just to avoid confrontation. I dip into the bathroom to give my brain a rest before heading back to class.

Stepping up to the sinks, I'm hit with a pang of disappointment. Class has already started but someone else is in here. Her red stringy hair droops down into her face. *Maisey.*

I make my way to the mirror next to hers and the same yellow slip from Ms. S.'s office sits on the corner of the sink, weighted by her glasses. Something nudges my brain to say something. I almost feel obligated. Like I should apologize. And I know it's horrible but I'm hoping like a maniac that no one comes in and sees me talking to her. I let my yellow slip fall from my fingers and do a quick sweep to see that no one's in any of the stalls before I pluck it from the floor. No feet. Clear.

"So, I uh, guess we're both taking advantage of these late slips, huh?" I wave it back into the pocket of my bag.

Maisey squints at the faucets. She's extra vulnerable without her glasses. Like a scared rabbit. Her eyes are swollen like they've been outlined in soft pink highlighter. "Yep. Guess so."

"Sooo," my voice shakes. "I know I don't really know you that well or anything but I just wanted to say sorry about the whole Prom thing. I'm not—I mean, well, it's not like I . . . I didn't nominate you or anything but I still feel like I should say something."

"Don't bother. It looks like you're all set." She nods at my PROM GUIDE paper. "You're on Prom Court now and you can do it with dignity. Tell all your friends and go home and tell your mom and dad the news." Her eyes get that shiny glossed over look as she clenches a wad of tissues in her fist.

"I'm not happy it happened like this and I'm not even—"

"Sure you're not." She exhales a short breathy laugh and swipes the tissue under her eyes. "Because no one would ever want to be Prom Queen, right? Yeah sure, it's nothing to be happy about. But really, you *try* to enjoy yourself. Just remember all the people you think you're not stepping on along the way."

"That's not true, I'm not even like that."

"Oh please, I've known you since elementary school. You've never talked to me. But you've laughed. Everybody does." As if a dam breaks, tears rush down her face. "You were sitting right next to me when someone left a dead mouse in my desk in sixth grade. The smell—" Her face crumples like tissue paper as she mops the tears into her wadded Kleenex. "The smell of it—for two whole days until I found it in the back corner in a sandwich bag. Don't tell me you didn't know about it. I remember like it was last week. You're the one who told me to check my desk, remember? There's no way you don't."

"Yeah, but I didn't. I—I . . ." I don't even want to finish because the look on her face takes me back to the way she looked when she pulled it out of her desk that day. Horrified, degraded, the tears, the face-slapping humiliation. I do remember. Our corner of the class was starting to get a weird stink. Kids were whispering and laughing at lunch and recess about someone putting something in her desk. "I didn't do that. I don't know who did either, I just heard about it—that's why I told you to look. I wasn't trying to be mean. I wasn't even sure if it was true." My heart's racing and the look on her face is killing me and I just want to leave. *Maisey Morgan isn't going to make me cry.* "I wasn't in on it and I really was trying to help."

"Whatever. I'd hardly call that helping. I'm sure you were laughing with everyone else. Just like you've laughed a million times at a million jokes about me. You think you're better than me with your perfect life. You get to walk down the hallway without wondering if someone's going to throw something, trip you, or squeak and sing when you're with friends or walking down the hall with your little sister who only just realized you were a loser once she got into high school with you."

"Listen, I'm sorry. I'm—"

"Just shut up. It doesn't matter anymore anyways. It's all done, it's over. I. Don't. Care. I'm more over it than you'd even believe."

My throat clenches tighter but somehow I push more words out. "Like I said, I'm sorry for anything I've ever said or done to make you feel like I thought I was better than you. That's crazy, but don't think my life is perfect either. I don't have a perfect life and everything isn't as easy for me as you think."

"Save the act of contrition, Bree Hughes," she says with such bite I can practically see the cold air coming from her mouth. Her smirk is so condescending that it resembles one I've seen many times on Jane Hulmes's face. "This isn't a confessional booth. You don't get to say sorry and everything goes away. You and the rest of this school are the least of my problems, anyway. I told you, it's done. Have fun on Prom Court and enjoy hanging out with all those assholes, seems like you'll fit in just fine."

She plucks her glasses from the sink, wipes her eyes with her sleeve, swoops up her books, and leaves me in her dust.

I can't believe that the first time I've ever really talked to Maisey just ended with her telling me off. Who would've thought she had it in her? Although a part of me is flattered for her thinking I'm perfect and leading some charmed, popular, happy family life, I mostly feel like an ass. I don't even know how I'd fix something like this. At least I said I was sorry. Maybe I can try to say something else to her another time. But definitely not right now. Right now, I have to get to class to turn in my assignment. Most importantly, I can't wait to tell the only person I'm hoping will care right now about my good news. Sean Mills.

SEVEN

Gripping my phone, I run through all the reasons why I should call Sean. Of course my seat was taken when I walked into Language Arts. Kallie didn't save it like she usually does so I had to sit in the front row, first seat in. Right in front of Maisey who was probably piercing me with sharper daggers than Kallie was. Being in front, I was also forced to leave class first when the bell rang. I didn't even have the nerve to turn around and wait for Sean. I was too worried that Maisey would have more stuff to say to me.

I jump onto my bed and relax into the pillows propped against the headboard. After tapping Sean's number into my phone, my finger hovers over the call button.

Just call him! Do it, do it. Okay . . . now. I pause. This is way different than last time when he had my notes and gave me his number. This is basically a "for no reason" call. *Okay, c'mon Bree . . . Now. Okay . . . Now.*

My finger is still frozen. I decide to recite the alphabet backward and once I get to "A" I'll call him. As I'm reversing LMNOP in my head, my phone startles me by ringing and buzzing in my hand.

CHIP RYAN.

"Uuuuuuugh." I shove the phone under my pillow but then rationalize that if I can handle talking to Chip, I can definitely manage a call to Sean afterward. I snatch my phone back and answer.

"Hello?"

"Hey Bree, it's Chip."

"Yeah, I know," I reply. "Your name's still programmed into my phone." *So I know when NOT to answer.* "What's up? Actually, how about this: Say everything you need to say and then we're going to be done with it. Got it?" In spite of my shaking hand and my heart beating right behind my uvula, I am empowered.

Silence.

"Chip?"

"Okay, sure," he says. His uncertainty is funny, considering he's had months to prepare. "Listen. I miss hanging out with you and I feel like you haven't let me apologize."

Another pause.

"Okay, fine. Go ahead."

"Really?" He exhales loudly into the phone. "I know I was a jerk but I had every right to be mad. You didn't call or answer my texts and you stood me up. What else was I supposed to think?"

"And?"

"Okay. Either way, I was an ass. I shouldn't have acted like that and I'm sorry, I really am. It's embarrassing. I had to tell my dad what happened because of the driver's side window and the fact that I broke my wrist. Then, of course he told my mom who made me see an anger management counselor every Thursday for the rest of the summer. It was all pretty stupid but I guess it was good. I'm not that guy. You know I'm not. I miss you."

I let the pause linger to make sure he's done.

"Thanks for apologizing and I'm sorry too. Sorry I had personal shit going on and avoided you and didn't call to give you a heads-up. I'm even more sorry that I had to witness you getting all psycho on me. Thanks for calling and I hope you enjoy the rest of your senior year. Okay?"

"Well, wait. Can we hang out and talk? Maybe this weekend? Prom is only two months away and I'm not sure if you got my message last week but I was thinking maybe we could go, just as friends, or whatever?"

"Chip. No. That's not happening."

"Is that also a no on meeting up to talk more?"

"Yes, Chip—."

"Yes?" he asks.

"No, Chip. I meant yes that it's a no. It's definitely a no. We're not going to be hanging out like old times or like friends or like *anything*. Thanks for the apology."

I click End Call before he can mansplain another second. I type Sean's number, pressing Send before I can change my mind. My heart is pumping hard but slows down as I finish my backward alphabet while waiting for him or his voicemail to pick up. I get to GF . . . ED and he answers.

Instead of "hello" he gives a long drawn out "yooooo." His voice is so cute and I stifle a nervous laugh.

"Hey Sean, it's Bree. Hughes."

"Bree, can I tell you something?"

"Um suuuure?"

"I have you programmed into my phone and I don't know any other Brees. You can use your first name. We're cool like that."

"Oh okay, got it."

"Funny you called, I was going to call you in a little bit."

My adrenaline is instantly leveled up. "You were?" I ask.

"Yes, is that okay? Or are you only allowed to call me?"

I flip the phone away from my mouth so he can't hear my long anxious exhale. I fan myself to keep the blood vessels beneath my face from flooding.

"Well, I called first so I win. I guess you owe me some sort of prize. I'll need to collect it by the end of the week. Anyway . . ."

"Sure, we'll see about that prize. So, what's up with Prom Court? Jane told me after school that you're taking Kallie's spot because she doesn't want to be with Molly. What's up with that?"

"Kallie's spot? No, actually I guess I'm taking Maisey's spot. Funny how fast rumors get twisted."

"Oh, that's kind of a bummer. I was pretty jazzed to see Molly get dethroned by the Morgan-ador."

"Yeah, me too, but I feel bad for her, she knew it was a joke." I want to go into everything that happened today but don't want to push it. I'm talking to someone way out of my social league here. I don't need to remind him.

"Yeah, you're probably right. That sucks."

"I know, right? So, what do I have to do? It says there's just one meeting and the pep rally. That's it? For some reason, I thought it'd be more than that."

"Nope, that's it. There's a meeting next Tuesday after school. I guess Prom Committee has a couple ideas that we have to yay or nay. Everyone knows it doesn't matter though, they're just going to do what they want. So, who cares? I don't even have a date yet. I gotta get on it—I'd sort of told Jane I'd go with her as friends but then she backed out because of some other guy. Don't you think it's pretty sad to be on Prom Court and not have a date?"

I think it's pretty sad that Jane's turning down Sean Mills. Naturally, this would be the part where I admit I don't have a date yet either. *Awk-weird.*

"Well, you have time, it's like two months away. If you get desperate you can always ask a cousin. I don't have a date yet either so that's probably what I'll do."

He laughs. "Oh okay, so you don't know who you're going with. That's cool."

He says it like it actually is a cool thing. As if it's by choice. I get another awkward don't-know-what-to-say-after-that feeling, so I change the subject to avoid more weirdness.

"So, next Tuesday after school. Guess I'll see you there."

"Sure, sounds good." He hangs up. One of these days I hope to tell him I hate that. I say good-bye to the air, then give my pillow a hug and whisper, "Sean Mills doesn't have a date." And then a little bit louder, "Woo-hoo!"

EIGHT

It's Wednesday after school. Less than a week till the Prom meeting, which means six days until Kallie and I are forced to interact since she's not budging on this silent treatment thing. It sucks. I want to be excited with her about being on court together. I want to ask her if she's inviting her parents to the pep rally. I want to be able to ask for boy advice—as long as she's not trying to pawn me off on a random friend of Todd's. At lunch, I almost spilled everything to Sam and Kendall, the girls I sit with, but it didn't feel right. They'd probably tell me I'm was out of my mind to think Sean would go for me anyways. Sam and Kendall are the kind of girls that talk about the really popular guys and girls as if they're the cast of an E! reality show. They hate worship them, and it's kind of uncomfortable. So instead of entertaining them with my first world guy problems, I listened to their dress shopping plans for the weekend. Sam's single because our school doesn't have enough out-lesbians or bi-girls to pick from, and Kendall just broke up with her boyfriend so they're putting a whole group thing together. It's something they're trying to make cool by calling it "Prom: Parties of One." I'm all for them debunking any stigmas about going solo, but I told them I'm holding out for a date.

****

After school I throw on a sweatshirt, grab my laptop, and head over to Java Joint to study for next week's Bio test.

47

For a coffee shop on a Wednesday night, this place is packed. I scan the room and spot an open seat to throw my stuff on before ordering. As I'm waiting for my order I get caught up in a daydream about Sean walking in wearing a tuxedo, playing his guitar. He walks toward me and the crowd and even the tables part in a red sea sort of fashion. He's singing that song "Will You Marry Me?" but changes the words to "Will You Go to Prom with Me." Molly Chapman, Jane Hulmes, Sam, and Kendall sit at one of the tables clapping and wiping tears because it's such a touching moment. The other coffee drinkers and employees do a cutesy flash mob dance that's sure to go viral. When he finishes, he kneels down with a rose. "Bree. Will you accept this promposal rose?" My coffeehouse fantasy has me deciding whether or not to ask Sean for an encore or just say, "Yes, Sean Mills, of course I'll go to Prom with you."

It's such a corny daydream that I have to bite back a smile. In real life, I'm gripping an iced latte, heading for my table, trying to give off a vibe that says I'm comfortable hanging out at a coffee shop by myself.

And out of nowhere there's a tight grip and tug on my ankle and I'm falling. Something breaks my fall and I'm knocked into the reality where a backpack strap has somehow weaved itself around my ankle. The harsher reality is Sean Mills's lap. Yes. Real-life Sean. With my latte. A *large* chai latte. On his lap. And me. I. Am. Mortified. For a quick second I wonder if I'm stuck in my daydream or it's a bad dream or something else, anything else. Nope. I'm still here on my knees staring at Sean's wet crotch. If I were in a sitcom, this is the part where I'd be all "Omigod I'm so sorry!" and try to dry his button fly with one napkin or the sleeve of my shirt.

But everything inside me stays doe-in-headlights as Sean winces and says, "I'm so glad this is iced." He laughs and grabs a pullover he had strewn over his seat to pat dry his pants. "Bree, are *you okay?*"

Silence. I want to say something but my mouth isn't working.

"Bree?"

"Um, omigod, I'm so sorry, are *you* okay?" I ask as he pulls me up to my feet. He uses his shoe to slide a few scattered ice cubes to the side. I glare at my feet as if the backpack on the floor owes me an apology. "I can't believe I did that. I'm really so sorry. What can I do, I mean, um . . ."

"I think I'll be all right. But you might have to promise me your firstborn in case I've lost my ability to procreate."

"Seriously? Are you really okay then because—"

"I'm just kidding, it's fine. These jeans are pretty heavy-duty, can't feel a thing. But since I don't have an extra pair of jeans, do you think you could drive me home?"

"Of course, I mean really, I should be offering you *my* jeans."

A barista sneers my way as she mops the coffee from the floor. I speed walk toward my table to grab my stuff and almost run right into Jane Hulmes, who, phone in hand, fingers and thumbs dancing away, is clearly walking and texting.

She lifts her head and sweeps over me with these gorgeous deep brown saucer eyes. If they weren't projecting that gleam of mean, I'd probably be offering to buy her a biscotti. "Ex*cuse* me Britney."

"Uhh-sorry?" I ask. I mean, really. She wasn't watching where she was going either. "Bree. My name's Bree."

"Oh yeah, I know that, my bad. Okay, well, excuse you. You *almost* ran into me."

"Sure. Sorry," I say with a tight smile as she turns on her high-heeled boot. I sigh and grab my stuff. As I'm walking back to Sean's table I realize I'm following Jane.

I hope she's not going where I think she's—

Both of us end up at Sean's table and, um, yeah, *awkward*. Sean tells Jane he's gotta go and is leaving with me. She shoots me another evil laser eye beam and I shrug, pretending to blend alongside two of the prettiest people at Belmont High.

Jane shifts her gaze from me to Sean. "You didn't drive? I can bring you."

"It's okay, I don't . . ." I say.

Sean says, "She's going my way anyway."

"Still. It's cool, Britta, I've got it."

My eyes bounce back and forth between Sean and Jane as I gnaw the inside of my cheek.

"Britta, like the water filters?" Sean asks Jane and rolls his eyes, "C'mon Jane. You know her name's Bree. I gotta get going. I'll see you in Geometry tomorrow."

"Fine." Her eyes bug out a little and she shrugs. "Well, try to have an answer for me by tomorrow please."

He slings his backpack over his shoulder and ushers me ahead using his free hand to hold open the door. I glimpse Jane out of my peripheral vision still standing at the table. I don't catch the look on her face, but in my mind it's a pretty sweet combination of pissed and envy.

Sean follows me to my car, an old silver Toyota Prius that Mom and Dad bought from Aunt Jen and gave me for Christmas my junior year. I slide into the front seat, and right before clicking the unlock door button a second time to let Sean in, I speed-throw a makeup bag, book of Shakespeare sonnets, plastic baggie of hair binders, and three water bottles into the backseat. I apologize to Sean for the messy car and again about the coffee, but he stops me and says he should be thanking me for getting him away from Jane.

"That girl thinks she can have what she wants just cause she's hot. She hijacked my study session with a sob story about how her supposed date is now backing out of Prom. Then says *she's free to go with me*—as if she's doing me a favor. I'm surprised she didn't slap me across the face when I told her I'd have to think about it. Her sense of entitlement is ridiculous." Sean directs me with a series of rights and lefts to get to his house.

"So, you didn't drive—what's up with that?" I ask.

Sean scoots the seat back and adjusts the seat belt. "My mom dropped me off. We share a car now, now that . . ." He looks out the window. "Since my dad lost his job last year and took off last month to . . . pffft, I don't know, I guess he's living with his sister in Wisconsin somewhere."

"That's funny," I say.

"Funny?"

"No, I mean funny because my parents just got divorced and my dad's living with his brother. It seems pretty lame."

"I guess. Lame. Yeah, if I was going to shirk my responsibilities and leave my family in the dust it'd have to be for something pretty badass, like joining a rock band or moving to LA to write music—not for my sister's basement."

"It really doesn't make sense if you think about it. Eff those guys," I say.

He laughs. "You're funny. It's this one," he says pointing to a small but cute ranch-style house only about five blocks away from my house.

"Did you know you lived so close to me? We're almost neighbors."

"Yeah," he answers. "I've seen you in your car a few times around here, so I figured you live close or deliver pizzas on the side."

"Sounds like you're kind of stalking me. Which is all fun and games until I see your fingers gripping my window on some dark rainy night."

"I might try that. Actually, we just moved here. Things got weird right before my dad left so we had to move and find somewhere to rent— long story, but we've been here about a month."

We make small talk in my car for a few more minutes. Then, as he gathers his backpack and sweatshirt and opens the car door, he turns toward me. "Do you want to hang out Friday?" The way he's squinting his eyes throws me off a little.

I squint back. "Are you *sure*?"

"Yeah," he answers, "it's just . . . um, I dunno, I didn't know if you already had plans or if you'd want to, I mean, it's okay if you don't, but, geez—I sound like an idiot, help me out here?"

I smile. "Yes, that sounds good. Friday. Got it."

"Okay, well thanks again for the ride and the free coffee for my pants."

"You're welcome—I aim to please."

"See ya later," he says and the car door squeaks to a thud.

Aim to please? Jesus. My stomach flutters anyway as I back out of his driveway and head home. A Maroon 5 song comes on and I crank the volume way up, popping my shoulders to the beat as I sing loud and slightly (okay, *way*) off-key all the way home.

NINE

Each day, Kallie's silence is louder and louder, and it seems forever until it's finally Friday. At our locker before last period, she's huffing as she bangs through her books and notebooks.

Her eyes rest on me for a split second then she lets out a long dramatic "Tsssssssst."

I'm tired of the tension, and feel bad for the things I said, but I'm still mad about what she said. I almost tell her to call me after school, or ask her to ride home with me instead of Todd. But five minutes in-between class is hardly enough time for any type of confrontation. Torn, anxious, yet pride intact, I leave our locker first and hold my poker face all the way to class. Score. I get my seat behind Sean and in front of Justin. For the first time since our fight, Kallie sits on the other side of the room, right behind Maisey.

Justin taps my shoulder and says, "Do I need to book you and Kallie on Dr. Phil? I heard you two are separated and she's cheating on you with Laura Rose, but only for now—while her and Chris are on another break."

"What*ever*. Mind your biz."

"Hey sorry," he says back, "I was just kidding. But if you need a new bestie, I'm more than happy to fill Kallie's spot—although I'm pretty sure her bra might be a liiittle too big for—"

Sean turns around. "Hey Conner, Dr. Phil just called and said he needs you for the 'my neighbor's a busybody' episode."

"Okay Mills," Justin says. "Point taken. But tell Phil I'll text him later for the deets." He leans back into his seat.

Sean flashes me a smile and looks like he's about to say something but Mr. Norderick taps his marker on the board. He assigns us sections to read aloud from Ginsberg's *Howl*. I've never read it before and it's pretty intense. Kallie throws me a scowl before reading with aggressive and hard-hitting inflections.

When Mr. N. looks to Maisey to read next, he walks over and taps on her desk with his highlighter.

Her head, resting on her hand and elbow, jerks up. "Don't!" She does a startled half jump out of her seat then sits back down. Her cheeks flush crimson and she mumbles, "Sorry, I fell asleep."

A hushed laughter waves through the room and someone squeaks from the back corner. Nord looks up with a quick glare then nods at Maisey. "No problem. I don't mind sleeping in my class but I can't imagine these desks are very comfortable. If you can please read your section Miss Morgan."

Maisey grabs her book and the bag at her feet. "Sorry, I gotta go. I'm not feeling good." She strides out of class head down, army green cargo pants frayed and skimming the floor as another squeak and a few laughs ring out from the class. The door slams behind her as Mr. N. crosses his arms and shakes his head. "I'm not sure what's going on here, but I'm assuming most of you are older than eight years old, so let's start acting like it."

Shandy Silvers finds a way to cut the tension by offering to read Maisey's section with a whiney baby voice that somehow sounds like she's reading a book about glittery ponies.

I look down to a folded piece of notebook paper on my desk. Kallie's two rows away and staring out the window so I turn to Justin who shoots me a blank stare from a doodle of an alien eating a sandwich. Biting my cheek, I unfold the paper. My eyes skim to the bottom. *Sean*. My heart does a quick hop and picks up speed.

Bree HUGHES—
Can I get a ride home

after school today?
Yes No Maybe
Circle one
PS—Yes = U will get the prize I owe U.
PS2—We still doing something tonight?
—Me (Sean Mills)

My face is a beet and even though his note is so seventh grade, it's also the cutest thing *ever*. I grab my pen and circle *Yes*, and then write, "Hope it's not coffee!!" I add a smiley face, and with confidence, I write *Yes* after his question about doing something tonight. I slide the note onto Sean's desk, brushing my wrist against his arm in the process. Mr. N. turns his back to write a couple notes on the whiteboard. He asks us to write down a few guidelines for a new assignment to free-write our own version of *Howl*.

When the bell rings, Sean and I walk the hallway together, which feels amazing except for the part about me wishing Kallie was excited for me too.

I get home after dropping Sean off and twist the rubber band around my wrist. He gave it to me on the car ride to his house saying it looks like a dumb prize but it's not and he'd tell me about it later. I slide the band between my thumb and forefinger and smile. I'm so into him that I'm kind of just content to just have a rubber band as a bracelet. Only Kallie would understand this so I lift my phone to call. I push a long exhale through my lips. My heart ticks faster and my nerves are harder to fight than the urge to call. Maybe tomorrow.

****

Sean holds the door open, and I duck into his maroon two-door Honda, trying to make sense of the whole friend zone vibe we've got going on tonight. It's kinda screwing with me.

Most guys I've hung out with never want to talk, or only talk about themselves or are just trying to figure out a way to give me a back massage at the end of the night that'll lead to *other stuff.* Apparently I've been hanging out with the wrong guys. Sean was actually looking at me when I talked, wasn't checking his phone every five minutes, and asked a lot of questions. Stuff about my summer job, my parents, and even about me and Kallie's fight.

"Thanks again for dinner," I say.

"You're welcome, again. I mean *De nada.* It's the first time I've ever been to Muy Mexicano. Maybe the last. Those Spanish guys with the sombreros and guitars really showed me up."

"I think they were Mexican though, not Spanish."

"Okay, got it." Sean nods but I can tell he has no idea what I'm talking about so I let him know that my dad's family is Mexican too, which means they're from Mexico, not Spain.

"Sorry, Dutch and Norwegian guy learning curve over here. But yeah, I speak English but I'm not from England. Makes sense."

Sean asks if I speak Spanish and then I give the whole spiel I always give after I tell people I'm Mexican. The whole thing where I'm all, "No, I don't speak Spanish, but it's not my fault! My dad almost always speaks English unless he's with my grandparents."

I shrug. "I learned more Spanish when I took it in tenth grade than I did growing up. Some people might think I'm a terrible Mexican, but whatever. It used to bother me but I'm over it."

He pulls the car into reverse and the curve of his forearm muscle is almost—no, it *is* distracting. I didn't even think I was into that sort of thing. But now, running my hand up his arm is close to the top of my to-do list. Right below kissing him.

Sean glances over. "You okay? Trust me, it doesn't bother me that your Spanish isn't fluent." He smiles and focuses back on the road.

"I know. I mean, yes. I'm fine. I was just thinking that *I* actually prefer your guitar playing over Muy Mexicano's, that's all."

"Thanks. You looked like you were thinking too hard. I thought maybe I offended you and you changed your mind about going to a movie."

"I haven't seen a movie at a theater in a long time. I'm still game."

"Good. So . . ."

"So," I say, trying to fill in the semi-awkward pause. "Were you serious about thinking I should call Kallie first?"

"Well, I wasn't saying you should forget everything, but it might be best to just, man up—or woman up—and call."

I sigh. "You're probably right. But I'm still gonna think about it. I hate being wrong, and it wasn't only my fault, but I guess I hate fighting even worse."

"Did your parents fight a lot before they got divorced?"

My stomach dips and I flick the button of my purse a few times. "Kind of. Well, yes. Or no, not kind of, but kind of *a lot*." I slide the vent of his fan to aim toward me but realize it's not on. The air got sort of warm in here.

"Mine too. They still do. I've heard my mom yelling at my dad over the phone a few times. It's always about money."

"Surprisingly, I haven't heard much between them since he left, except for the time my mom left a message saying he better pick his stuff up or she was going to sell it. I'm sure they're both happier. I think my mom got tired of my dad being tired of her. Something like that." The stupid sad feeling scrapes at the bottom of my gut, so I push it further into a corner. "You know what though, I'm just glad our toilet seat is always down and I can walk around in a bra."

He laughs and says, "You're lucky it's so simple."

"It has to be, otherwise I'd just be mad or sad about it all the time."

Sean pulls into the parking lot, his eyebrows scrunched. He studies the rows of cars driving up and down looking for an open space. "Sometimes I'm tired of being mad and sad about everything." He turns his head, locking eyes with me for a second before turning back to the lot. "Anything I say's between us, right?"

"Yes." The seriousness and vulnerability in his gaze catches my breath and pulls off another layer of my own unease. "Of course."

"Well . . ." He drums his fingers on the steering wheel. "My dad has a gambling problem and probably pills too, and it got bad after he lost

56

his job. My mom didn't even know how bad until our house got fore-closed on because he was supposed to be in charge of all the bills. I guess he hadn't paid on the house for almost a year or some shit like that. My mom freaked. She didn't even give him a chance. Nothing. She told him that dealing with his crap wasn't worth it if he was going to be lying and stealing too. That's why we moved."

"Oh gosh. I'm sorry, that sounds crazy. Is that when your dad moved to his sister's?"

"Yep. He hasn't called or texted since. Nothing."

"And he has your number?"

"Sure does."

"I'm sorry," I say. "What's the deal with dads anyway? It's not the same, but my dad kind of pulled that after he left. You'd think that living with someone all their life would make you want to call all the time to check in. I know my mom would. It took my dad almost a month to see how I was doing."

"Maybe our dads are in a secret club or something."

"Sounds like a cool club. I'll have to Google it."

"I think it's under d-bag meet-ups." Sean laughs, then nods as a car pulls out of a spot front and center to the theater marquee. "Hope nobody minds if I take the best damn spot in the lot."

I'm sitting in a movie theater next to Sean Mills, and he's not wearing a football uniform or swim trunks so this must be real. At first, I wasn't even sure if this was a date or not, but now I'm pretty sure it is. He paid for my tacos at Muy Mexicano and insisted on buying my movie ticket as well. I almost had to hire a lawyer to convince him to let me buy the popcorn and candy.

The movie sucks. It keeps shifting back and forth between some CIA agent's past and present and then flashing to some unrelated story about some unshowered teen-mom and her crying kid. Instead of trying to fig-ure out how the agent is related to the mom and boy, my head spins with the possibility of kissing Sean at the end of the night.

I hate first kisses. Or rather, I hate all the stress that leads up to a first kiss. I've never been kissed first. It's not that I'm some kiss-crazed control freak, but it's more about just wanting to get it over with. I'd rather not deal with that whole crazy "is he going to kiss me?" anxiety or the end of the night awkwardness with him wondering whether he should or shouldn't. My preference is to alleviate any anxieties on both parts. But, Sean's different. I've never really been on a date with someone I like this much already.

As I scoop a handful of popcorn and this CIA lady dashes through a parking garage with a briefcase in high heels, I second-guess myself for telling Sean so much. Maybe he thinks I'm a baby for fighting with Kallie. His issues are way worse than mine. Before my negative what-ifs start reproducing, I'm jolted back to the movie as a car spins and screeches after the woman who's still running.

"Why is she not kicking those heels off?" I whisper.

Sean smiles and slides his hand over the top of my thigh and under my hand, sending a wave of goose bumps up my calf.

"Hey, let's get out of here," he whispers. He clasps my hand.

I don't care if the movie lady drops her briefcase or makes it out of the parking garage, I just want *more Sean*. The palm of my hand gets hotter beneath the pads of his fingers. As he pulls me through the dark theater, I wonder who'll let go first. He answers the thought by dropping my hand, but it's a somewhat graceful transition into him pushing open the bulky theater door for me.

"I hope you weren't into that movie," Sean says. "I'm sorry. I told you, you should've picked it."

"Yeah, for a thriller, it wasn't very thrilling. As soon as my hot tamales were gone, I had nothing left to care about," I say. "I'm not sure I'll be able to sleep tonight knowing whether the lady gives the briefcase to the scientist or her grandma's bingo rival or whoever it belonged to."

Sean laughs as his phone buzzes and he reaches into his pocket for it. "Hmmmm . . . We could go to Monroe's? I guess he's having people over. That could be interesting or obnoxious, depending on how you look at it."

I get an anxious pit in my stomach that's inscribed *Not so good with the parties*. Ergh. *Fake it 'til you make it* flashes in my brain like a neon 7–Eleven sign.

58

I say, "Yeah, that sounds cool."

In Sean's car, I do a quick hair check and reapply my lip gloss—the shiny sticky, bubblegum smelling one reserved for special occasions like this. Sean calls Chris and asks for a reminder on where he lives and asks me to write down the directions. On our way, Sean looks over and asks me if I'm wearing the rubber band.

"I am and I will never take it off. Seriously, though, it's really just a rubber band, right? You totally cheated me out of a real prize."

"Aaaah ya got me. Well, sort of. I don't even know where it came from. It's been in my jacket pocket for a year or so. I couldn't throw it away, for some reason I kept thinking I'd need one day. So, it's kind of like a lucky rubber band."

He glances over and I hold his eye for a quick skeptical second.

"You got me. I guess I still owe you," he says.

"Actually maybe it is lucky. I better keep it. Don't even think about trying to take it back now." I start to feel a little more comfortable about the party as we get closer to Chris's house. Maybe it'd be good to talk to these people considering I have to meet with some of them this week at school for Prom stuff anyway. If Kallie's there maybe she'll talk to me, too.

We pull up to at least ten cars parked alongside the street leading up to Chris's house.

"Jesus," I mutter, "I guess his parents are out of town."

"Yeah, this is definitely more than a couple people over. You're still cool with going, right?" Sean asks.

"Yeah, of course," I say.

As we walk in, there are clusters of kids from school everywhere, including the corners and lining the walls. Not just the Molly/Jane clique that I figured would be running the party. We squeeze through a crowd by the door and two girls from school say hi so I let my guard down, smile back, and scan the room for anyone else I might know. Mainly Kallie. But there's no sign of her glossy black hair that usually shines so hard it bounces the light off it. Chris Monroe catches my eye from across the room, looks at Sean next to me and walks over.

"Hey guys," he says slapping Sean on the side of the arm. "Bree. You're in my Bio class. You never talk though."

Sean smirks and slaps Chris's shoulder. "Maybe you should shower more. At least every other day, bro. Then you too, can get your very own . . ." Sean trails off.

I interject to save him while taking a split second to bask in the idea that I am Sean's *very own something*. "Yeah, I do try to talk to the *showered ones* only. Sure are a lotta people here," I say tiptoeing over the crowd.

"I know," Chris says. "For every one guy I told, an extra five showed up. I'm gonna hafta start kickin' people outta here if it gets any crazier."

Sean tells him to let him know if he needs any help and Chris says there's beer and soda in the kitchen if we can make our way through the masses. We squeeze through a bunch of people barraging Sean with fist bumps and high fives. The kitchen's a bright yellow room that'd be pretty spacious if it weren't sardine-packed with high schoolers and probably some guys from the community college.

Sean rifles through a chunky blue cooler. "Any requests?"

"Coke or a bottle of water is fine." I do not pride myself on my alcohol tolerance. No way I'm going to drink anything that could lead to me singing show tunes on the coffee table or getting sick in front of him and his friends.

He passes me a Coke and grabs one for himself. "I guess we're both sober tonight huh?"

"The last time I drank didn't end well for any of the parties involved, so I'm sitting this one out."

"Yeah, makes sense. Last time I drank, I woke up with a hangover and—"

Someone yells across the kitchen. "Yo Mills—you D.D. tonight?" It's Todd White. Molly Chapman is leaning on him, wearing a tight pink T-shirt and equally tight jean skirt. If he moves, she'll fall down, big red cup and all.

"Nah, man," Sean yells back, "I'm not gonna be good for a sober cab tonight—sorry bro."

Molly yells, "Don't worry, I'm not drunk! I can drive him home. I can drive everyone home. Call me a bus!" She ruffles his hair.

Kallie's definitely at work. No way would this be happening if she was here.

"Oh shit, I hope he doesn't let her drive." Sean laughs.

"Yeah, good call," I say, "but by the looks of it, I think she'd give Todd a piggyback ride home, if he asked for it."

We laugh and head outside. There are a few people around a fire pit and some empty chairs so we grab two.

"So, is this everything you dreamed it'd be?" I ask.

"Not sure yet. The night's young." His eyes give off that smiley vibe and his smile looks like trouble. The good kind. "What do you think? Do you think our drunk friends are more exciting than a lady, a briefcase, and her long lost son?"

Instead of telling him that these are more his than *our* friends, I laugh. "I had no idea that kid was supposed to be her long lost son."

We talk for a little bit until I realize my Coke's empty and it's been a while since I've used the restroom. It feels like I've been holding it since last Wednesday.

"I'm going to find a ladies' room and I'll be right back."

"Okay. Don't get lost." He raises his Coke and winks.

"Excuse me. Just gotta squeeze through here. *Sorry.*" My shoulder leads me sideways through the kitchen group and thankfully I don't run into Todd again or Molly stuck on him like one of his chauncy little bow ties. I scan the crowded rooms for a bathroom. All I find is a coat closet and a bathroom already taken by two girls sharing a cigarette. "Oops," I say, closing the door. At the end of the hall is a staircase. I check my blind spots to make sure no one's watching, and rush upstairs where there has to be a clean, unoccupied bathroom. Voices are muffled behind one of the doors so I twist the knob of the next one.

Yes. A bathroom. Clean. Vanilla candle scent wafting through the air. No pee on the seat. Score.

As I'm washing my hands, a girl's sobs muffle through the wall. A guy speaks in-between her sobs. I dry my hands and tilt my ear against the wall. The guy is arguing something about waiting for a better time. The rise and fall of their voices, her crying, and the familiarity of his voice has me pressing my ear even harder against the wall.

The girl asks, "Then why'd we just do that again?" She ends the question with a rising whimper.

The guy answers her by telling her to calm down. "People are gonna hear you," he says.

She speaks again, "I love you and it's not fair we're hiding everything." And then she's muffled again under the sobs. *Did she say secrets and promises or seasons and Prom dresses?*

I can hear him again. "Not yet. I told you. Just let me figure it out." *Damn, who is that?*

"Before Prom, right? That's what you said," the girl says.

"Shit, I didn't know it was gonna be so complicated. She's got everything all planned out already. It sucks," he says.

"Everything in my life sucks right now. You have no idea. What about me?" Her words get louder and bitchier, and a little slurry. Her voice is familiar too but I can't quite place it.

I step back from the wall because being nosey is only worth it if it's something good. This is some kind of tortured breakup makeup relationship. But just as I'm double-checking my reflection, the guy's voice says something that sounds way too much like "Kallie." My eyebrows scrunch as I press my ear against the wall.

"If Kallie finds out . . ." He *is* talking about Kallie. There's only one that I know of in our school. "She's going through a tough time right now and the last thing I can do is break up with someone whose mom's really sick. Let's just wait a little longer. You better not say anything."

Wait. Mrs. Vate—sick? What's he talking about? Todd. It's Todd. And it must be Molly in there. Oh. My. God. Todd's cheating on Kallie with Molly. He just slept with her and it doesn't sound like it was the first time. In a matter of five seconds I go from listening to teen TV show drama through a wall to hearing way more than I'd ever want to know.

I bolt from the bathroom to the stairs and shove my hand into my purse. I rush down the stairs, my eyes darting back and forth as my fingers flip through lip balms, receipts, and keys for my phone. This is going to crush Kallie. Right as I lift the phone from my bag, my whole body is jolted as I slam into something. My breath is knocked out of my chest with a loud gasp. A blur of silky blonde hair and pink screams and tumbles down the stairs. I stare in horror at the pink heap at the bottom of the stairs. It's Molly. How could she have been coming *up* the stairs when—

"What the hell's going on?" I turn and a puffy tiger-eyed Jane's coming down the stairs behind me, twisting messy tangles of wavy dark hair into her fists, the light catching her auburn highlights. "Shit, are you okay Moll?"

Todd's head appears over her shoulder. "Jane, wait. I'm not even finished talking to you."

Molly jumps up, dusts herself off, and starts laughing. "Can't feel a thing. Oh yeah!"

"I'm so sorry," I say. "I was just coming down the stairs."

"Doing what?" Jane asks, "Eavesdropping?" She glances over her shoulder at Todd. "I told you I heard something." She meets my eyes with a sneer, "It's your little friend Kallie's BFF."

Todd tugs at the collar of his black shirt and smooths his hands over his jeans. "Bree?" asks Todd, "What are *you* doing here?"

"Yeah, no kidding, what are you doing here *Brittney*?" Jane slurs, "Just because you're on Prom Court doesn't mean you're all of a sudden invited to our parties."

Anger and embarrassment rise in my chest and heat my face. If I could melt through the stairs and somehow end up back in my movie seat, that'd be great.

"Where the heck have you guys been? I've been looking aaaall over for you." Molly laughs. "I am *so* not going to be able to drive us home. I shouldn't've had those beer coolers."

Todd rolls his eyes. "For fuck's sake, seriously, Molly? You need to get out more. You've had *a* beer and *half* a HotShotz."

Molly curves her goofy smile into a fake pout. "Stop yelling at me."

Todd looks to me, "Bree, can we talk for a sec?" He pushes a sandy blond curl off his forehead sounding more like I'm the one in trouble, not him.

"What the hell would you need to talk to her for?" asks Jane.

Before I can respond to any of them, Sean appears at the bottom of the stairs, meeting my eyes with a smile held up by one corner of his mouth.

"Sean!"

"Sean."

"SEEEEEAN!" All three of them say in unison.

"Hey, guess this is where the party's at, huh?" says Sean.

Clearing my throat, I prepare for some kind of magical word formation to tumble out. "Ummmm . . ."

Clearly, dealing with cheating love triangles isn't one of my hidden talents.

Jane shuffles past me on the stairs and throws her arm over Sean's shoulder. "We were just wondering how Britta got here? Don't tell me she's with you again?"

"Again?" asks Todd. "Where've I been? You guys dating or something?"

Sean ducks out from under Jane's arm and smiles, "Yeah Bree, how did you get here? First you're sitting by me at the movies, now we're at the same party. Something's up."

I know he's kidding and sure, laughing seems logical, but just standing here has me feeling like I'm in a crowded, sweaty, everybody's-carrying-bags-and-babies kind of elevator. I'm on the top floor, out of breath, and all the floor buttons are lit up.

My heart is ticking with furious beats that are way too close together. The ticking becomes a thud and I can't slow it down. There's a fist punching my throat from the inside and I can't breathe with everyone looking at me.

My feet kick into flight mode and I'm down the last two steps, bumping Molly's shoulder as she's straightening her skirt. I push past Sean and Jane taking extra care not to make any more eye contact. Squeezing and turning my body through conversations and red cups, I weave my way back toward the front door.

Sean's voice calls out, "Bree. Where're you goin'?"

My body doesn't stop moving until Chris Monroe's door is shut behind me and a line of cars are at my back. I collapse onto the curb by Sean's car, and squeeze my eyes shut. My nails dig into my forearms and I wanna tuck all the different thoughts and ideas rushing my brain into the corner pocket of my stomach, but it feels like there's not enough room. I suck air through my nose and out of my mouth in a slow stream but everything's all jerky and jagged as *don't cry don't cry don't cry* loops in and out.

My breathing slows and I congratulate myself for not getting too deep in the curbside air-heaving dramatics. I can breathe again. I'm fine. I'm okay.

Saying yes to this party was a mistake. I don't know who I'm the most mad at right now. Jane for being such a shithead or Todd for being a slimy cheating dog pig? And then there's Kallie who's been so oblivious. Molly too. And that whole deal about Kallie's mom. *What is wrong with these people?* And where is Sean? He probably should've run out here after me. Would I even want him to? I rake my hand through my hair. It's tangly and slightly wet at my hairline from sweat. No, I'm glad he can't see me like this. I'm a mess. I'm the one I should be most mad at. I'm the idiot. I should be back there calling those guys out on all their bullshit, instead of punking out with some crybaby move.

A rhythmic swish and the sound of heels clicking the pavement slices through my neurosis.

Palming the coarse concrete of the curb with one hand, I peer from the side of Sean's car. Immediately my body jerks back, freezing into hiding as Jane's figure passes by. The clicking of her heels gets farther away but then she spins around and paces the street, peering into car windows.

She settles on a red car in front of Sean's and leans against the driver's side checking herself out in the side view mirror, then pulling a phone from her oversized sparkly silver bag.

"Sean. Where'd you say your car was?" She pauses. "Nothing. I'm fine. It's red, right? Maroon? Oh. Okay, same difference. Bye."

She clicks her heel into the bottom ridge of the red car's tire and dials another number. "What're you doing there? Oh. Can I talk to my mom, please?" Jane pushes herself off the car. She exhales a low growl and begins pacing again. Back and forth from the red car to the blue one across the street. Her breathing is loud and clipped, almost like mine just was.

Damn, this girl gets so worked up about everything.

"Mom, what're you doing? . . . Okaaaay, well, why's Dad over? . . . Yeah, I know—I just—" She wipes away a line of tears though her voice doesn't give away that she's even crying. "*Mom*. Right, I know. But you said you'd stay at his place when you wanted to spend time together. Well, I *was* sleeping over but now I'm not. I'm coming home. No, like, now. Tonight—in like an half hour . . . No, I can't. Molly's aunt's in town or something. I just want to come home. No, I'm not being a bitch, I just thought—it's only been a couple weeks and we had an agreement. You said he wouldn't be at our house. I'm trying *too*, Okay? Plus, I had a dumb fight with my boyfriend. No, I'm fine, I just want to come home. Fine, but he'll be gone before I get there, right? Okay, thanks . . . Love you too." She stuffs the phone back into her purse, walks up and kicks the tire of the blue car. "Ow. Sunuvabitch." She yanks her foot out of her strappy silver heel, wiggles her toes, then shoves them back into the shoe. Slipping down into a squat, she screams into her handbag, "Fuck you. Fuck my life. Just fuck it." There's a couple short sobs and then Jane jumps back up, wipes her eyes, and brushes her jeans off with renewed energy. She adjusts the shoulder strap of her bag and walks back toward Chris's house with a final, fiery drawn-out growl.

My phone vibrates into a ring in my bag. I pull it out, poking the silence button before it shouts me out to Jane and her wrath.

SEAN MILLS.

I pause as Jane steps back into the house.

"Hello?" I whisper into my phone.

"Bree. Where'd you go? Why'd you leave like that?"

"Ugh, I don't know. I don't even want to know. That's the problem. I know those guys are your friends, but what jerks."

"Wait. You don't know where you are?" Sean asks.

"Oh sorry, um . . . I'm outside. By your car."

He sighs loudly into the phone. "On my way."

Click.

Definitely not a good time to confront Todd or Jane. I have no idea what's going on. Can't even call Kallie right now. Maybe when I get home or in the morning so I can decide what to say. Okay. Definitely in the morning.

Sean steps out of the house and jogs my way. I swipe my hands over the ass of my jeans to brush off any dirt or debris from the curb. Sean clicks the doors of his car unlocked and opens mine. I slide in and hope he'll talk first. There's not really a way to explain why I threw a mini-tantrum without exposing Todd and Jane. It's really best friend code that I tell Kallie first.

Insert twenty to thirty seconds of silence that feels like five minutes.

Sean clears his throat as he clicks on his seat belt. "Bree, I hope you don't mind, but we have to give 'those jerk' friends of mine rides home. I'm kind of stuck. All three of them. Is that cool?" He sounds annoyed and I'm hoping it's not directed at me *entirely*.

"Yeah, of course."

Sean drives up the street, parks in front of Chris's door and honks twice. "If we have to wait longer than a minute, we can ditch them," he says with a short laugh.

Instead of saying *"One can only hope,"* I lean back against my seat, a little more relaxed because he's actually laughing a little. I tell him he's a good friend and next time I'm wasted I'll call him for a ride too. He smiles.

"Sorry for calling them jerks. I know they're your friends."

He says we'll talk about it after we drop them off, but then adds, "Is it okay for me to drop you off last. I think I'll need some sober company."

I say, "No problem," as Todd, Jane, and Molly amble down the walkway of Chris's house. Sean presses his palm against the horn again and Molly jumps. Jane walks ahead of Todd and Molly, piercing eye holes into Sean's car.

Jane swings my door open and asks, "Hon, is it okay if I sit in the front? I get *so* carsick and I'd hate to throw up in Sean's car."

She's gotta be fucking kidding me. "Yeah, sure. Fine." I grab my handbag so I can move to the back.

"Wait," says Sean. "Actually, no. Bree stays up front. There's grocery bags back there so if anyone pukes, they can use those. She's the only other sober one here, so I need her to help me navigate." He winks. So, so glad he's not mad at me.

Jane huffs as I slide my seat forward. She squeezes in behind me with another obnoxious sigh. Molly and Todd hop in on Sean's side.

I tap Sean's knee and mouth "Thank you."

He throws me a quick smile and says, "All right, who's going where first?"

"You can drop me off last or well . . . whatever," Jane says. "Just not first. That should be good, I mean, it makes the most sense."

Sean and I laugh the majority of the ride. The three of them are pretty funny in a sloppy entertaining kind of way. Molly makes a big gag out of trying to sound intellectual while talking about old *iCarly* reruns. They're like hyenas back there reenacting an episode about pranking that I must've missed back in middle school. While Molly racks her brain for more plots to what she deems "serious *classic* comedy, you guys" we drop Todd off.

When Sean finally reaches Jane's house, after she directs us the wrong way twice, she gets all bitchy again.

"What the hell, don't pull in the driveway!" Jane yells from the back. "Go to the curb."

"What's the big deal?" asks Molly.

In the driveway, a man and woman are lip-locked and leaning up against the side of a black SUV. The man, tall with dark wavy hair, hops into the driver's side, and the woman heads back toward the house, then turns and waves.

"Back up, hurry, *back up*," says Jane.

"I am, I was about to," says Sean. "Chill out, you guys are the drunk ones. I can drive just fine. My lights are on, it's not like the guy's gonna hit me." Sean backs the car out of the driveway and pulls over to the curb as the car backs out, then drives away.

"Holy shit," laughs Molly. "You didn't tell me your mom has a boyfriend. Finally she's getting some action."

"Seriously, Molly. Shut *up*. That's the last thing I want to think about right now."

"Wait, that's not your dad?" I ask over my shoulder.

"No, what do you care?"

I turn around and Molly subtly shakes her head "no." The urgency in her eyes stops me from asking another question. Molly flicks me in the shoulder.

"Well, I'd love to sit here and discuss my family tree and my mom's social life, but I'm fucking tired. Can you unlock the door and let me out?"

"No problem." I push the unlock button and barely lean forward so she can squeeze out.

Jane oozes sappy good-byes to everyone but me.

Sean yells after her, "Britta said good-bye *Jaaane*!"

Without turning around or looking back, she sticks up her middle finger and waves it back and forth in one of those pageant-style waves.

"Wow, she's really into you," says Sean.

"Her name's *Bree*," slurs Molly. "Don't you know uughhh, my stomach hurts, try not to go so fast."

"So, that wasn't Jane's dad?" I ask.

"No, that's why I stopped you. She never talks about him. She told me her dad died when she was in kindergarten but then once a few years ago, her older sister said he left when they were kids. Jane's funny like that so I never ask personal stuff."

"Funny?" I snort. "More like bitchy. Whatevs."

Molly moans again. "Do we—where are those bags?" the pep in her voice wilts away with each word.

"Oh no, hell no. I don't do vomit." Sean swerves over to the curb, slams the brakes and opens his door.

I jump out and help Sean usher Molly out of the car. "Just wait here," I tell him. "I got this." I guide Molly to the edge of someone's lawn.

Molly groans. A waft of crisp green grass reaches my nose at the same moment she heaves a supersize vomity sludge onto the curb, the grass, and my purple Converse. I jump back and stop inhaling before I get a whiff of Homecoming Queen and Class Veep barf.

She gags, "I'm so sorry. Oh God, I'm being punished."

I kneel down and flip my hair back, feeling more like I'm the one being punished. Molly's hair is strewn about and stuck to the sides of her puke slobbery mouth. Using my own bare ungloved fingers, I peel the half-silky, half-slimy wet mattes of hair stuck to her cheeks. I reach for the black ponytail holder that's usually on my wrist. Shit. I'd replaced it with my "lucky" rubber band.

"Hey Molly, do you have a hair tie?"

"You're so—uuugghhhehh-buuuugh ughhh, BLECH. Ohhhh, God. Here, take this." She slides a yellow-corded tie off her wrist. I wrap it twice around her sticky hair and it snaps. *Figures.* I take my Sean Mills rubber band off my wrist, sigh, and tie it into her hair.

In-between the next and last hurl of green slush, she tells me in a drippy slur, "You're so pretty Bree, we should hang out more."

Molly finishes her last heave, wipes the corners of her mouth—then a "fuck it" thought bubble pretty much appears over her head because she pulls her shirt up past her neck and does a full swipe of her face and chin. I try not to stare at the neon pink bra and her two perfect—nope, not perfect, boobs. Yay. One is totally bigger than the other. *Cool girls. They're just like us!* Molly drops her shirt and hiccups. Well, it sounds like little hiccups but then I realize it's the crescendo unto a full-on sob. Oh wow. Molly's drunk crying about Todd. And how he's her first love and they're *hiccup* supposed to be, should be, *sob* planning Prom and college, and *long-drawn-out wail* getting engaged.

I should be the one crying here. So much for kissing Sean—or Sean kissing me. Molly's cries vibrate her whole body and I wish she knew who she was really crying about. I doubt she'd even remember if I interjected in-between her sobs that the love of her life is not only dating Kallie, but also screwing Jane, the girl who's supposed to be her best friend. Instead of saving Molly with a truth bomb, I throw in a few "Yeah, that's toughs" and "Oh, you'll be okays" while half carrying her back to the car.

TEN

Saturday morning. I wake up with a mental hangover. And Mom peeking her head through my creaky door.

"Get up. Let's get brunch and do some shopping."

"C'mon Mom." I hug my knees under my blanket.

"We need some girl time," she sings. I roll over and grab my phone. 11:09 a.m. Feels like 6:30.

"Sure. Give me twenty minutes and I'll be down." I'm pretty sure that I haven't gone shopping with Mom since . . . I'm not even sure. Maybe tenth grade.

As she closes the door, an ever so faint gust of Molly Chapman's puke slivers past my nostrils.

What a shitty night. Instead of spending more time with Sean and maybe, just maybe, learning what his lips would feel like on mine, my lips got to feel what it would be like to get puked on. No, seriously. Molly puked in my face when she hugged me at the car door. So, as Sean walked Molly to her door, unlocking it for her and practically pushing her into her house, I realized—no, *smelled*—that no one was going to be hanging out with me anymore. The night was over. Aside from having to wipe my own face with my shirt, somehow my hair had sprayed puke in it, my shoes were inside a canvas grocery bag in the backseat, and my head kept reeling about the whole scene at the party and my next move.

As Sean got back into the car I said, "I guess my house should be your next stop—I'm a mess."

"I figured, you gotta lay off the booze."

"Yeah, I smell like beer and Hotshotz had a baby that was born in a sweat sock."

We laughed a little and he even apologized for bringing me to the party as he opened my door to let me out of his car. This was the part where I would've been stressing about the kiss. Now I just wondered how bad he thought I reeked as I tried to get the hell out of his smell-line.

"Thanks for everything. The night wasn't so bad, really," I called over my shoulder, speed walking so he wouldn't try to walk me to my door or anything.

In the shower, I realize my arm muscles are sore from lugging Molly around. As soon as I pop the cap from my shampoo bottle, I gag. The sweet apple scent is way too reminiscent of hurl. I end up grabbing an unscented bar of soap instead.

First thing I do after my shower is check my phone. No call or text from Sean, not that I care. I mean, he did say he'd call today but I hate the idea of waiting around for him, or any guy, to call.

"Breeeeee! You ready?" My mom calls up the stairs.

"Just a minute, trying to find a shirt." I yell back. I'm glad I have her to occupy my time today. As I rifle through my drawers, a framed picture of Kallie and me stares me down. We're goofing around, holding up fish we'd caught the summer before seventh grade. Dad took the picture while we pretended we were going to kiss the fish. Kallie's fish did a floppy bounce out of her fingers and she actually did end up kissing it. We laughed so hard and Mom had tears running down her face.

I'm calling Kallie as soon as I get back home today.

Over omelets and orange juice my mom asks how things went with Sean last night. Maybe the smell of vomit was some sort of truth serum because I spill everything: The Jane and Todd cheating scandal, Drunk Molly, and my puke-soaked shoes. Mom gives me a short lecture on hanging out with drunk kids mixed in with an "I'm proud of you for making some good choices" speech.

"So can we look at some Prom dresses today or what? You can't be a Prom Queen wearing jeans and tennis shoes."

"Why not? I mean, I don't even have a date."

"Hmmm," she says. "When is this Sean guy going to ask you? I'm guessing he doesn't have a date if he's taking you to the movies and on drunk driver ride-alongs."

"I don't think he has a date but that doesn't mean he's going to ask me, and if he doesn't, it's not the end of the world."

"Are you sure about that?"

"Okay, maybe it would suck a little. A lot. But if I don't have a date, I'll just go with Sam, Kendall, and some other kids as a group. It'll be fun.

"That sounds fun, but if he doesn't ask you," she smiles, "*you* should ask *him*."

"Just thinking about asking him gives me hives. I don't want to put myself out there like that, plus it's *Prom*. I want to be asked."

"Yeah, you're right hon, you deserve it. There's still time, so I'll keep my fingers crossed."

We thumb through a few racks of dresses at Macy's but I don't try any on. Instead, Mom buys me a new pair of purple Converse and says it's my "Good Choice" award. I give a short acceptance speech at the counter. The cashier looks confused when I thank the alcohol industry and Molly for eating something green for dinner.

It's really, really nice to see my mom laugh.

As we drive the forty-minute ride home from the mall, I practice a hundred different ways to tell my estranged best friend that her hot and amazing boyfriend is a dog-pig. Unfortunately no matter how I recite it, it all sounds the same.

The second I get home, I run upstairs to my room to check my phone. I'd purposely left it on my nightstand to charge. It seemed like a strategic plan that wouldn't have me checking it every two minutes at the mall. Six missed calls, one voicemail, and two texts. One missed call is from my dad, and the other five are from an unknown number. I click the voicemail button.

"Hey Bree, it's Todd. Can you please call me back. I think there was some sort of misunderstanding about last night. I'm not sure, but give me a call. Okay, well, *just call me*. Thanks." Even though my messages are over, I wait to see if there's an extra one that didn't get listed. One from Dad. My stomach pangs with missing him.

Both texts are from Todd.

Bree its Todd. CALL ME ASAP

The other one:

BREE CALL ME WHEN U GET THIS THX

Call when I get this? Pffft. Don't mind if I don't.

I scroll through my recent calls and look at Dad's number instead, but my phone vibrates, playing the song I programmed last night for Sean.

"Hello?" *Please ask me to do something please, please, please, ask me out tonight.*

"Bree. Hey, is it too late to see if you wanna do something tonight? Or do you have plans already?"

"Nope, I don't. I mean, well I don't have plans. I can. Yes. I can do something."

"Are you suuuuuure?" he asks. "I think it's against the rules to accept a date on the same night a guy asks."

"I'm sure," I say. "That's so nineteen hundreds anyway. Plus, I was hoping we could get drunk and puke all over each other in your car tonight."

"That sounds really hot. I didn't know you were into that sort of thing. Cool. But can you drive? My car's all puked out." His laugh is so *charmingly sexy*.

"No problem," I say into my phone as I tell the fluttering in my stomach to calm the hell down.

"Hey," Sean says. "Have you talked to Todd?"

"Todd? No, why?"

"He called me to ask if the number he had for you was the same one I had. I guess Kallie gave him your number but he said you weren't answering."

"Yeah, I saw that he called but didn't call him back and probably won't. For reasons."

"Sounds mysterious. Tell me about it tonight. What do you want to do?"

We do the whole "I don't know, what do you want to do?" bit and in the end decide that I'll just pick him up around seven and we'll see what happens. After he hangs up, I hold the phone with a big nerdy smile on my face. My head falls onto my pillow and I yawn. "Sean Mills asking me out for two nights in a row . . . mmmmhmmmmmmm," I murmur.

ELEVEN

Breeeeeeeeeeeeeee!" My mom's yell echoes from downstairs.

My eyes dart to the clock on my wall. 6:44 p.m. Shit. *Shit!* I gotta go. I'm supposed to pick Sean up in fifteen minutes. I should've made some phone calls by now, too. I slide and hop off my bed, and am maybe a little relieved there's no time for confrontational phone calls. I'll call Kallie later and Dad too.

Mom yells again. "You want me to order pizza?" Her footsteps pound up the stairs.

"Sorry Mom!" I peek my head out the door. "Sean called. I'm picking him up in like five minutes."

"Back-to-back Sean dates? Good for you. Sounds better than pizza. Have fun. Maybe I'll call one of my girlfriends and get out too."

"Just make sure you act like you don't know me if we end up at the same bar," I say.

I manage to put my hair back, brush my teeth, wash my face, and throw on some mascara in ten point five minutes. *Good thing Sean lives so close.* As I pull into his driveway, I slather on lip gloss, wondering if I should wait or knock on his door. Even though my heart rate most definitely picks up with each step, I decide to go to the door. I'm not trying to look like some creep sitting in the driveway in case his mom's home. A petite woman, maybe in her late forties, with big brown hair and Sean's blue eyes greets me.

"Hi, you must be . . . Bree? Right?" She smiles as I nod. "I'm Beth."

"Yes, that's me, nice to meet you." I shake her extended hand.

Sean's mom invites me into the house that opens right into the living room area. The house is small, the furniture and decor are modern and take up a lot of the space. It smells clean, like lemons and fresh laundry.

"Sean! Bree's here," she yells toward the hallway behind her. "He'll be ready in a minute—probably changing again, you know how boys are," she jokes. I laugh, imagining Sean trying on T-shirt after T-shirt.

"Sooooo, you're the girl that Sean's going to Prom with?"

Sean steps into the room as soon as she says it.

I stumble over my words as heat radiates beneath my cheekbones. My cheeks are constantly flushing, which is why I never wear blush. "Um, no, uh . . . um . . ."

"Mom, this is Bree. She's on *Prom Court* with me."

"But she's the one you're bringing as your date right?"

Sean stares past her at the oven. Maybe he's thinking he wants to crawl in there. I know I am.

Beth's eyes widen and she bites her lip. "Yes, that's what I meant, the Prom Court. Right. It's going to be so fun. I'll never forget my own Senior Prom."

"Well, we better go so we're not late." Sean escorts me back through the door I came in.

"Nice meeting you!" I say as the door closes.

Neither of us speak as we walk out to my car. I can't think of anything good to change the subject with. My stomach turns at the idea of him accepting Jane's invite to Prom. No way. Maybe he has another date already. I try to fight it, but that stupid "let down" feeling stirs around in my gut as I adjust my seat belt once in the car. My anxiousness is tiny little soda bubbles, starting from the bottom of my stomach and rising up, up, up.

My mouth stretches into the tiniest most uncomfortable smile. "Your mom seems nice—she's cute," I say.

"Yeah, she's cute all right." Sean answers as I pull out of the driveway. "And yeah, she's just, um, weird. So, where're we going? Whattaya wanna do?"

I have no choice but to let him off the hook. I can tell he's embarrassed and doesn't want to talk about it. Maybe he really is going with someone else. There's Jane and a ton of other options he could've had in the last week or so. My mom's right. I should've been the one to ask.

"Well," I say, "I heard there's a really good movie out right now, it's about some lady trying to find her car in a parking ramp. I bet it's amazing. Wanna see it?"

"Oh, I've seen it," Sean says. "But the only good thing about it was my hot date." The heat returns to my cheeks but I keep my eyes on the road as if he won't notice.

"Aaaanyway, enough about your hot dates, are you hungry? Are you thirsty? Are you in the mood for a party? The beach? A concert? A carnival? A pony ride—what?"

He responds, "A pony ride? That could be interesting."

I smile and smack his knee.

"Just kidding," he says. "Actually horses and ponies and donkeys and anything else like a horse freaks me out. Long story. Let's get something to eat. Azumi?"

"Sounds good to me," I reply, glad to have a plan. "But hold on. Horses freak you out, really?"

"Yeah, don't tell anyone though. I don't want to ruin the image I've tried to maintain. You know how people are these days, always assuming every football player loves a good ole-fashioned pony ride."

I laugh again and attempt to stifle my giddiness. His flirting pushes aside my thoughts about his potential Prom dates. As he tells me a story about his dad forcing him to ride one of those depressed donkeys at the state fair, I try not to miss any turns to Azumi. I also rally myself back into thinking my chances of him asking me to Prom might still be pretty good.

He finishes his story and I let out another giggle. "That was really shitty of your dad, but a photo op is a photo op."

"Hey, can I get a little sympathy here? I was traumatized by a burrow with a bum knee."

I stifle another laugh. I cannot keep laughing at everything he says. I'm being way too easy. "I'm sorry, that's awful. Are you also afraid of— Oh my god—I'm sorry, but are you—" And now I'm laughing at my own stupid joke. One I can't even say because I'm laughing too hard. If there's anything worse than overlaughing at a guy's jokes, it's laughing at your own. I finally manage to ask him if he's also afraid of unicorns.

He laughs with me and says, "I guess that'd be a yes. Hopefully we don't run into any tonight."

When we pull in to Azumi, Sean jumps out, rushes to my side of the car to finish opening my door and closes it behind me.

"Thank you," and then again when we get to the restaurant door.

Sean slides his hand across my lower back, almost gripping my waist as we walk toward the hostess. I lose a breath as a spine-tingly warmth waves down my torso.

The hostess smiles, "Hello Sean. Are you playing tonight?"

"Nope, off duty for the night. We came for dinner. Is there a wait for a booth?"

"For you, no wait." She waves for us to follow. "Right this way Mr. Mills."

As I slide into the booth, a scene from last time I was here flashes in my head—me trying to avoid Chip's stare and listening to Sean sing and play guitar. Ugh.

"Who's this guy?" I point over to the longhaired guy in an ACDC T-shirt singing about dust in the wind.

"That's the regular guy, Ace," Sean says. "He's pretty badass on the acoustic and electric. He's in a band that actually does gigs. Pretty cool."

"What about you? Are you going to do more with your music or football next year?"

"I only got offered a couple partial scholarships for football, so I'm not going anywhere. Just L.C.C."

"I'd hardly call Lakeville Community College 'anywhere,' since that's where I'll be too."

"Nice." His face brightens as he leans back into the booth. "It seems like everyone's doing their best to get out of here. I plan on it, but I'm not in a rush. I'll get my associate's and maybe move to Nashville where I can make music contacts and hopefully get a good internship."

"Nashville? Does that mean you want to be a country singer?"

"I'm not sure. I'm more rock with a pop, country, and blues influence. I'm into a lot of different styles right now but I have a lot to learn. One thing I do know is that I want to write music. Guitar and singing, sure, but I want to write songs for everyone, write across genres—and maybe a few that my mom will sing along to on KDWB."

"That's really cool. Do you write a lot of stuff now?"

"Yep. I'm not saying it's Grammy material or anything, but I've written a lot lately."

"Oh, okay. Hmmmm," I say, running my finger back and forth between the sushi and entrée menus, remembering how he asked for help with his poetry assignment. If he can write songs, there is no way he needed my help for Nord's class. The only thing I can do to hide the gigantic smile pulling on the corners of my mouth is to keep talking. "Well, maybe I can be your manager or at least the girl screaming all the words in the front row. I like your plan better than mine. My big plan is to not have a plan right now. But I'm okay with it. And I'm glad I'll see you in school."

After dinner, I drive us to my house. The first thing I see when I click our garage door open is that Mom's car is gone.

"Guess my mom actually did go out. Wow." I dial Mom's number as we head inside. I leave a message saying that Sean and I are hanging out here. "So don't come home and embarrass me," I whisper into the receiver and hang up.

There's a yellow Post-it stuck to the counter:

Bree!
Went out with work friends.
Be home later.
Hope you had fun with Sean!!!! ☺♥
Love, Mom

Next to Sean's name she's drawn a heart and smiley face. Of course my face gets hot and I quickly flip the note over.

"A heart and a smiley face? Guess your mom has a crush on me," Sean says as I glance up to him hovering over my shoulder.

"Oh ummm, yeah, I guess she just figures, um that, yeah whatever. She's totally embarrassing."

"Guess we're even on embarrassing moms, right?" Sean asks, then continues, "Well, the reason my mom said that stuff about Prom was because, well . . ."

My phone interrupts. *Kallie's ringtone.* My heart jumps. The fire engine ringtone gets louder as I rummage for my phone. Ridiculous. My purse is big but not that big. I look like a moron, not being able to find a loud blaring vibrating phone. Sean's half smiling with his eyebrows raised. My phone stops singing the exact second I pull it out of my purse.

"Got it!"

One Missed Call

KALLIE VATE.

"Missed it," I say. "I'll call her later."

"It's okay," Sean says. "I don't care if you want to call her back now. Go ahead."

"I don't know. I kind of need to—want to—well, it'd be best if I heard what she has to say first."

Sean's mouth crinkles. "That makes sense. But not."

The urge to get his opinion on the whole Kallie stuff overrides my whole "wait until you tell Kallie first" plan. "I'm going to tell you something but you can't tell anyone, okay?"

Sean's mouth stays crinkled. "Um, okay."

"Do you want something to drink first?" I ask.

"Sure."

"Well," I say rummaging through the fridge, "I got Diet Coke, organic green tea, almond milk, or OJ? Or water?"

"Coke is fine."

I grab two Cokes and give him the whole story of Todd and Jane, omitting the visual of my ear suctioned to the wall for every detail. I let him know that Todd trying to call me was most likely him trying to save his ass.

Sean pauses for a minute. "Interesting, and kind of gross. I guess that's why Todd called me asking if we wanted to hang with him and Kallie tonight. I didn't think Todd was like that. And Jane. I knew she was obnoxious and had some issues, but not like that. If any of the guys were ever messing with my girlfriend . . . shit. Molly would go crazy if she found out."

"Molly?" I ask. "That's nothing. Kallie's gonna snap. If it weren't for Molly still being so hung up on Todd, Jane would've told everyone. She'd love to throw that in Kal's face. Jane was so pissed that night—from the sounds of it, Todd's been sort of leading her on. So, yeah, you're right. Gross."

Sean and I try to come up with a crazy scheme to have it all come out without me having to be the bad news bearer. We come up with a couple of ideas that, when examined further, would never work unless we were in a movie. Like, what if we send an anonymous note to Kallie and Molly. Or somehow get Jane, Molly, and Kallie into an elevator together; lock them in, until Jane tells everything. After realizing that I'm pretty much forced to tell Kallie, we decide to watch a movie. As we look through the shelved movies, I punch Sean lightly in the shoulder.

"Thanks for trying to help me out with the Kallie drama. Sorry you're kinda in the middle with your friends."

"No worries," Sean laughs. "It's my fault. I was the one who wanted to go to that party. But I guess that's the way it is. Sometimes you go to a Belmont High party and it's fun and sometimes you go and find out that the idiots you hang out with *are actual* idiots. And then they puke on you."

We decide on an old movie, *Stand By Me*, when Sean says he's never seen it. We sit on the couch leaving enough space for two people to sit in-between us. As the movie starts I alternate between ideas on how to scoot closer to Sean and ideas on how to talk to Kallie. After laughing at a few of the spots where I usually laugh (I've seen this movie about fourteen times) I ask Sean if he wants popcorn. I'm sure we'd have to sit closer if we're sharing a bowl of popcorn.

"No, that's okay. I'm fine, unless you want some."

"No, it's fine. I just didn't want to be a crappy movie host." My shoulders slump in defeat as I pull my legs up on the couch to cross them. Might as well get comfortable. Way over here. My lips twitch as I force myself not to frown.

"Total change of subject here," Sean says, "but what kind of cat do you have?"

"Cat?" I ask. "I don't have a—ohhhh yeah, *that* cat. Yeah, ummm . . ."

"—Because I'm allergic to cats but my eyes aren't itchy or anything. I just realized that I'm not sneezing either."

The only lies I can come up with would be that my cat died and we had the carpets deep cleaned or I have one of those scary looking hairless cats. I run my palms, already sweating, along the sides of my jeans.

"Well," I start, "actually, maybe you'll find this funny." I meet his eyes for a second before taking special interest in the seam of the pillow I've stuffed into my lap. "I don't even have a cat. I was trying to leave a . . . I wanted to change my message and can we just say that I'm horrible with leaving voicemails?" Clamping my mouth shut, I lift my head for his reaction.

He laughs. "Sure. I should confess something too. If I do we'll call it even?" He thrusts his hand forward for a handshake.

Any kind of touching is better than none, so I take it. "Ummmm, yeah, okay. Deal."

He pulls our linked hands into the space between us. "I didn't really need any help with the poetry writing stuff."

"Really? Why?" I ask. In my best interest, I hold back using my fake surprised face.

"I was just trying to hang out with you."

"Well, I did think it was interesting when you told me earlier *that you write songs*."

Sean squeezes my hand tighter and looks up with a smile that makes me want to just lean in a little farther and—

"I wasn't sure how to ask you out. You're not the most approachable girl in the school, you know."

"Yeah, I've heard that line before. *Sorry?*" I really don't know how to respond. He's so damn cute, even though his eyes, like aquamarines, are practically pulling off the layers of my cornea, begging for some sort of answer. Which is unnerving. I mean, maybe he's right about me being unapproachable, but there's also practically a mini-airplane flying overhead pulling a sign that reads: *She's so into you.*

My stomach is aerial-cartwheeling while my bottom lip is clamped between my teeth so I don't say the wrong thing. The only way to delete some of the weirdness going on right now is if we kiss.

Wetting my lips without being super noticeable, I scoot my legs and butt over. *Going for it.* I pull my hand from his and move it to his shoulder, feeling the warmth beneath his snug gray T-shirt against my palm. He reaches out and cups the curve of my waist. The background noise from a movie we're not watching fades into nonexistence. Our eyes lock like magnets as the space between us gets smaller. The excitement, the anxiety, the neediness burns and tingles through my core. I grip the couch cushion as I continue leaning forward while his eyes shine, then blur as they move parallel to mine. My eyelids fall and a spark rushes through me as our lips meet.

The slam of my kitchen door being closed from the garage echoes into the living room. As if our lips actually *are* on fire, Sean and I jerk back.

I jump up. "Omigod, *my mom.*" I whisper, "Um, sorry. Sorry." I do a backward jog and dive into the chair next to the couch. "Moooom?" I call. "You home?"

She appears in the doorway between the kitchen and the living room. "Hey, you forgot to close the garage, hon. Good thing I'm not some serial killer looking for teenagers to—"

"Okay Mom, *sorry.*" I say. "This is Sean."

Sean rises from the couch and walks over to her, extending his hand.

"Sean. Nice to meet you Mrs. Hughes."

"Nice to meet you, too. I remember you. The singing guy from Azumi. I'm in-between last names right now, you can call me Brenda. You guys watching a movie?"

"*Stand By Me*," I answer, with a slight nod, making urgent eye contact with her. "Unfortunately you've already seen it, sooooo?"

"You bet. I'll be upstairs if you need anything. Just right *upstairs*," she points upward as she walks up the stairway.

Sean stifles a laugh. "Your mom's pretty cool. She's funny, like you."

"Thanks. Cool, funny, and yet, so embarrassing." The assertiveness I had just before my mom got home fades into a light shade of shy, which freezes me on the chair I'd jumped into.

Out of the corner of my eye, Sean shuffles around on the couch, moving his leg, tapping the armrest, but he doesn't say anything. I talk myself into getting out of my seat and going back to the couch about twelve more times, but my body never actually moves.

The movie eventually fades to the main character in a scene as an adult, hanging out with his kids, and then the credits roll.

Sean stands and leans against the armrest. "That was a good movie. I'm officially appointing you to be in charge of picking out movies for us from now on."

From now on. Pretty sure my heart just skipped and swooned heavily to the right.

"Too bad you hung out on that chair the rest of the movie. It was kind of cold over here."

"Sorry," I say. "I just got kind of thrown off by *my mom walking in* when I was trying to kiss you."

"Whoa, hey. I was trying to kiss you."

I smile. "No, I'm pretty sure that was all me. I was about to kiss you."

"Well, I guess it's not how you start but how you finish. Something like that."

I smile and imagine jumping on him, pushing him back onto the couch, and finishing the kiss. Instead, I make my way over to the bottom of the staircase.

"Hey Mom," I call up. "I'm going to drive Sean home, okay? Be home in a little bit."

"Drive safe!" she calls from her room.

After I put my car into park in Sean's driveway, he lays his hand on mine. "I had fun tonight. Sorry about all your drama."

"I'll figure it out," I say. "I had fun too. Sorry my mom came home so early."

"Soooo," Sean says, "About that. I think I owe you."

"Yes," I say. "My prize. You do owe me. That lucky rubber band was stolen by Molly's stinky hair."

"That's on you, Bree." The way he says my name pulls me, kills me, grips my heart something crazy. "You better get that back." He grins. Then he does a sideways lean into me from the passenger seat. He slides his hand down my hair, then beneath my ponytail at the nape of my neck. His lips press against my bottom lip and my body *sighs*. My lips melt into his. It's like tiny sparklers are shooting around inside my body. I try to keep my breathing steady although my heart races as his hand moves down my back, probably leaving fire-prints beneath my shirt. His lips are smooth and light across mine. He inhales deeply as he slowly pulls away.

Exhaling, he says, "I guess I better go. Before my mom comes out here asking if we want a snack or something."

"See you in school Monday?"

"Yep. Maybe I'll give you a call tomorrow too, if that's okay?"

"Yes. Have a good night," I say to his back as he exits the car.

He turns and winks, "You too, Breezy."

He waves one last time before going into his house. My lips stretch into a smile that lasts me all the way home and into Sunday morning. Best. Night. Best. Weekend. Ever.

TWELVE

Still inhaling the glow left over from my time with Sean, this morning has me refreshed and ready to conquer my phone call with Kallie.

"Finally, you call me back," Kallie says without even saying hello first.

"Well hi to you, too."

"Hi. What's up?" Kallie asks.

"Kal. You called last night and didn't leave a message. You go first."

"Okay, but only because it's been a while since I've said it first." She half whispers, "*Sorry*."

"Who said that? Do you have a tiny little mouse over there? I barely heard the guy. What'd he say?"

"Omigod Bree," she laughs. "I'll kill you. You heard me."

"I know, I'm kidding. I'm sorry too. Really."

I think we both sigh into our phones at the same time.

"So," I say, not wanting to get into anything good or off topic until I spit it out. "I have to tell you something."

"Ugh. I already know. Todd told me."

"Really? About Jane?"

"You mean Molly. Yep. He said you guys were at Monroe's Friday and she was all over him and you probably saw. Todd said you guys were all pretty wasted so he hoped you didn't get the wrong idea. It was all Molly. It might've looked bad but Todd swears he didn't touch her. I believe him. *I should believe him, right?*"

"Um, yes and no." I take a deep breath and begin pacing my bedroom. "What're you doing right now? Wanna come over? I bet I can get my mom to make us pancakes?"

"I can't. I gotta work. I swear every kid and their cousin has a birthday party this weekend. I need to get in early and help set up."

"Okay, well . . ."

"Dude," she says. "Just tell me."

"Okay, first thing, you'd tell me if your mom was sick right?"

"Omigod, of course. I'm not like you, Bree. If shit's going down, you'll hear about it. My mom's fine. What does that have to do with anything?"

"I know. Here's the thing, I didn't have anything to drink at the party, just so you know. But, I heard Todd tell, okay, well, Todd and Jane were talking and . . . Okay, not so much as talking but—"

"Wait. You mean Todd and Molly, right?"

"No. I mean Jane. Jane fucking Hulmes. So, I overheard them and apparently they have a thing going on."

"Wait," Kallie's voice cuts through the phone. "Todd and Jane would never have a thing. He can't stand her. He's always talking about how crazy and bitchy she is. He actually avoids hanging out anywhere she's at. Plus, what about Molly? She's still in love with him. Jane knows that. Best girlfriends don't fuck with each other like that. C'mon—I think you're reaching here," she says.

"No, I'm not. I heard them. Jane doesn't care about girl code and I'm pretty sure they had sex and Todd told her that your mom's dying so he can't break up with you."

"Bree, that's nuts. Todd would never say anything like that about my mom. It's psycho. Did you actually see them together?"

"Not exactly, but I heard them."

"Right. There were so many people there and it was someone else. Jane probably sleeps with a lot of guys and I wouldn't put it past her to be screwing someone else's boyfriend. But not mine."

"No, it was def—"

"Listen, I gotta get going. I'll ask Todd if you want, but I know you're wrong. I feel like you think the worst about people just because of who they hang out with. Todd actually likes you."

"Well, why would he be calling me yesterday then?"

"Because of *me*. You know what? He told me you and *Sean Mills* were hanging out at that party, and are, like, dating, or something. It was real shitty to hear that kind of news from someone else besides you. Because, since Todd is such an *evil person*, he said you and I shouldn't be fighting. And that we should call to see if you guys wanted to double date."

"I know. I wanted to tell you so bad. Trust me, I'd rather be talking about Sean than having to call you about this."

"Good. I just want my friend back. So, no hard feelings, man?"

I force a fake laugh through the phone. "Nope. No way man. We're good."

"Good. I'm calling you on my break and I wanna talk Prom and most importantly, get all the nasty details on Sean finally growing the ovaries to ask you out."

When we hang up, I drop my phone, grab a furry orange pillow, and hurl it. It smacks and slides down the wall of old records that Kallie and I spent the whole summer collecting and hanging before our junior year. We did the same to her room, but her mom freaked and had all the nail holes filled and the whole wall repainted within the week. I snatch the pillow, lean up and slide down the wall, too. Sigh. At least I have my friend back. Best friends again, but with limits.

Sean calls before I'm about to go to bed and I tell him about the convo with Kallie. Not that I expect him to, but he doesn't really get it.

"Hey at least you laid it out there. They'll figure it out. Just be glad to have your friend again."

We talk a little more and he says he'll see me in class tomorrow.

Maybe he's right about Kallie and the others, I think. Guess I'll just let them all work it out.

****

I drop my Howl free-writing assignment on Mr. Norderick's desk.

"Looks like you had some stuff you needed to get off your chest, Ms. Hughes." I look down at my paper and nod. I can see how my sharp, heavy strokes and a handful of all-caps fuck-bombs jumping off the page might have tipped him off.

I shrug. "Maybe a little."

"Hey," I say to Sean as I slide into my chair. I'm really talking to Sean in class and making eye contact. I don't drown, but my heart definitely kicks up a notch.

"Hey." He smiles. Glad you two are cool again." Sean turns to Kallie and asks where she was Friday. "You missed out on our sober taxi. Maybe next time."

When we leave class and run into Todd, he punches Sean in the shoulder and says "Hi" to me like Friday never happened. I raise my eyebrow but say hi back. The four of us walk out to the parking lot and part ways to go to our cars. When I get in my car, my phone rings. *Sean Mills.*

"Hey," he says, "I know I just saw you a minute ago but wanted to tell you that you look nice today and . . . I want to ask you something but I'm not sure if it's too soon. So maybe we could hang out again on Friday and we'll talk about it then."

"Sure," I say. *Please God let him be talking about Prom.* "And thanks."

THIRTEEN

Prom In Paradise
An Evening With The Stars
Twilight Memories
Jungle Boogie Nights

It's Tuesday after school and everyone on Prom Court is sitting at one of the cafeteria tables.

Brian's texting on his phone, Chris and Laura are on opposite ends of the table, which means they're broken up *again*, and the rest of us are passing around poster boards and the list of Prom theme ideas.

"Are they kidding me?" Molly says. "This is awful." She shoves a neon green poster board back to the middle of the table. "Jungle Boogie Nights? What the heck? How does the committee come up with this crap? So lame."

"Easy," says Sean. "They know what they want and present it in such a way that you have to pick, hmmmm . . . pick . . ." He sets the boards up side by side. "None. They all suck."

"Twilight Memories?" Laura asks. "Someone is going too far celebrating their cultish book love."

"They can't be for real," I say. "We can't pick a theme that includes cutouts of vampires and werewolves, can we?"

Clearly, Twilight Memories is what the Prom Committee wanted us to like. The presentation board is pretty professional. Beautiful calligraphy, crisp gothic magazine cutouts and detailed illustrations of fancy punches, satin streamers in blood red, smoky gray, and jet black. Not going to lie, it's sharp. But they lose me at the werewolf and vampire cutouts. The other themes are totally thrown together like afterthoughts. A few magazine and Google images glued onto tag board. A generic beach scene with a sunset, a map of constellations with the promise of star confetti, and a monkey in a tuxedo hanging from a jungle vine.

Jane straightens her gold headband and frowns. "I'm not trying to be mean, but should anything Breanne says count? I mean, you guys, she's not *originally* on court."

"Really Jane?" snaps Kallie. "I'm pretty sure Bree *is* on court. I'm also sure *Bree* was voted in fair and square and *not* as a joke like Maisey was, which was probably your asshole idea. Furthermore, she's going to feel the same way as the rest of us. Right, Bree?"

"Um, yeah," I say. The same knots that were in my stomach at the party tie themselves tighter.

"Ladies, ladies," says Todd. "How 'bout we just figure this out. It's not that serious. Everyone, just be cool."

"I'm always cool," Kallie says and kisses Todd on the mouth.

Jane twists and pulls the gold bangles on her wrist, her mouth twitching.

"He's right," says Justin. "I, for one, have always wanted to have my Prom pic taken with a monkey in a tux."

"It might not be the end of the world to have the werewolves and vampires at Prom because everything else they have is worse," says Laura.

Justin's eyes widen and he slaps the table. "Hey, maybe once we get to Prom, we can steal the cutouts or something. We could decapitate them or hide 'em in Shandy's locker."

"Good idea, Conner," says Brian, standing up and shoving his phone into his pocket. "As much fun as this is, I have things to do. Twilight Memories is fine. Dress the cutouts in boxer briefs for all I care. Everyone agreed?" He looks to Molly who is cross-armed and crinkly faced.

"Well, the color scheme is pretty complimentary so . . . *fine*. I guess," she says.

Jane's hand comes up. "Hang on. I don't think we should just give up like this."

"I'm in," says Sean.

The rest of us nod.

Except Jane who glares at Kallie. "Obviously I don't matter all of a sudden. So fuck it, do whatever you want."

"Agreed," says Brian. "It's all set. Twilight Memories. I'm off to meet my boyfriend who's home *from college* tonight. No more time for high school shit."

"Call me tonight, Moll, or *anyone else* who cares about *anything,*" Jane slaps the table in front of Molly and sashays out of the room.

"Sure, I'll call you." Kallie laughs.

Molly stands, "She's in a crap mood lately so we should go easy on her."

"Thanks for the tip, Molly. I'll see what I can do," Kallie turns to Todd. "I told Bree I'd ride with her today, okay?"

I shrug. "Yep, let's go."

Sean squeezes my shoulder sending a warm flutter up my neck as we all part ways.

"Getting hot in here," whispers Kallie as we walk to our locker. "Thanks for covering. I'm just tired and not in the mood for hanging out with anyone today."

"So, I don't count?" I smile. "Good to know."

"You know what I mean. Ugh. Speaking of someone who doesn't count. What the hell is she doing? She was such a bitch today. I'm going to say something."

Jane's down the hall by the library doors, hovering over someone, and talking all over the place with her hands.

Kallie flips her hair behind her shoulder and moves ahead of me.

"What are you gonna say?" I take long strides to keep up.

"I'm asking what her problem is with you and why she was being such a bitch in there."

We get closer and Jane's so engrossed in her bitching that she doesn't see us to the left of the giant column near the library entrance.

Jane's voice is almost pleading. "But there's nothing I can do. It's not my fault he's trying to apologize."

The other voice says, "Yeah, but he's your—"

"*Shut up*," Jane hisses. "*Please*. I'm not talking to him and I have nothing to do with any of it. I just need it to go away. He's not part of my life anymore. At all. *Ever*."

And a familiar voice with the same bite, "*Please*. You're just worried about people finding out."

Jane lowers her voice, "You're not the only one it happened to, you know."

Maisey Morgan looks past Jane's shoulder and meets my eye. Jane spins around following her gaze.

"What the hell?" Jane's face reads red hot horror as her fingers flare in and out of her palms.

"What the hell's your problem?" Kallie shoves Jane in the shoulder. "You better not even be talking about my boyfriend."

I grab Kallie's wrist, squaring off in front of Jane. "You need to leave Maisey alone, she didn't do anything."

Maisey stares at Jane, tears in her eyes. "For the record, Janie, I never thought I was the only one, and that's the worst part of all." Maisey runs down the hall toward the main doors. She does a trip slash half stumble but keeps on going.

Jane steps forward. "Maisey!" She stops, takes a deep breath, and faces us. Her mouth is pulled into a tight line and her eyes look ready to release a serious stream of tears. She huffs. "Whatever. What a loser. That rat doesn't even know what she's talking about."

Kallie tugs her wrist out of my grip and steps back up to Jane. "You've got some serious issues, Hulmes. You've been picking on Maisey since elementary school, grow up. Everyone's tired of your shit. You need to stay out of our way, cause if you haven't figured it out yet, no one actually likes you, they're pretending. Just like you, with all your fake gold tiaras and pageant shit."

"Screw you," Jane says as she tries to walk past, but Kallie sticks out her boot.

"Easy there, Grand Supreme. Listen to me. If your name comes up in anymore rumors or if you try starting shit that has to do with me, Todd, Bree, or anyone—"

A librarian peeks her head out the door, "Ladies, keep it down, please."

"Oh, get over yourself." Jane shoves past Kallie, whipping me with her thick braid.

"Did she just bitch slap you with her hair?"

"Just let it go. I'm over it," I say, actually relieved she's gone.

"Same. I think we made our point."

Jane runs down the hall and out the door, her braid swinging from side to side.

Kallie locks her arm through my elbow. "Let's forget about this and get donuts. And most definitely discuss the *real* issue from that Prom theme meeting. Sean Mills was staring at you like it was a life drawing class."

We exchange the after school drama for glazed donuts, Sean talk, Prom dress image viewing, and absolutely no more mentions of Todd.

****

At dinner I give my mom an abbreviated recap of my day and the meeting. I tell her how ridiculous Jane was but that Kallie and I seem to be cool again.

"That's great, what a relief." She sighs and leans over her grilled chicken. "Soooo . . . speaking of 'being cool again', do you owe your dad a phone call?"

"Why? It's not like we're in a fight."

"Hon, your dad says you've been distant since the divorce was finalized and he said you haven't returned his calls and he hasn't talked to you in weeks."

"Not on purpose. And funny you should mention it, I was thinking of calling him this month. Maybe even this week."

"Don't be cute. I'm sure you know, but the divorce wasn't all his fault," she says.

It's been like half a year since the divorce was final and she's talking to me about it now? "Yeah mom, I know. I'm sure there's a reason why Dad didn't feel like hanging around here all the time. Maybe all the yelling got on his nerves. Trust me, I get it."

She opens her mouth like she's about to say something but takes a drink of water instead.

"Like I said, I'm going to call him. Why's he calling you about me anyway? I didn't even know you guys still talk."

"Of course we still talk," she says. "He loves and cares about you like I do. He worries too. He wants to know what you're up to, how you're doing. And hey, if you're not calling him," she narrows her eyes, "then he's going to have to call *somebody* to get that info."

"Point taken. I'll call him. Promise."

She looks relieved and goes back to her chicken. As I choke down a mouthful of bland broccoli, I make a mental note to call Dad by Friday after school. *Before my date with Sean.*

FOURTEEN

Late Thursday morning I'm called from Biology to the office again. Second time in the past month. My heart and stomach do all their signature moves. Jumping, flipping, racing, and all to a horrible tune of "what-if this or what-if that?" Maybe Maisey wants back in Prom Court. Or maybe Mom called Ms. Selinski about me not calling Dad. Convinced Mom ratted me out on my lingering divorce issues, I take longer, faster strides down the hall. *Who does she think she is, anyway?* Either she's sweeping shit under the rug or making mountains out of it. I veer to the wall, lean against it and pull my phone out of my bag to text her.

Really Mom?! I said I would call—FOR SURE TMRW! ☺

Send.

As soon as I step into the office, I'm confused. My mom is standing in front of the main desk, still dressed in her work clothes.

"Mom. What's going on? Is everything okay?" I start to feel jittery.

"I don't think so." She glances down to her gray leather pumps. "Not really."

I get a sick stab in my gut and bubbles of fear burst upward. I gasp. "Is it Dad? Is he okay—is everything okay with Dad? He's okay, right?"

She hugs my shoulder with her arm. "Honey, calm down."

"You two can step back into Ms. Selinski's office now," says the school secretary, waving us toward the back of the office.

My body stiffens and refuses to move. "Mom. Tell me right now. What's going on?"

"I promise. Your dad's fine. It's . . . well, let's just get in here and sit down." Her tone is low, somber, and offers no reassurance.

As we settle into our chairs, Ms. Selinski shuffles papers beneath a strained smile as I run through every person I care about in my head. Then, I tick through each class and my grades. Not failing anything. Maybe Nord thought my Howl poem had too many fucks and was a cry for help. Actually, I doubt Nord would care about swearing in an assignment. It still might be Dad. I wish I'd called him this past weekend, like I'd originally *sort of* planned. My right knee bobs up and down in short, sharp jolts.

"Bree, hello?" My mom grips my shoulder. "Honey, relax. Listen."

"Bree, are you okay?" asks Ms. Selinski.

"Yes," I say evenly, "I'm okay. Just tell me why I'm here."

"I'm so sorry to be delivering this news, but I wanted you to know that one of your classmates has passed away."

I take a deep breath, press my hand on my knee and beg my heart to slow down. I hate this feeling. The speeding heartbeat and the blur that rushes in and out of my head and past my eyes. My breaths are too short. Just gotta breathe. *Onetwothreefourfivesixseveneightnine . . . ten.*

Ms. Selinksi runs her hand back and forth over her chin. "It was Maisey Morgan."

"What?" I ask.

"She took her own life. I'm sorry. Were you, um, close or friendly with her?" Ms. S. asks.

"No, I mean, *what?*" My face crinkles. "Maisey? Are you sure? She was just here the other day. Wait. But is she okay?" I stutter.

My mom's hand clenches my knee. "No babe, she's not okay. Ms. Selinski is asking if you knew her."

I stare at my lap. My jeans are dark blue. They look clean. They're one of my more expensive pairs. I don't want them to fade so I rarely wash them. I probably haven't washed them in three months. I bought them with my first paycheck over the summer. I wonder if I'll work all the time now, and not just summers, now that school's almost over.

"Bree?" Mom's hand is patting my knee again.

I shake my head. "Friends? No, we weren't. I've talked to her once or twice. Well, I guess we're . . . acquaintances? Why?"

"I know this is hard, but her parents wanted me to ask. She left a few good-bye letters, one for her parents, and a couple others for her friends. One has your name on it but her parents didn't know who you were. Did she ever say anything to you, about wanting to hurt herself?"

"About being suicidal? No." *I'm pretty sure she told me I was an asshole and called it a day.* I add, "I know she didn't have the easiest time at school, but I mean, I didn't think it was that bad. That doesn't sound right. I guess I mean, no. No. She never said anything like that. Do her parents think it's because of me?"

"Oh, honey, no, not at all. They're just trying to make sense of something that will probably never make sense." Ms. Selinski says.

Things get blurrier. There's a whooshing whurr in my head that sounds like the roar of the cafeteria at lunchtime. And then I'm pushed into the feeling I get when giving a presentation in front of a class. The feeling that I'm not really here.

My mom sniffs and wipes tears from her eyes. "Thank you so much for being here for Bree and letting us know. This is awful and so devastating for everyone. Her parents. No one is supposed to lose a child, especially like this."

Like this. Thoughts pound through my head, invading like quick flashes of light. *Why? Was she scared? Where were her friends? How'd she do it? Did it hurt? Did her parents find her?*

Ms. Selinski looks at me, softening her eyes. "Here's her parents' address." She hands Mom a yellow Post-it. "They have the letter. I'm sure it's all really confusing. But Bree, whenever you're ready, they'd really like you to have it. I'm really sorry. This is a big loss for all of us. Friends, acquaintances, *everyone*."

Everyone? I can picture Jane up against her locker, screaming at Maisey's back whenever she'd walk by, "Eek, you guys! I just saw a mouse. Somebody kill it!"

"We're going to miss her."

Even the kids that used to sing Maisey Mouse to her in the hallways? The song ribbons through my brain and I can't stop it before it sashays around in my head. Almost taunting me. *C'mon everybody, on one, two, one two three . . . M-A-I-S-E-Y M-O-U-S-E.*

It feels like smoke billows around me, like a cloud trying to suffocate me. Ms. Selinski escorts us to the door and shakes Mom's hand again. "If either of you need anything, please, please let me know."

Walking through the main office, things get foggier. I feel like I'm walking through water, but I'm all the way in. Over my head. Immersed in it. Everything is hazy and sounds are faded echoes in my ears. I watch in a daze as Mom signs me out and smiles politely to the staff.

I follow her voice to her car in the parking lot but I can't make out what she's saying. The words are so muffled. Is she talking too fast or too slow? I try to focus, and slow down my breath. Maybe I can't hear her because my heart's beating so loud in my ear. It's fast, too fast. It's moving up in my chest. The ba-dum, ba-dum, bad-dum gets closer and closer together until it catches in my throat and I can't breathe. Can't. Breathe. Pushing myself against the car, I grasp the door handle. It's not opening. I tug harder.

Slow down. Slow down. Stop freaking out. Calm down. Dad isn't dead. I'm fine. Fine, fine, fine. Aunt Jen is still here. Mom's okay. C'mon, relax. Count to ten. One, two, three . . . four . . . You're not even friends with her . . . five . . . six.

My body sinks to the ground in a heap next to the car. Then Mom's pulling me into her and cradling my head to her chest. I'm shaking, heaving, and sobbing. The tears pour out of my eyes and my heart is a fist trying to break out of my chest. I'd let it out if I could.

****

Mom backs out of Maisey's driveway. Even though I'd convinced her I wanted to get it over with, as soon as Mom knocked on the Morgans' door, I wanted to run. I could literally feel pangs of their torment as I stood next to my own mother in their doorway. The way Maisey's parents looked at me, stoic, searching, and still in shock.

A scene from *Stand By Me* flashed through my head. The part where the dad tells Gordy that he wished he would've died instead of his older brother. *It shoulda been you, Bree.* I tried to shake the thought out of my head as soon as it arrived, but it hung around for a few more minutes, taunting me. Maybe Maisey's parents aren't in that kind of place. But I am. I feel guilty. Guilty for not being some kind of savior. Like in the movies, the girl who takes the unpopular girl under her wing, gives her a makeover, the one where I'd convinced her to be on Prom Court, and she'd win. Not as a joke, but because everyone would be so amazed at her transformation. She'd stand tall and proud instead of gangly armed and slouchy, her tiny sunken eyes would pop with the right shade of eye shadow and a thick coat of mascara. Instead of laughing when she'd get her crown, everyone would cheer and pat themselves on the back for realizing the errors of their ways. And they all live happily ever after, smiling, shopping. *Alive.* The End.

Hindsight and regret suck the breath out of me, leaving me empty and motionless.

Mom grips the steering wheel and shakes her head. She mimics my thoughts, "I felt guilty for even standing there, with my daughter. My living daughter."

I felt it too. Mrs. Morgan was in her own house, but she seemed so lost. It felt so intrusive to show up with nothing to give and asking for a letter I didn't want. I couldn't even say I was sorry, because that felt too small. I was squeezing mom's hand so tight, lest I were to disappear down the same dark hole Maisey did.

My mom, taking her hand off the steering wheel to wipe a tear and pat my leg, asks, once more, if I'm okay.

Silence. I grip the envelope I wish wasn't addressed to me, haunted by the sad smile her mom had when she said, "She didn't reach out, but she still wanted to say good-bye. We had no idea she was still hurting."

I'd sat in their foyer while Maisey's mom and mine spoke in low hushes in the den. Her dad's eyes were glossy and vacant, his tie loosened around his neck, his beard the same shade of burnt red as Maisey's hair.

"Take it easy," he said, disappearing upstairs with a can of beer.

I strained to hear the conversation I wasn't asked to join. The details or backstory that Mrs. Morgan assumed I was too young for. Words jumped out of the hushed tones.

Devastated.
Abused.
Prison.
So long ago.
Happy.
Friends.
Released.
We didn't realize.

My mom's voice is a little clearer. Her "I'm so sorrys" ended with a trailing off of "If there's anything I can do."

Mom pulls me back into the present with a quick pat on my knee. "So, I texted your dad. He's meeting us at the house."

"What? Mom, really? Why?"

"This is a big deal, Bree. You were so upset at school that you could barely breathe. You need us. You just lost your friend."

"Mom, she wasn't my friend. Don't you get it? If I was her friend, maybe . . . maybe . . ." I trail off. I don't even know how to finish.

"She had a lot going on, things a kid shouldn't have to deal with. Whether she was your best friend or your worst enemy, it's not your fault. Suicide is tragic and hard to comprehend for most people. You're pretty shaken up and you've been going through a lot lately too and I'm sorry. I think I forget sometimes that you're still a kid too."

"A kid? Oh God, Mom. Come *on*. And what's Dad gonna do? Sit there and lecture me about not calling him? Sounds fun. Thanks."

She shakes her head as if it'll shake out whatever thoughts or images are plaguing her, keeping her eyes on the road. "I just don't ever want anything to happen where . . . I need you to know no matter what, you can talk to me about anything."

If only it were that easy. Mom hasn't even stopped crying yet and is trying to pretend she's not wiping snot and tears from her face with her sleeve. "I don't know the plan, but let's be glad that for once in his life your dad is trying." She sighs.

I answer with only a sigh to softly mimic hers. The rest of the ride home I think of the places I'd rather be. I'd rather be on the hill, with the sun heating my back. Lying on a blanket at the park by my house, with earphones, listening to music louder than my thoughts. Or at home in bed, wrapped in the blue cornflowers of my comforter. Or kissing Sean again. Or maybe even in my bed kissing Sean again. Anywhere but on my way to talk to my dad about a dead girl from school.

As we drive up to our house, Dad's truck is parked along the curb. My stomach gets that sinking feeling because Mom was always annoyed when he'd park it there instead of the driveway. She takes a lot of pride in our home, and the loon and lake scene she hand-painted on our mailbox is a big part of that. She touches it up at the beginning of every summer.

"It looks so trashy to have extra vehicles parked along the curb. Besides," she'd say, "I worked hard on that mailbox, *Nicholas*. It's like you're hiding it." He'd joke and tell her he *was* hiding it. But only because he didn't want anyone to steal it.

"Oh geez. Why is he parking in the street?" Mom asks.

There's a car in our driveway. Sean's. My heart skips and then sinks again. I don't want him to see me after I've been crying. Sean's sitting on our step about a foot away from my dad who's in his police uniform.

"Mom, look at me. I can't see him like this."

"Who? Your dad or Sean?"

"*Sean*. Do I look crazy?"

Her eyes scan me from hair to my one red and one yellow tennis shoe. "If you want, you can go right in through the garage and I'll get rid of him. Only if you want. You don't look terrible but I can tell you've been crying if that's what you're worried about. You're still cute, though."

"Thanks Mom." I flip the sun visor and peek at my reflection. Puffy, blotchy, not great. My eyes flit down to Maisey's envelope on my lap. I've folded it in half so many times that it's now a fat tiny square. I push it into my back pocket and step out of the car.

My dad and Sean stand up as I walk over.

"Hey kiddo," Dad says, giving me a big hug.

"Hey Dad." Trying not to encourage the tears lining back up behind my eyes, I pull away and shrug with a small smile at Sean. "What is this, like a surprise party?"

Sean smiles, "If it's your birthday, yes. If it's not, no."

"A few months early, buddy," says Dad looking over to Sean.

Mom walks up behind me. "Come on into the house Nick, let's give them a few minutes to talk." She smiles at Sean then looks me in the eye. "See you in here in two minutes, all right?"

"Fine. Two minutes."

Dad shakes Sean's hand saying it was nice meeting him and follows behind Mom.

Sean rests his hands on my shoulders. "I got worried. I waited by your car after you missed class. No one knew where you were and I kept getting your voicemail."

I tuck a strand of hair behind my ear. "Sorry, I guess my phone's off."

"What's going on? Are you okay? I'm not going to pretend I didn't freak out when I saw a cop hanging out in front of your door."

My lips form a tiny smile. "I guess I never mentioned my dad's a cop. Was he nice?"

"He had a lot of questions, but he was nice. He said your mom called and asked him to meet you guys here and then he was trying to see what I knew and I didn't know anything. Nobody knew anything."

"I'm fine, really," I insist, gently lifting his hands from my shoulders. I press the pads of my fingers into his palms. Resisting the flame that flickers amidst *everything else* in my chest, I let them go. "I don't know, it's all really overdramatic. My dad called my mom about me not calling him lately so my mom was worried and I guess now because of some other stuff, I guess it's a good time to talk to him. But I really was going to call him."

He looks down at me, his mouth the slightest curve away from a frown. "But you've been crying? Is that really all that's wrong?"

Sean stares into my eyes and for a second I don't know where I am. I have to lower my head because a stupid tear forms in my eye. It falls in slow motion, then hits the top of my sneaker, stretching into a tiny splat against the red canvas making me think of blood. Maisey's face flashes my brain and there's a barrage of bad thoughts stacked up, ready to push their way in but I push right back and they disappear.

"Can we talk about it later?" I ask. "I want to talk to you. And I'm sorry, but I should probably deal with the two parents behind door number one." I half laugh, waving my hand toward the door.

Sean wipes beneath my eye with the edge of his sleeve. He leans in, presses his lips to my forehead, and then my eyelid. I pull back and open my eyes, letting another tear run down my cheek.

"Sorry I'm such a baby," I say. "I better go. Thanks for coming by and I'm sorry you were worried. Thanks for that."

"Hey, you're not a baby. You've had a tough day. Text me later, okay?"

I nod and disappear into my house before I start crying again. I take a deep breath and make my way toward Mom's and Dad's voices coming from the kitchen. They're talking about Maisey.

Dad steps away from the table and wraps me in another hug. He speaks a few Spanish words, the way he always has when he's trying to comfort me. "It's okay, *mi hija. Esta bien, esta bien.*" This time I hug him back and my shoulders shake as I release all of the tears I have left.

****

My eyes crack open to bright light and silence. I grab my phone that still hasn't been turned back on. My cat clock says I've slept till 10:23 a.m. but it still doesn't feel like enough.

When my phone powers on, it immediately buzzes in my hand. Missed calls and texts from Kallie and Sean pop up like reminders of why my head is throbbing. My eyes are pulled to the window, the sun extending its arms, beckoning, promising a new day.

If only the light were enough. My head sinks back into the pillow and I hug another between my knees. I drift back to sleep, waking in and out of dreams of Maisey pulling the mouse out of her desk, and nightmares splattered with dark images of her limp body, skin paled in blues and grays, hanging from a rope in the halls of Belmont High. My classmates hum the Maisey song, pushing her dangling body out of their way as they rush through the halls. My waking moments are no better, taunting me with what the letter I've tucked into my pillowcase might say.

I wake again to Mom, calling because the school's automated system left her a message saying I was absent this morning. Shit. It's already quarter to twelve.

"I'm tired, my head hurts, but I'm going."

"You can forget about school if you want. Go back to sleep and I'll see you when I get home."

"I don't know what I want to do," I say, almost whining.

"Well, it's up to you," she says, like it's no big deal and says good-bye. The consolation that it's Friday taps my shoulder and reminds me that I've made plans with Sean. I look back out the window and the golden rays win, pulling me out of bed.

Fresh out of the shower, jeans from yesterday and a long-sleeved Jane Eyre T-shirt, I sit back on the bed, reach into my pillowcase and pull out the creased and folded white envelope.

Bree Hughes. The hollow echo of her saying my name in the school bathroom replays in my head, like an encore I didn't ask for. The way she'd said it. Patronizing. The envelope unfolds itself into my hands, as does the letter. Sloppy wispy script, blatantly screaming that she was tired and didn't care. I unfold it, letting my eyes drift to the top heading and right back off the page. Again, it's there. *Bree Hughes.* Like she's taunting me. My throat gets rushed by my heart, so hard and so rapid that I just can't. I flip the letter over, refolding it with swift sloppy hands and stuffing it back into the envelope and my pillowcase. I can't read this right now. Not today. Not when I'm trying to get to school, to walk through the hallways looking like my shit's so together I can be a fucking Prom Queen.

FIFTEEN

I get to school at lunchtime and everyone is chirping and buzzing with the news of Maisey. I hear snippets of the tragedy passing each lunch table. I can't even stand in the lunch line without hearing about it.

"It's crazy. Everyone treated her like ass."

"At least she'll go to heaven because all dogs go to heaven."

"No, dude, she was a mouse. Where the hell do mice go?"

"The moon?"

"That doesn't make sense."

"Sure it does, moon's made of cheese, dipshit."

I clank my tray back onto the line and shove through the two assholes. "*Excuse* you." I grab a bottle of water and walk right to the cashier.

"That's all you're getting today?" asks Kendall. "Prom Queen diet, huh?"

"I had a big breakfast."

"Did you hear what happened?" asks Sam, mouth agape. Kendall leans in, eyes wide, waiting to hear a story she's obviously heard a hundred times today. "Maisey Morgan committed suicide. *Suicide.* How sad. Can you believe it?"

I inhale slowly through my nose and as I exhale, I use every ounce of energy I have into fighting the urge to cry. To scream. To run. "Yeah, I can believe it," I say. "Our class pretty much made her life a living hell. So why not? Maybe she's in a better place."

"Well, I'm Christian and I know this sounds wrong, but suicide is a sin. So that means she would be—."

"Kendall. Don't even. *That* is just wrong. You didn't know her," Sam says.

"Heaven or hell, either one sounds better than high school. I don't want to talk about it, okay," I say. "And none of us knew her, so get over it."

"Damn," says Sam holding her hands up. "Sorry."

"Fine," says Kendall. "New subject. Bree, what's up with Prom? You going with us or not? It's gonna be fun. We're renting an SUV limo instead of a regular limo. And taking a road trip to Valley Fair the next day, too."

"*Prom: Parties of One* is the hottest ticket." Sam brushes her fingers through the edge of her fro-hawk. "You could even match your corsage to the pink streak I'm putting in my hair. So far we have six of us going . . . you really should come."

"Breeeeee!" Someone steps up behind me. "I had no idea. This queen doesn't have a date?" Justin Conner plants his ass on the seat next to me and hangs his arm on my shoulder. "Neither do I, we should probably go together then."

"Sounds like a blast." I pull his hand off my shoulder, dropping it like a dirty pair of underwear. "I think I'll pass. You have a better chance of getting with Jane. As a matter of fact, I heard she doesn't have a date either. You should ask her."

He shrugs. "Maybe I will. Anyway, I was coming over here to see how many haikus are due for Nord's class. I did three but can't remember if we're supposed to have three or four?"

"Haikus today? Oh crap, I forgot. Talk to you guys later." I grab my water and rush to my locker for a pen and paper. Writing a few haikus is a lot more tolerable than dodging Prom inquisitions and Maisey gossip in the cafeteria.

My eyes stay dry but I bleed my emotions into my haikus. Funneling my feelings onto the paper is the next best thing to skipping the rest of the school day.

When I drop the poems onto Mr. N.'s desk as the bell rings, he hands them right back. "No, you can go ahead and take this to your desk, Ms. Hughes. Unless you have the one you'll be reading memorized?"

"Oh right," I say, shaking my head as if I'd just remembered. Like I knew all along we'd be reading them aloud. As if it's no big deal and I hadn't made the poems so personal.

Mr. Norderick leans against the whiteboard. "I'm sure everyone's heard it by now, in the hallways, if not from the morning announcement, but we've lost one of—" Mr. N. swallows, clears his throat, and pauses long enough for me to worry that he's going to cry. "We've lost one of our classmates. Miss Morgan was smart, polite, kind, and respectful. It's a tremendous loss for her family and friends, but for our school as a whole. Whether she was a friend or not, I offer my own condolences, and if any-one needs anything let me know. I also hope her loss is one that'll remind us to reach out to our friends and family in uncertain times."

Justin's hand creeps up behind me. "I'm reaching out," he whispers.

Kallie giggles as I elbow his hand back and glare. "Could you be any more awful?"

Mr. Norderick unbuttons his navy blue Friday blazer and sits on his desk. "In life, death is one of the hardest things to deal with. Did anyone have any questions or anything to add?"

Everyone glances around and shrugs or just stares at the tops of their desks. I chew the inside of my cheek, wishing I could think about anything but Maisey. And how I barely noticed her in class, but she was here. Now she's not here and I can see her. Her eyes are still just as sad and her posture is even more defeated. And I can feel it in my bones.

"Are we reading one or all of our poems today?" Shandy asks.

"Good call, Miss Silvers. Since no one has anything to add, let's get to work."

Shandy recites a poem about a cold winter snow without even glancing at her paper. Ready to submit her work to the Pulitzer judges, she ends her poem with a proud display of her teeth, braces banded in maroon and white.

Nord calls on me next.

Without the energy to even attempt to improvise something less personal, I read the first one I wrote.

Flames blaze over tears
Ashes search, clawing black skies
New wings make her dance

"Very nice," says Mr. N.

Kallie reads hers about a cherry blossom in a snowstorm. She leans across the aisle and whispers, "I found mine online."

Justin pokes me in the back with a pencil. "Oh you just came up with that today? Doubt it. You didn't have to bail on us at lunch. It's cool, though, I'm over you. Do you really think I have a chance with Jane?"

Mr. Norderick interrupts. "Mr. Conner, I guess you're volunteering yourself to go next. Please do us a favor by delighting us with all three of your haikus." Justin stands and reads about video games, bacon, and something about a breakfast burrito, all three sounding like he's inviting us to a mattress sale.

Maisey's seat, screaming its emptiness, keeps dancing in my peripheral vision. A lump forms in my throat, and I zone in and out until Nord calls on Sean.

"Mr. Mills, do you have something for us today?"

Sean straightens his back against the seat.

Gray diamonds sparkle
Breezy smile alluring laugh
Drives me past crazy

. . . He clears his throat. "I hope she says yes when I ask her to Prom."

Mr. Norderick adjusts his eyeglasses, looking down his nose at Sean, "Impressive, had it not been for the last line. A haiku is only three lines."

"I know," says Sean. "I just threw that last line in there on impulse. For fun."

"Okay, gotchya Mr. Mills. Good luck, we all hope she says yes too."

The class laughs. I blush a rushing wave of hot crimson as I run through the lines he'd read over again in my head. Is he talking about my eyes? Breezy? *He's talking about me?*

Kallie pumps her fist and mouths "Yes!" as I run through Sean's lines once more. I shrug. Another classmate reads his haiku and she kicks me sideways from her desk across the aisle.

Of course he's talking about me. He kissed me last night. On the fore-head. And for real kissed me this past weekend. And he's amazing. And he likes me. And he's going to ask me to Prom. I smile back at Kallie.

The bell rings and everyone jumps up, pre-armed with books and folders to rush the door, as if the school's on fire. It's the sound and adren-aline pumped vibe of "it's finally Friday."

Justin Conner sings from behind me, "You're sooooo vain, you prob-ably think that haiku's about you, don't chew don't chew."

Sean looks back with a smile. "You're a real riot, Conner. Stop flirt-ing with my girl, 'kay?"

Sean clasps my free hand with his, "See ya later Kallie. Todd." He nods to Todd, leaning against the door frame, waiting for Kallie.

I raise my eyebrows and give Kallie a "See you later. Call me!" look. I hasten with Sean's pull, trying to keep up, focusing on the back of his neck, slightly flushed, as he leads me through the maze of students ready to start the weekend.

I weave through the cars in our school parking lot and pull up next to Sean's, as he'd instructed before we parted ways to go to our lockers. He's leaning on the passenger side door, a guitar slung over his shoulder with a black and white strap. He bends toward my window, signaling me to roll it down. As I do, the smell of cedar and spearmint kiss my nose. A dimple appears beneath his right cheekbone as he smiles.

"Hey there. Thanks for making it all the way here to parking spot 128. I'll be here, every Monday through Friday until the end of May.

However, I'm only singing this song once. One time and one time only. Feel free to step out of the car, Miss." His blue eyes twinkle in a way that makes me all at once: nervous, giddy, and a little embarrassed. I am *so* not the only one left in the school parking lot.

I hop out of the car, closing the door with the back of my heel.

Sean fans himself with the tip of his T-shirt collar, beneath his sweatshirt. Then as if that's not enough, unzips his gray hoodie, exposing a blue faded T-shirt that lightly hugs the muscle definition in his chest. Not that I notice that type of thing, or really care, but if I did, I'd be impressed. Who am I kidding? He looks totally hot. Guitar in hand, he strums slow, then fast, and looks directly at me until he starts to sing. He alternates eye contact between my eyes and the hood of my car.

> *Gray diamonds sparkle*
> *Breezy smile alluring laugh*
> *Drives me past crazy*
> *Oh don't you think*
> *Don't you think*
> *Don't you think maybe*
> *You could*
> *You would*
> *Well I think you should*

His fingers tap the guitar a few times before he speaks in a monotone:

"Ever since I started hearing your laugh in Language Arts. Ever since your crazy ex-boyfriend requested I sing you a song. Ever since I told my mom how cute you are when you blush. And ever since I started imagining you wearing vampire teeth to the Prom. Just kidding about the vampire teeth. Unless you wanna."

Covering my face in my hands, I laugh as he strums the guitar faster.

> *Ever since I started hanging out with a cool pretty funny*
> *smart girl like you I just wanted to ask you, ask you, ask you . . .*

114

to the Prom. Please don't say no because I didn't work as hard or
maybe work as long, on the rest of this song, or as
I did on the haiku, as I did on the haiku, the haiku.
Because I worked really hard on that haiku, that haiku,
that haiku. I'm really only improvising the last lines of this song.

I stare at him, trying to focus on keeping my laugh to a loud giggle, but soon I can't stop and I'm wiping tears from my face.

And I'm just gonna keep making up more words until
you tell me you'll go to Prom with me. I hope you say yes.
It's gonna be a freakin' awesome Prom. Hey, please don't forget,
I can't stop singing until you say yes . . . Please say yes—

"Oh my God, Sean. Please stop." I say holding my side, which has literally started cramping. "Yes, I'll go to Prom with you."

"Are you *sure?*" Sean asks, his fingers hovering over his guitar strings. "I could keep playing."

A few girls in a red pick-up truck parked behind me are clapping, saying things like "Ooooh, how sweet" and "Omigod that is the cutest."

"Yes, I'm sure." Throwing out my insecurities, the heaviness of the morning, the afternoon, and without a care as to who may or may not be looking, I take a giant step forward and plant a kiss on Sean's soft crooked smile. He pushes his body against the guitar between us, slightly opening his mouth, and kisses me back. A shiver travels up my spine, and a sigh escapes my mouth into his. The cars disappear into the sky, and the parking lot falls into the earth. All I can think about is the warmth of Sean's arms and the taste of spearmint on his tongue, kissing away the aches of the last two days.

****

Mom sits on my bed Saturday morning with her phone and an unsteady gaze. "Hey hon. Good morning. I have a couple things to run by you."

Something's up.

"What is it? Are you and Dad getting a divorce?" I smirk.

"You can be such a smart ass, ya know?" She smacks my leg with the phone. "Well, two things. Your friend from school, Maisey, her obituary is online. It says the wake is tomorrow evening and the funeral is Monday. I think we should at least go to the wake; it looks like the funeral is closed to family." She looks to me for a response.

I can't even face the letter Maisey left me. But to actually go to her wake? Shame jolts through my body in such a rush that I shudder.

"Okay, I guess you're right. I should be there. What's the other thing?"

She purses her lips together, inhales and speaks quickly. "I was wondering if you wanted to talk to someone about what happened the other day?"

"Someone?"

"I made you an appointment for a therapist. It's in a couple weeks on Saturday morning. I know you have a lot going on right now so I thought—"

"You thought what? It's the end of my senior year, Mom. I have a lot of crap going on and the last thing I need is someone who thinks they know who I am because they read a bunch of books in college. *No.* I'm not going. You can cancel it, or better yet, maybe you should go. You're the one who seems to have issues with *me*."

My mom does the thing where she lowers her voice to act calm, but I can tell she's mad. "I don't know what you're talking about and why you're getting so worked up. It's a counselor. Someone like Ms. Selinski. Listen, you had a panic attack on Thursday. You might also have some issues with me and your dad. I thought it might be easier to talk to someone else about it, rather than us."

I narrow my eyes. "Easier for you, you mean?"

"I'm not sure what you mean by that." The look on her face tells me she knows *exactly* what I mean.

We sit in silence for a few moments, and I wait for her to say something else. I've said my part. Mom sighs and attempts a half hug. My body is stiff as I sit on the edge of my bed, rubbing my toes into the soft shags of my carpet.

"I love you, Bree Ella. I'm trying here. I've made some mistakes and I'm not sure how to say it all without rehashing a whole lot of junk and talking about stuff you don't need to hear about. I know I'm not perfect. I seem to have skipped over this chapter in the mom manual."

"Really Mom?" I roll my eyes and try not to smile. "The mom manual? That's so corny."

She cracks a smile and we both giggle. But then I tell her I'm still not going to any counselor.

That night I stay home. No call from Kallie, Sean's playing guitar at Azumi, and when he texted to see if I wanted to meet up, I wrote that I was tired but maybe tomorrow.

I decide to do some of the studying I've been neglecting the last couple weeks. As I'm jotting down some definitions for sociology class, my phone rings and it's Dad, checking in to see how I'm doing.

"Making sure I'm not having another *said panic attack* or making plans to jump out of a window?" I ask.

"Your sarcasm is charming and a pain in the ass at the same time."

I don't disagree. We make small talk about his current beat partner at work (rookie cop), how Uncle Mike's doing (same ole same ole), and my grades at school (mostly Bs).

"I hear you're giving your mom a hard time," my dad says.

"Dad, come on. You too? I'm not going to a therapist. I've had to talk to the one at school, like a million times this year."

"*Escuchame*, Bree Ella," he says. He says my name the way he always did when I was little, putting Bree and Ella together but with a Spanish accent. Bree-a-ya. "We didn't really get into it the other night because of the circumstances, but I think that with everything that's happened this past year, your mom might have a good point."

"Really? How come you guys never went to counseling?"

"We did."

"Oh." Anxiety bubbles zip through my core. "Well," I say, "I didn't know that and now that I do, it's not a very good sell. I'm really okay and I don't feel like talking about any of this with some stranger."

"Well, what about talking about it—or talking about *anything* with your dad? Regularly. How come you haven't called lately? I moved out in July and I've only talked to you a handful of times."

"I don't know," I say.

"Do you think you're upset about the divorce?"

"Nooo, Dad. It's not that. Or maybe it is. It's . . . I don't know. I'm just pissed sometimes when I think about it, that's all."

"Why?"

"Because it was kind of shitty how everything went down." I take a deep breath and continue, "A few years of listening to you and Mom fighting all the time, you leaving whenever you felt like it, which was like all the time, and then it's over, just like that. Then you leave for good. No one even asked me what I thought or said anything about it until it was all over with."

A moment of silence.

"*Si.*" He sighs. "*Entiendo.*" Another pause. "I'm sorry it happened that way. Maybe it was a lousy way to go about it." His voice is pained.

"So maybe I shouldn't even care because you guys didn't."

"It's not that we didn't care. We thought we were doing what was best by keeping you out of it. Bree, I'll do what I can to get your mom off your back about the counseling, but we need to talk about this more, is that a deal?"

"Yes, deal. But I'm kind of over it right now so how 'bout another time?"

"Sure, no problem," Although he doesn't let on, I'm positive he's sighing with relief. "I'd rather talk about the guy waiting on my daughter's doorstep the other day like a lost puppy. I forgot to run his license plates."

I laugh, grateful he's broken a bit of the tension.

"He's not a puppy, Dad. He's an ex–drug dealer. He just got out of jail a couple weeks ago. Nothing serious though, he was only trying to make enough money to rent a tux so he can take me to Prom."

"Not even funny, Bree. Not even funny."

SIXTEEN

The Lord opens his arms,
The heavenly choir sings,
For today, a soul rises up
To soar on angel wings . . .

I read this over and over in my seat, flexing my calves as the backs of my heels dig into the stiff, bristly carpet. Mom sits next to me, in silence, on a scratchy cushioned chair in a funeral parlor that feels like the basement of some old lady's house.

Apparently, Maisey's here too, at the front of the room in a fancy blue marbled box atop a table. A picture sits on each side of the box. One's of Maisey as a baby, eyes laughing, wearing a bright yellow tutu and a smile that lights up her whole face. The other is a lousy generic senior picture from this year. I can tell by the corny way she's cupping her face with both hands, our school flag, the maroon and white shield, and a picture of our signature Bengal snarling behind her. Mom has the same picture of me on the fireplace mantle. Maisey's eyes are nowhere near laughing and her smile is just lips forced and stretched open over her bucked-white teeth. It's like she knew the pose was corny too, knew that a smile wouldn't make her look happy, just pushed through, long enough for them to get a couple shots.

The box she's in looks like a jewelry box, which is kind of surprising. I thought when people were cremated they went into some sort of vase-like urn or a jar. I wonder if ashes in a box were her parents' wishes or hers. Or maybe whatever happened gave them no choice. The way she died is still just a montage of rumors and graphic "what-if" images flashing in my brain.

Not that I want to know the truth. Either way I still can see her face, the pissed off glare permeating her eyes, glossy and swollen. When Mom and I walked up to Maisey's box, her parents stood there like statues, taking almost a full minute before they remembered us from Thursday's visit. Her dad gave me a "hello" head nod, and shook my hand. Mrs. Morgan gave me a starchy hug as I felt her body resist a convulsion into tears.

"Thank you for coming. It means a lot," she said.

I could barely eke out an "I'm sorry." I walked away, choking back a sob before my mom even finished her hug.

We're next to an aisle, making it easier to leave. Mom said we wouldn't have to stay long, just about a half hour or so. I open my purse and click my phone. 6:12. It doesn't seem right that we just sit in these chairs, doing and saying nothing while people come and go. My body is swarming with anxiety bees. The buzzing is like it was the day I found out about Maisey. Just keep breathing. That's all I have to do. Try not to cry, don't let my thoughts run all over the place and just slow down. Not that I want to slow down any of this. Being here is awful. Is this what Maisey imagined when she thought about killing herself? Did she weigh her pain with the pain she'd be leaving behind for her family? Her family is unraveling and she is somewhere else. Did she even think this far ahead and if she did, was she thinking about how her mom would look? Standing in a shitty room, lost, tortured, crying her eyes out, with her daughter gone. *Forever.*

This does *not* feel the way it looks in movies. In the movies, it's sad, tragic, and almost beautiful. Violins and soft piano, pretty people gliding around in black, dark sunglasses hiding their eyes. But this shit? Right here, right now is nothing close to an easy state of melancholy. The music comes from overhead in a static whisper, the same kind they play at Bev's Grocery. The room is dingy and drab, even with the scattered floral arrangements that barely give off any scent. It smells like wet concrete and bar soap. The yellowed walls have seen so much that they just don't care anymore. Feet shuffling, hands looking for things to do, no one, not one person wants to be here. Staring back at Maisey's box, I know, just know that if she saw this, she wouldn't have wanted any of it. She wouldn't have left them behind.

Tears pool and I press my knuckles into my eyes. And just when I think it's *not* like the movies in here, Jane walks in. Jane Hulmes, but with a reluctant air, lagging behind her mom and the guy from her driveway the night of Chris's party. He's thin, stiff suited, with Jane's dark hair and eyes. Her mom's a plump, pretty bleached blonde wearing too many layers for the spring and more than enough eyeliner rimming her eyes. Jane's in a short black dress with her hair pulled into a low bun. Her eyes are blank, alternating her stare between straight ahead and the ground in front of her. I shrink a few inches lower in my seat.

Why on earth is she here? Mean girl with a heart of gold? An overwhelmingly guilty conscience? It must be the latter. If *I* feel bad, surely Belmont's biggest bitch and Maisey's nastiest critic must be rotting inside.

I "hmph" quietly. *Too late on this one, Jane. Maybe next time.*

They walk the aisle, and the eyes of Maisey's parents quickly register their presence. A sudden flash of anger flashes in Mr. Morgan's eyes. Mrs. Morgan sways and steps back.

They must have known what a bully Jane was.

Mr. Morgan lunges forward, stalking up to the Hulmes with such vengeance that I flinch. Collective gasps come from the mourners, seated and standing. Mrs. Morgan is frozen next to Maisey's box, wringing her hands.

Mr. Morgan grabs the guy's arm, spewing into his face, "Joe, you don't belong here. The laws haven't changed just because it's a funeral. You have no right. No right. You're an abomination."

Mrs. Morgan steps up, her voice shakes. "Please leave before we notify the police."

"I'm sorry," the man mutters as he lowers his head and walks straight out without looking back. Mrs. Morgan turns to Jane and her mother. Jane's head is down, her body shivering while her mom stands like a statue clasping Jane's hand. Mrs. Morgan steps directly into Ms. Hulmes's gaze. "*You*. You can leave with your husband."

Ms. Hulmes shakes her head, chin quivering, tears falling from her eyes. "Please . . ."

Mr. Morgan puts his arm around his wife pulling her back, then addresses Ms. Hulmes as Jane studies the tops of her own shoes. "Janice, you need to go. Now."

"Enough said, Charles. We're leaving."

"Oh jeez, let's go too." I poke Mom's arm.

"Just hang on, it'd be rude to get up right now." She rests her hand on my knee to stop me from rising.

"I need to go to the bathroom," I say.

"Bree." She presses harder on my knee.

"I'm serious. I promise. I'll be right back."

As I pass the window of the front doors, I see Ms. Hulmes and Joe walking back out into the parking lot. Jane isn't behind them but three guys are at their heels as if making sure they're leaving. Ms. Hulmes turns back toward the funeral home but the tallest guy blocks her as she argues, waving her hands around and pointing back my way. One of the guys turns and heads back as Jane's mom and Joe are escorted to the black SUV from the other night. I step away from the door and head down the hallway looking for a restroom sign.

"Excuse me, Miss."

I spin around and the tall guy from outside is waving me down.

"Um, yes?" I raise my eyebrows as my heart drops at the idea of being caught semi-eavesdropping.

"I hate to bother you but do you mind checking the ladies room for a small brunette in a black dress? Her name's Jane."

Uh, yeah, I do mind. I didn't really want to see Jane here. "Sure, no problem. But I don't know where the restrooms are."

"Last door on the right. If she's in there, please tell her to make it quick. Her ride's in a hurry to leave."

I push the bathroom door open, hoping to find it empty, but it's not. Right away I notice Jane's black heels and her voice echoing a whispered screech over a bathroom stall. "I'm not going back with you guys. I'll find my own ride. I told you this was a bad idea. You're so fucking delusional, Mom. No. I'm not getting back in the car with him. I have a ride. Just go. I'm hanging up now. Bye."

I open the door again, and shake it a little and cough as I pretend to walk back in. "Hello? Is somebody in here? Jane?"

"Shit." She whispers. "Hang on a second," she calls out. A few seconds later, the stall door opens. Jane adjusts the thin black strap of a tiny black leather bag over her shoulder and speaks into her phone. "Hey, It's me. I just texted you. I need you to pick me up from the SA gas station in about ten minutes. Call or text me as soon as you get this."

She steps up to the sink and turns on the faucet. Her face is snide as hell as she yanks a towel to dry her hands. "What're you doing here?"

"What do you think?"

Her lip twitches a little and she raises an eyebrow. "You just get here?" Her fear is way too easy to read. If I was half the asshole she is, I'd let her know the spectacle I just witnessed or at least make her sweat a little.

"Yep. Just got here. About to go pay my respects. What do you care?"

"No reason," she exhales, relaxing just barely. "Well, whatever. This was—nothing. Forget it."

She pushes past me and waltzes out the bathroom door.

"You didn't even use soap," I say to the door flapping past the frame.

A minute later I'm falling back into my chair next to Mom, silently processing the scene that just unfolded. When I watched Jane walk through the parking lot, the SUV was already gone.

"Let's sit for a few more minutes or until Mrs. Morgan comes back so we can say good-bye," Mom whispers.

Rifling through the junk in my purse, I'm checking my phone, watching the time, and hoping for a missed call or text from Sean. To add a bright shard of happy to this dark and mind-fucktacular day. For the next few minutes, people walk up and down the aisle like an assembly line of slow-moving head nodders, head shakers, and huggers. I'd feel like a zombie too, but my brain is way too busy for that. Finally, Mrs. Morgan returns, elbows locked with the lady who passed me the little flyer when me and Mom got here.

I slide my fingers beneath my eye to catch what I hope will be the last of today's teardrops. Then I grab Mom's hand and whisper, "Okay, please, can we go? I can't take anymore. I need to go home."

"Okay, yes. Let's go."

Mom swings by the gas station on our way home and asks me to run in and grab her a Diet Coke.

Sitting on a bench to the left of the door is Jane; knees locked, feet jutted out and her head in her hands.

I stroll through the door, eyes straight ahead, hoping she's gone when I walk back out.

Aaaaaaand she's not. Sigh. "Jane?"

Her head jerks up and she's got two serious lines of black mascara running down each cheek. "You again? What?"

"Do you need a ride or something?" I ask.

"No, I don't need any more of your fucking charity rides," she says glancing down at her phone and clicks it a couple times.

"What's your problem? You're obviously stranded because you didn't want to ride with your mom and dad or whoever those people were."

"I'm not sure what you're talking about. Someone's picking me up any minute now so if you'd pull your head out of my biz-n*ass* that'd be great."

Glancing back at my mom waiting in the car, I consider my options. In spite of the world's bitchiest tone, Jane's eyes bleed desperation. Whatever was going on at the funeral home has freaked her out. Jane is the last person I'd ever expect to lose her shit, but she's definitely on the edge.

"Really? It doesn't look like it. We can drop you off somewhere else to wait if you want?"

"What do you care if I . . ." her voice trails off as she clicks through her phone again. "I mean, thanks for the offer and I can probably just—"

"Just come on."

And she does. She follows me to Mom's car and hops in the backseat without a word.

Mom raises an eyebrow as she grabs the pop from my hand.

"This is Jane, from school, she needs a ride home if that's okay."

"Actually I can't," Jane's voice cracks, "go home. I mean, I'm not going home and if you don't mind, the coffee shop or diner would work better. If it's okay?"

"No problem," says Mom. "It's on our way."

Jane's phone doesn't ring the whole way there although she makes a series of about two hundred thirty-eight unanswered calls. When we drop her off she tells my mom thanks but doesn't look my way.

"Poor girl," says Mom. "I can't believe her parents left without her in all that drama."

Yep, poor little bitch girl. "Yeah, poor Jane. Let's go home now. I just want to curl up in my bed."

SEVENTEEN

"Sorry you're still sick. You missed out on Tuna Melt Tuesday," says Sean.

"Tuna melts," I say. "Yeah, I'm going to pass on being sad about missing TMT. Tuna shouldn't be allowed anywhere but the ocean. The smell would've made me worse. Hopefully I'll be better by tomorrow."

"Hope so. That's what you said yesterday and I ended up crying over my desk 'cause I didn't have you breathing on me in Norderick's class."

"Crying, huh?"

"Almost."

"I don't breathe on you." A short laugh falls from my lips.

"Guess it's better you don't breathe on me if you're sick, right?"

"I'll be fine by tomorrow. It's just a virus. Something my mom picked up from those little germ hoarders from her school."

"You sure I can't come by? I could bring you soup or crayons?"

"Crayons?" I twirl the drawstring of the pilly gray sweats I've had on since Sunday night.

"When I was little and I'd get sick, my mom would make soup and my dad would bring me home a new coloring book."

"That's cute. Thanks, but I'm fine. I don't want you to catch anything and I'm still really tired." *Really tired and sad. Plus, I haven't showered since Sunday.*

"All right, but if you're not back by tomorrow, I'm going to climb a ladder into your window. I'm not afraid of your germs."

"Okay, you've got a deal."

I hang up, slide the phone to the other side of my bed, and pull my pillow into the curve of my neck. I grind my fist into the mattress, wishing the thought of being back in school dealing with people again didn't feel so heavy, like so much work.

My phone buzzes my eyes back open about an hour later.

SEAN MILLS.

Just wanted to say good night.

I smile and write back, **G'night. :)**

I get that liquid rush feeling through my veins, just remembering Sean's kiss and his hand on my neck. I fall asleep, thoughts of Maisey fading out and focusing, instead, on the memory of Sean's lips sliding into mine, warming my body beneath my sheets.

****

Wednesday morning eventually creeps into my room and just opening my eyes feels like a major feat. The alarm blares and Mom's words from the night before ring just as loud, "You're going to school tomorrow or I'm bringing you to the doctor."

I pull myself out of bed and into the shower for the first time since the wake. After scrubbing my face, my shower caddy unsuctions from the wall, spilling everything onto the floor. In defeat, I slide down onto the warmed tiles, letting the scalding water run over my knees. I grab my razor from the floor, not even trying to shake the image of what Maisey might've looked like on her last day. *Was this how she did it?* I slide the pad of my middle finger over the razor's smooth edge, tears springing to my eyes. The pain in Mom's eyes as she'd gripped my hand on the Morgans' doorstep and at the funeral parlor. She didn't say it but I knew what she was thinking. She couldn't handle losing me. If Maisey's parents were ever okay before this, I can't imagine that they'll ever be okay again. I think of Anne and Tera, sitting as two in the library after school, instead of the trio they once were. They'll never be the same, either.

I wonder if they both got letters from Maisey. Did they read them right away or are they like me? Afraid of knowing the truth about the kind of pain that could kill you Afraid of finding out if it really is all my fault.

Once the water runs lukewarm, I rise. *Fake it 'til you make it.* I got this.

When I get to my locker at school, Sean's leaned up against it, a smile spreading on his face that I can't help but return.

"Hey, you made it." He reaches out and brushes his fingers along my wrist.

"Yep. I'm all clear, still a little tired but totally not contagious."

The warning bell rings, lockers slam, kids start pushing and piling toward the halls as Sean leans in and kisses me on the mouth. His lips linger long enough to make me want to go back home and cuddle up in bed, this time bringing him with me.

Maisey's empty chair in last period, untouched like a plague, is another cold reminder of her absence—like the rumors, unraveling in the hallways.

Kallie nods toward the empty seat and starts with the same rumor Kendall had brought up at lunch. "Did you hear that her sister found her naked in the bathtub? I'm sure it's not true but like, who's saying this shit?"

I cringe. "I don't know, but as long as we're willing to listen, why not just keep making the stories crazier and crazier?"

"Right. People are sick."

Justin leans in, "I heard her friend Anne and the private-school-looking girl are going to pull a double suicide at Prom."

"Sure," says Sean. "But only if you do it first, Conner."

Shandy shushes us over her shoulder.

"Did she just shush us?" Kallie asks loud enough for her to hear. "Class hasn't even started yet. Simmer down, Shandy. No one's going to ruin your Prom."

Shandy rolls her eyes and jerks back around.

Sean sets his hand on my desk just as Nord starts tapping his high-lighter. "Call me tonight," he says. "Maybe we can grab dinner or go study?"

"Sure," I say, pulling the edges of my mouth into a smile. He turns back in his seat as I nurse the anxiety in my gut. Half of me wants to spend any second I can with him and the other half wants to roll into a ball in my bed and sleep until tomorrow.

EIGHTEEN

W hat about this one?" Kallie asks, rifling through a rack of dresses at Main Street Formals, Belmont's only option for formal wear.

I shake my head. "Nothing red. That's too showy for me."

"Hey! My dress is red." Kallie swats my arm with the dress hanger.

"Exactly. I don't wanna show you up."

"I wonder what colors the other girls are wearing. Maybe we should check. I ordered mine online, but if anyone even comes close to matching me—"

"You sound like one of them. You're scaring me, Kal." I laugh.

"Just grab at least one more dress to try on. I cannot believe you've waited this long. When you're on Prom Court you have to represent. Plus, Sean Mills. How crazy is that? If anyone would've told us last year that we'd be up for Prom Queens and our dates are the hottest guys in school, we'd have laughed our asses off."

"I wish I'd have known. I would've been able to hold out and skip the whole 'Chip Ryan' debacle. Yeesh!" I grab a couple dresses off the rack and we head into the dressing room. Two black dresses and one silver. As I'm holding up the embellished top of a short, shiny black number, Kallie strains to zip me up. The zipper pinches me right as we hear the *bing bong* of the store's front door.

"Ouch!" I flinch.

"Oops, sorry," Kallie says.

A familiar voice takes over the whole shop.

"I cannot believe you stood me up last night. You said as soon as you dropped her off, you'd be over."

No question about it. The high, sharp, on the edge tone belongs to Jane. *I don't have to guess who she's talking to.* Kallie and I stare at each other like we've driven over a dead skunk pile.

Kallie tugs the zipper to the top. Her reflection behind me scowls. "Ew, what's she doing here? There's no way she doesn't already have her dress." We both peek our heads out of the curtain.

"Shut up for a second," Jane spits into the phone, then moves it away from her face to address the sales lady. "I'm here for a pickup. I have a pageant dress that should be ready and a Prom dress here for alterations, so if you can check on that too. Last name is Hulmes."

The lady nods and disappears behind a set of double doors. Jane gets back to her phone, "You took her to dinner last night so it shouldn't be tough to cancel tonight. I can't keep doing this. You promised we'd start spending more time together. Figure your shit out and call me back." Jane sighs and hangs up the phone, wiping an angry tear off her cheek.

Kallie's cheeks flush with a warm pink Her facial expression goes from livid to embarrassed to . . . nothing.

"I have to go to the bathroom, I'll be right back." She races through the curtain and disappears. Jane stands at the counter tapping her foot, oblivious to her eavesdroppers.

Buzzzz. Buzzzz. Kallie's phone vibrates from the top of her purse. A flash of light highlights a text on her oversized screen.

TODD.

Hey Lover, don't hate me but I have to babysit my cousins tonight—just found out! I'll try to come by ur house after! XOXO-TDubs

Lover? T Dubs? Ugh. What a douche bag. Actually, a douche bag is too good for him. He shouldn't be allowed anywhere near vaginas. Todd White is an enema bag. At least I'm here for Kallie and hopefully I won't need to hold her back from fighting Jane.

I eye my reflection and frown. This dress is so not me. The top is like an explosion of taffeta and little wires of shiny black beads. The bottom's way too short and it's so tight on my hips that it's bunching at my waist.

"Psst, it's me. Hide your ass, hide your twins!" Kallie swooshes back into the dressing room with a grin. "That dress is a no. It's like hooker meets . . ."

"Nineteen eighties stripper?" I ask.

"Exactly. Try the silver one. It's hot without looking strippery."

I watch from the corner of my eye as she picks up her phone and lets out a long hiss between her teeth.

"Don't tell me," I say, "Todd?"

"What? No," she says fumbling around in her bag. "Just my mom wanting to know if I'll be home in time for dinner." She zips me into the silver dress with a strained smile. "This is the one. You're stunning."

"I think you're right," I agree, juggling my enthusiasm for the dress with the reality that my best friend is most definitely getting dicked around by this jerk. And there's nothing I can do about it. Not to mention the fact that she just lied to me. This Prom thing has really become a pain in the ass. She's right about one thing though. This dress *is* the one. I can't help but wonder what Sean will think. It's form fitting, long and slinky, showing off the golden tone of my skin and the random spray of beauty marks across my bare shoulders. Best of all, it accentuates the curve of my hips that I used to try to hide.

All I can do now is follow Kallie's lead and act like I don't care about what we just witnessed. If Todd and Jane aren't going to ruin Prom for Kallie, they're not going to ruin mine either. I pile my hair up onto my head, strike my best model pose in the mirror, and wink at Kallie. Click. No problems here. Prom Court ready.

****

"So, let me see that dress you bought last weekend." Sean walks over to my closet door.

"Don't *even*." I jump from my beanbag and sashay in-between the closet door and Sean. He bounds over to my wide-open bedroom door instead and closes it with quiet stealth.

"You're gonna get in trouble." I smile and push him onto my bed.

"Feels like you're the one looking to get in trouble." Sean bounces back up and props a pillow between him and my headboard.

It's the first time Sean and I have been together in my room. In any room, alone. I can see why my mom told me to leave my door open. Rather, I can feel it. *Horny teenagers.*

"So, what do you want to do? Hang out here or go somewhere?" I ignore the ache.

"I don't care—whatever you want. I'm just glad you're hanging out with me. And not sick, tired, or maybe blowing me off. I almost thought I was going to take Justin Conner to Prom. You had me worried."

"Yeah well . . ."

"Yeah well, what?" Sean pats the space next to him on my bed.

"Scoot over." I sit, leaning up against the headboard next to him, extending my legs, and feeling a warm blaze as his thigh brushes against mine. "It's silver."

"What?"

"My dress. It's silver."

"Oh. Okay. I guess we're back to talking about your dress."

"Well, supposedly it's an important detail. Kallie says you're s'posed to match it to some of your tux accessories and the corsage."

"Oh, right. My mom asked me about that. Hey, stop trying to distract me from the real issue here. Why haven't you wanted to hang out? I don't think any of our phone conversations lately have been longer than five minutes."

I drum my fingers on my knee. "I've been lame, I know. To be honest . . ." As if I can really be honest. Tell him I've spent the last two weeks since Maisey's wake beating myself up with worry, anxiety, and regrets. How I'm not sure I deserve to be with someone so great, getting ready for Prom when all this other fucked up stuff is buzzing in my head. Tell him how Maisey's eyes have been haunting me, staring, lifeless and bitter. Ask him to read me the letter she wrote that's still hiding, unread, in the pillowcase just inches away from him. Or tell him that because of all this, I feel like I want him even more than I'd care to admit. Tell him that I'm over my head, beyond crushed and crazy about him. That it's something that means and feels more than I can explain as the warmest meltiest loveliest ball of *good feelings* swishing around my stomach, my brain, in my everything, everywhere and I'm not looking to get hurt in the end.

"You were saying? To be honest?" Sean smiles, waiting for me to fill the silence I've created and filled with tension.

"This whole Prom thing is getting mega stressful, that's all. I guess I have a hard time knowing where I fit in. Because I don't."

"What do you mean, you don't fit in? That doesn't make sense. You have friends. Everyone likes you."

"*Everyone?*"

"Except maybe Jane. Like she matters. But how does one fit in to Prom Court per se? Do you need bigger hair? Maybe if your eyes were brown instead of smoldering gray. Or if you drove a Mustang or an Audi? Don't take this the wrong way, but none of this stuff is that serious." He slides his hand over my thigh.

"Smoldering gray, huh? Now that you put it that way, I'm fine. Thanks for the pep talk."

"Don't get smart with me, Hughes."

"Don't boss me, Mills. And hey, if it means anything, I missed you."

"It does mean something." He smiles shyly, his eyes dipping from my gaze to our now-clasped hands. Some of the tension in my shoulders releases.

"I better open that door before you get any ideas." I lean in to kiss him quickly but stop to inhale where his neck and shoulder meet. He turns to meet my mouth. My lips rest on his, and the kiss is gentle and intense. With a pained, slow exhale, I pull away, then grab a pillow and hit him in the side. "I'm hungry. Let's go get something to eat." As if food could satiate me.

"Probably a good idea." He tosses the pillow to the side and kisses the bottom of my ear.

"Do you wear cologne?" I ask.

"No, should I?" His low voice at my ear sends a tiny shiver down my neck and down to like, *everywhere.*

"I just love how—" I lean back into him. "The way you smell, it's good. I could just . . ." I inhale and exhale breathing into his neck, beneath his ear.

"It's soap. Sandalwood." He pulls back ever so slightly, holding my gaze, "Yeah we better get something to eat."

My breath hitches. "Good idea." Obviously we are on the same page.

****

"A-ha. I knew something was up" I say. "This place should be called 21/7. Look, it's closed from three until five in the morning." I point to the diner's business hours sign as Sean and I hover behind a group of other high school kids waiting to be seated.

"I better talk to the manager about this. This place is a sham. Let's leave." Sean turns pretending to leave.

I laugh but then see something that makes me want to follow through. Molly and Jane. Strutting through the parking lot hand in hand. Jane's perfectly slicked back ponytail is topped off with a sparkly tiara. Seriously.

"Great." *Here comes Beauty and the Barf.*

Sean follows my gaze and spots them. "Look, our colleagues. Let's dodge 'em." Sean weaves his way to the hostess stand. "Two for a booth, please. If you have one."

"No problem, right this way," the hostess says, grabbing two menus and leading us toward the other end of the restaurant. We scoot in and she rests her hand on the table leaning over Sean, her boobs practically falling onto his place setting. "Can I start you off with something to drink before your server arrives?"

"Two Cokes and if you could do me a huge favor—don't seat that tiara girl next to us. She's my sister and I told her I was working all day so I couldn't make it to her pageant. She's pretty intense. I don't want her to start flipping tables in here, if you know what I mean."

The hostess giggles and blushes. "No problem. I'll make sure she doesn't see you." She flips her gaze to me. "Did you want something to drink too?"

"I'll probably have one of the two Cokes he ordered."

She blinks a few times and giggles. "Oh yeah. Right. Of course. Got it." She rushes off.

"You sure have a way with the ladies."

"Guess so. *You're* sitting here, right?"

"Ha. I'm only here for the cheeseburgers," I say.

"Good to know." Sean glances at his menu, slides it to the edge and drums his fingers on the table. "So, I have to ask you something. Todd wants us to go to Prom with them, as a group. Did Kallie mention that?"

"No, that's weird. Anybody else in this group I should know about?"

"I don't know, it got complicated. Chris and Laura are going with Molly and Brian, and Molly's supposed to be doubling with Jane and whoever her date is. Todd said anything with Molly won't go over well with Kallie, which means Todd and Kallie are on their own unless—"

"Unless we go with them. Ugh. I need a Venn diagram to keep track of everyone who can and can't stand each other." I pretend to scrutinize the menu rather than the decision. "Well gosh, I don't know why Todd wouldn't want to go to Prom with his current girlfriend, ex-girlfriend, and his side piece. What a missed opportunity for him." I roll my eyes.

"Yeah," Sean laughs. "He must not be one for drama."

"Sure, we can go with them, it just . . . I don't know. To be honest, it sucks. She's my best friend and I have to watch her hanging out with such a . . . such a—"

"Fuckwad. I believe that's the politically correct term."

Smiling, I put the menu down. Then back up, over my face. "Shit. Speaking of fuckwads, guess who just walked in? Don't turn around."

Sean turns around, then raises an eyebrow and smirks. "Ahemmmm, Chip Ryan. Your ex-lover."

"Gross. Hardly my lover."

"Really? Meaning you weren't in love with him, or you never—*you know*? You two were dating for a while, right?"

"Ugh. Not that I want to get into it right now, but we were only dating for a couple months and we never . . ."

Our server bounces up to the table, popping his head over my menu. "Hey there, I'm Jake, I'll be your server. You two ready to order or ya need more time?"

Good save. *Thanks Jake.* We order and Sean leaves for the bathroom. Of course Chip sees me. Of course. He's probably got an app that alerts him whenever we're within a hundred feet of each other. As he glides my way, I chant over and over in my head: *please don't come up to me, please don't come up to me, please don't.*

"Bree?" he yells. "Hey Bree!" He sidles right up against the table. "How's it goin'? I see you're here with that football player guitar guy. Interesting."

"His name's Sean."

"I knew that. So, is *Sean* your new boyfriend or something? He takin' you to Prom?"

"Chip, I'm pretty sure I've told you that I'm not really trying to be friends, okay? It's not your business."

"Oh, sure. I get it. I can't talk to you in front of your new friends. Give me a break. You know these guys are idiots."

And then as if it wasn't bad enough, Jane slides up next to Chip. I shoot him a dagger. *Thanks for shouting me out Chip.*

"Well, look what the cat drug in. With Chip Ryan. Am I interrupting a drug deal or something?"

I glare. "Sorry Jane, we're out of Go-Go Juice this week. Did you need another ride somewhere?"

"So, you two are hanging out now too?" asks Chip.

"I was just coming over here to congratulate Bree here on officially stealing my Prom date. Guess all's fair in love and war, right?"

I narrow my eyes at her. "Love?"

Chip pushes Sean's sweatshirt over and sits across from me. "You're really going to Prom with him?"

Jane leans in over the table, gripping the edge with both hands. "She sure is. After he already said he'd go with me. You two haven't even been hanging out that long. Have you had sex with him yet?" She blinks her chunky spider leggy lashes.

Chip watches us like a movie.

My anger steamrolls the anxiety that's been fizzing in my stomach since Chip walked up. My teeth unclench as I glare into Jane's eyes. "Are you done here?"

"Just what I thought," she says. "You know, I'm a big contender for Prom Queen and I don't even have a fucking date now. Which smells a lot like horseshit if you ask me. I'm not trying to be mean, but you don't stand a chance so there's no reason for you to use up one of our king nominees, especially one of the good ones."

"Not trying to be mean." Chip laughs.

"Use up?" The anger pushes me to my feet as I leer back at her. "It's not my fault that no one wants to go with you. I mean, you're walking *into a diner* with a tiara on your head. Your attention whoring is so goddamned sad."

Jane sighs, shaking her head slowly. "Really? Ouch. That hurts right here." She makes a duckface and cups her left boob.

"It's not my fault the guy you're screwing has a girlfriend he obviously isn't going to leave. At least not before Prom."

Jane squishes her lips into a tight "O" and raises her chin.

I continue, "You and Todd do have something in common, though. You don't give a shit about anyone else, and he doesn't give a shit about you." The permabitch grin leaves her face for another split second so I smile, "Maybe you should decline your nomination like Maisey did."

"Good call," says Chip. "Yeah Jane, how about you off yourself the way Maisey did, too."

Jane's face falls and her words come out in almost a whisper. "Screw you, Chip."

"No, screw you," he answers. "Everyone knows Maisey killed herself because you're such a bitch."

Jane's eyes glisten as she pulls her shoulders back, and the way her fists open and close have me worried she might throw a punch.

"What's up, guys?" Sean steps between me and Jane and there's a wave of *Thank God*, as he places a hand on each of our shoulders.

Jane adjusts her crown and faces Sean. "Just talking to Bree here, you know, details about Prom, your sex life. All sorts of TMI, but don't worry, *my* lips are sealed." She narrows her eyes, "For now, anyway. Later, guys." She walks off.

"You sittin' here?" Chip asks Sean from the booth.

"Yep," answers Sean. "Pretty sure that's my sweatshirt you're sitting on."

"Sorry man. My bad." Chip gets up and Sean moves past him to sit back down in the booth.

"You okay over here?" Sean says looking from Chip to me.

"Yeah, I'm fine." I slide back into my seat.

"Yeah, man, she's all right. I was just saying hi." He turns to me. "See ya Bree."

I exhale as Chip walks away. "Oh my god. I don't get why he can't leave me alone. I'm beginning to think I can't go anywhere with you without running into my two favorite people."

"Hang on a second, okay?" Sean asks.

"Sure."

He slides out of the booth, takes a few long strides up to Chip and grabs his shoulder.

Chip's bony shoulder hunches beneath Sean's hand. He looks as skinny as he's always been, but for the first time I notice the way his spine wears his T-shirt. He faces Sean and they have an exchange that I can't make out, but Chip looks intimidated and a little pissed as he looks back and forth from Sean to where I'm sitting. I feign a deep interest in the white marbled tabletop.

Sean returns as Chip leaves my sightline, not looking back.

"What was that all about?" I ask.

"Just guy to guy stuff, but I think we're okay now. You sure you're all right?"

"Now that you're back, yes."

"So what'd I miss?" he asks.

"You missed out on a really great time, great friends, great conversation. Just three besties catching up."

"Sounds like it. Care to give me the scoop on what Jane meant by 'our sex life'? Must be pretty racy if even Jane couldn't stand it."

****

"Woooooooohooooo!" Kallie shouts through my receiver. "You, me, Todd, and Sean doubling for Prom? We're going to have the best time ever. I was scared for a minute 'cause no way did I want to triple or quadruple date with Molly and Jane. Hell's no."

"Well, when Sean told me your options I knew there was no way you'd let that fly."

"It was probably Molly's idea. She's still totally in love with him."

"She's crazy. And not funny crazy."

"Yeah, she's *bananas* crazy." I hear Kal suck air through the phone and then a short silence. "Bree?"

"Yeah?"

"You're going to be nice to Todd, right? I know he's not your favorite person, but I really don't want it to be awkward."

Too late for that. "Um, yeah, c'mon, what do you think I'm going to do? Bring out a lie detector and strap him into a chair?"

"Ha ha, I hope not. Maybe you can let that stuff go? I just don't want it to be weird between everyone."

"Kallie, I'm not going to ruin anyone's night if that's what you're thinking. I want to have fun too. This is supposed to be the most magical night of our teenagerdom, isn't it? Who am I to mess with that?"

****

NINETEEN

Something about dealing with Jane today, seeing Sean handle Chip, and me letting Kallie's stuff go makes me feel brave or *clearer headed*. Or maybe I'm just over being scared. When I lay my head down, like every night, the crinkle of Maisey's envelope in my pillow-case sends my heart racing, the back of my neck gets hot and prickly, and tears spring to my eyes. My breath usually slows down once I tell myself, *I'll read it tomorrow, for sure*. But this time I don't say that. *Tonight I'm reading it.*

The cool cotton of the pillowcase meets the warmth of my palm. Trying to relax, I breathe until the air isn't shallow in my throat. I pull the envelope all the way out, sit up cross-legged, and click my lamp on.

My heart thumps like bass in my chest. I read it through fast, like summer's first jump off the dock at Crystal Wood Beach.

My mouth is knocked open by her emotion and I gasp out loud. Everything on this page is fresh and raw. Maisey's pain is carved into each and every word. Each sentence. Each revelation of who she was and everything she was hiding.

I pull a tissue from the Kleenex box on my nightstand, wipe away my tears and blow my nose. Everyone thinks they knew her. They didn't. And they didn't know this. They didn't know what she's been through. With the bullying. With her life beyond school. We all have lives beyond school. And Maisey's was beyond awful.

What the hell is wrong with me that I never thought about who she really was? Why didn't it ever occur to me that she had a life beyond our Belmont High? It's selfish. She was just a character in scenes from my life at school, just someone walking through the hallways, offering comedic relief for me and my class.

My heart races, longs, then aches in vain for a second chance. *If I would have cared. If I would've really known her.* I read it through once more, slower this time.

This definitely explains Jane and Maisey's relationship. The fear, secrecy, the bullying. Jane's straight-up bitchiness.

Jane has somehow made it this far and is still standing, so Maisey should be too. Maisey was tough. I wish she would've known that she was strong enough to get through this. I fold the letter back into the envelope, clutching it to my heart as if it'll calm me. My sheet is splotched with tears and I can't stop shaking.

This explains so much more than I can even handle. No one needs to know everything, but they sure as hell need to know how much they hurt her.

TWENTY

Sean grabs my hand across the center console of his car. "So you're my girlfriend, right?"

"I don't know," I say with a smile, butterflies rushing my chest. "We haven't really discussed anything official like that. I don't know how all that stuff works, do you?"

"Sure. First, I tell Chip Ryan that you are, and then realize I might need to ask you first. So, the next day I ask if you're my girlfriend, you say yes and then we kiss."

"Oh okay. Um, yes?"

"Are you *sure*?" He jokes.

"Good question. Glad you double-checked because I'm not sure. Maybe I should kiss you first. Then I'll decide."

Sean unlocks his hand from mine, places it behind my neck, pulling me closer, making me forget about the movie we weren't really watching anyway. Sherwood Forest is the only drive-in movie theater within five hundred miles. Probably one of the last ones left in Minnesota. The movie playing is definitely better than the CIA lady movie but not better than this. His lips are warm and I lose my breath and maybe a piece of my heart in his kiss. His hands grip the hair at the nape of my neck and send a shiver into me. I pull away and tell him we should leave. Or go in the backseat.

"The backseat, huh? Whoa, Miss Hughes. You're trying to seduce me."

I lean back into him. "I'm your girlfriend, that's kind of my job now."

143

Sean touches his nose to mine. Then tilts his head and kisses my neck, scraping his teeth against my skin. I squeeze my eyelids closed and inhale sharply.

"Let's go," he says, as he shifts the car into reverse and flips the car lights back on. "You're killin me, Breezy, *killing* me."

"Where we goin'?"

"Definitely somewhere classier than the backseat."

****

A few porch lights brighten the houses lining the streets, but other than that, everything is dark, still, and cricket chirpingly quiet. But my hands are sweaty anyway. "This is crazy," I say. "Someone's going to call the cops. And that could be my dad."

Shoulder to shoulder, Sean and I walk up the long driveway of a big house with dark gray siding. "No, they're not gonna call your dad. I hope not, anyway. Everyone in the neighborhood is out or sleeping. No one lives here yet. The bank put a "For Sale" sign out last week. I promise," Sean whispers, squeezing my hand tighter. "Plus, we're not actually going inside—just the backyard."

He reaches through a slat in the fence and fumbles around, unhooking a latch. The door creaks and lets us in.

Clutching Sean's hand, I follow him into the backyard of the house. The overgrown grass swishes against my ankles as we pass a pond on the side of a large deck and up to a prim green and gray storage shed in the corner. Brushing my hand over my ankles, I cringe, hoping not to run into any crickets or spiders preparing to crawl up my cuffed jeans. I turn to the house and ask, "So, this was your old house? It's nice."

"Yep. It was nice. It's twice as big as our house now, but I'd rather be there than back here with my dad. I only miss this place." He slaps his hand on the shed's door.

"Right. That makes sense and I didn't mean that your house now isn't nice or anything." I fumble for something better to say but nothing comes out.

"I know. I know you're not like that." He reaches under the ledge of the shed's window and pulls out a small box and slides out a key.

"A secret key? Should I be worried?" I ask, more excited than worried but also feeling a little worried that I'm so excited.

"About what? That someone's going to report us for trespassing?"

"No, that you're about to take me into a creepy shed for . . .?"

"For what? To show you my old favorite hangout?" He unlocks the door and faces me, "I'm not going to try to get you to *you know*—"

"Sleep with me in a creepy shed?" I ask biting my smile.

"Um, wow. Sometimes you surprise me. But yes, I mean no. No, I'm not trying to sleep with you in a creepy shed. I think more of you than that. But I did see how you were looking at me at the drive-in so hopefully you're not disappointed about that. Even though I'm not trying to 'you know,' I hope you'll come check it out in here anyway." He pushes the door open and grabs my hand again. "Unless you're really not comfortable. I'm not trying to make you feel like—"

"Sean." I drop his hand, slide my fingers up his shoulder and give him a quick kiss. "I'm just messing with you. I'm fine."

Once we're inside, carpet squishes beneath my shoes and it's pitch-black as soon as Sean shuts the door behind us. He clicks on the flash-light of his phone, pulls a piece of cardboard off the wall and slides it over the windowpane.

"What's that for?"

"It covers the light." He reaches up and pulls a string that lights up the room. "I used to put that board there so my dad wouldn't know I was in here at night when—or if—he'd come home late."

"Oh. That's kind of . . . depressing."

"Not really. This is where I'd play guitar and hang out. Wanna sit? The carpet's not that dirty."

"Sure." I sit next to him on the floor. "So . . ."

"I'm sorry." Sean frowns. "I guess this isn't that fun. It was cooler in here with posters on the wall, my amp, and the mini fridge."

"It doesn't matter. It's still a neat hangout. What if you played your guitar?"

"What, like air guitar?" The side of his mouth curves into a half smile.

"No, your real guitar. The one I saw in your backseat." I pierce his eyes with my stare. "Pleeeeease?"

"Can I really say no to you?"

"Nope." My smile widens.

"All right." He jumps up. "I'll be right back."

He leaves and returns after a few minutes, the guitar slung over his shoulder. "I can't believe you're making me do this."

"Stop. Just play something."

"Requests?" He sits across from me, adjusting the strap over his shoulder and the guitar in his lap. I'd take a picture of him with my phone if it wouldn't make me look like a creeper. My daydreams never could've come up with something this good.

"Can you play something of yours?"

He taps quietly on the guitar with a grin. "That's pushing it."

"Just a *little* something?" I stare him down again, this time adding a pouty smile. "*Please?*"

He starts strumming something kinda slow, hip, and mellow. "Only because I can't say no to those little freckles by the corner of your mouth." He fumbles a little, glances up at me, then back to his guitar. "This is something I'm working on but don't have the lyrics sorted out yet." He continues to play, his hands focused, fingers moving fast, back and forth across the strings and sliding up and down. His eyes rest on the movements of his hands, while I marvel at the shy confidence in his . . . everything.

I get up and sit next to him, admiring his profile, feeling almost drunk with his woodsy scent, his music, his just being here.

He slows down, "So?"

"I love it. It's different but familiar in a cozy kind of wrap me up in blankets and—"

I lean in and kiss him, and he kisses me back. "Thanks," he says. "You're cozy."

He sets the guitar on the floor and we're kissing, like really, really kissing. The kind that feels like everything could just go on forever like this but then *whoosh,* there's something different. The kind of kissing that feels like it should be something more, that it would only be right and perfect to be more. Because in spite of everything that's so *not right* in my life, this feeling right now is so *right.* It doesn't feel like I'm trying so hard to fit into his world. It's like I just do, and he fits into mine. He's this guy that really looks at me, and listens, and I care about what he has to say and what he thinks about.

My hands slide under his shirt and curve over the muscles of his back. I want to put my hands everywhere. I pull away, scrunching my eyebrows in. "Do you think about me?" I ask. "Like when we're not hanging out?"

"Too much," he smiles. "Way too much. You?"

"Same."

He presses his lips against mine again and soon we're on the floor and I don't care, I don't care, I don't care. It doesn't matter where we are because I'm in Sean's arms and as scared as I am to feel like this, I don't want to let go of this feeling because it's too safe, warm, and good.

****

"Care to tell me how sending a text that says *'on my way'* constitutes as an hour and a half extension on your curfew?" My mom stands at the top of the stairs, arms crossed over her chest.

"Sorry Mom, I just lost track of time, I guess." I make my way up to the top of the steps, avoiding eye contact. I grab the handle of my door.

"Whoa, stop right there. You're not done here. It's two o'clock in the morning. Do you think I can sleep when I know you're out this late? C'mon Bree, have some respect. What do you think is going through my head when my teenage daughter is out until two in the morning?"

"Well I'm not drunk or high, Mom. I'm *fine.*"

"Yes well, that's only one of the places my head goes. I was your age once too. And you know, I'm not dumb, there are other things you could be doing." She raises her voice an octave when she says "other things."

"Like breaking into houses?"

"Stop making a joke out of everything. This is serious and I'm tired. You know what I'm talking about. Sex. We haven't had this conversation in a while."

"No Mom, I wasn't having sex." *I was almost having sex. Madly, passionately, wildly almost having sex.* I rub the goose bumps off my arms. "Maybe we can talk about this some other time."

"No, not maybe. We will. I'm going back to bed. This time to sleep. We can have a nice chat about this tomorrow, okay?" She hugs me quick and tight. "I love you. I'm glad you're home safe. Now go to bed."

TWENTY-ONE

D ing Ding! The doorbell rings me awake.

"Moooooooooooom! Dooooooor!" No answer. I check my phone for a clue and the time. 10:15. Saturday morning. No missed calls or texts. Kicking off the sheets, I yawn and jump out of bed to overly bright morning rays seeping through my blinds. I peer through the wooden slats. Sean's car is in my driveway.

I rush into my bathroom and do a quick swish with mouthwash.

Ding Ding! I rush down the stairs, balancing my phone between my chin and shoulder as I throw my hair into a ponytail.

"Good morning," I say to a face I wouldn't mind waking up every morning to. "This is kind of a surprise."

"I know, I hope that's okay. I wanted to drop these off and—" He hands me a bouquet of yellow and purple gerbera daisies. His eyes skim my body from head to toe, then he studies my face, twisting his smile into a question: "I woke you up, didn't I? I should've texted first. I'm sorry."

"No, it's fine. Thanks," I say plucking the flowers from his hand.

"They reminded me of your shoes."

I drop my gaze and study my bare feet. "That's cute, I mean, thanks. I love them. C'mon, let's put these in water."

We head to the kitchen and see a blue Post-it stuck to the table from Mom.

B—
Got called into school for mtg!!
Should be back before 12.
WE'LL DO BRUNCH.
XO Mom

"Last night was fun," Sean says as I arrange the flowers into a vase. "I stopped by to see if you wanted to get breakfast."

We're interrupted by the sound of the garage door opening. A minute later, Mom appears, in a navy blue blazer and her heels already in her hand. "I'm so tired of these parents. Oh, hi." Her eyes meet us at the table. "Good morning. I can't believe you're up so early."

"Hi Miss Hughes. I mean Brenda. Good morning." Sean gives my mom an awkward wave.

"Good morning, what are you two up to?" Mom eyes the flowers, then me. "You're not trying to get out of going to brunch with me are you?"

Sean says, "I was just stopping by to say—"

"To say he wants to take me to brunch. So we could, uh, work on our poetry assignment together."

Mom puckers her lips to the side. "Well, I have been up since 5:30 this morning. Had to meet with admin, and another teacher and then the parents of—well, you know, helicopter parent stuff. It's been a long day already. I'd actually appreciate you filling in for me, Sean."

Sean shrugs. "No problem."

"Pretty flowers. Maybe you can make sure she gets home at a reasonable hour though. Sometime before two a.m.?"

Sean winces and adjusts the neck of his white T-shirt. "I apologize for that."

"It's fine, Mom. We'll be back in a couple hours." I tug at my sweatpants and notice my shirt is hugging me a little too close and way too sheerly. My face heats up as I cross my arms over my chest. I move my eyes from Mom to Sean. "Can you wait here while I change?"

I have no problem wearing my sweatpants and a T-shirt to grab something to eat, but I definitely need to put on a bra.

****

"If we run into Chip or Jane, I'm officially leaving this town," I say to Sean, handing my 24/7 menu back to the waitress.

"I'm leaving this town if she forgets our order. I never trust a server when they don't write it down."

"I know." I lean across the table, "Now we're gonna have anxiety until our food comes. Will they scramble the eggs or bring 'em over easy? And if they're scrambled are they gonna be scrambled well or runny? And if they're scrambled well is she gonna forget the cheese? And if the cheese is there, is it gonna be Swiss instead of American?"

"Yes," Sean smiles. "We should probably leave town right now."

"Where would we go?" I ask, almost serious.

"I wonder how far we'd have to go to help Chip get over you?" Sean asks.

"I'm sorry about that. I'm not trying to pull you into some ABC family series called *The Boy Who Wouldn't Go Away*."

"Now that he knows we're together, he should be fine. Guys are usually good like that."

"Hope so, thanks again for that. Anyway." I pluck my straw from its wrapper and drop it into my water. "Let's talk about anything else but exes."

"Sure." Sean's eyes meet mine and his gaze lowers to my chest. "How about we talk about that T-shirt you were wearing this morning. Wow."

"Are you sexually harassing me?" I pick up my fork pointing the prongs at him.

"Yes. Yes, I am." He snatches the fork and lays it in the middle of the table. "I might be scared of you holding a cup of coffee but I'm not worried about your forking skills."

"Don't remind me about the coffee. Forking skills, huh? Maybe you *should* be worried about my forking skills."

"Whoa. Now who's harassing who?" Sean leans in, squinting his eyes with a small smile. "First you wanna make out in the backseat, then that very little, very thin blue T-shirt and now you're discussing your forking skills in a diner."

The lilt in his voice kills me, it really does.

"I'm not, um, well . . . I'm . . . I haven't technically . . ."

Sean shifts his eyes from the fork to my eyes. "Are you still talking about forks?"

I reach across and move his fork on top of the one between us. "See what these two forks are doing?" I check my peripheral vision to make sure no one is within earshot of my whisper. "I haven't *technically* done that."

"Oh *that*. Really? You haven't?"

I'm not sure if he's asking because he thinks I'm lying or that I'm some sort of freak. My face burns. My heart rate has bumped up to the fat burning zone right now. "Yeah, really."

"Even with Chip?" Sean asks.

"Do you want me to be honest?" I fumble with my straw before taking a long sip of water.

"Uh, yes. That's one of the things I like most about you."

"We almost did but we didn't. He wasn't happy about it either."

"It's not a big deal," he shrugs. "If you had or hadn't. But he's a jerk. If I'm being honest, I'm glad you didn't make that mistake."

"So," I say placing the forks back on each of our paper napkins. I fidget with mine, making sure it's perfectly straight. "What about you? How many?" I ask even though I'm not sure if I want the answer.

"Three. Nothing obscene. Do you think that's bad or good?"

"No," I ignore the little pit in my stomach that wishes he would've said zero. "As long as they're not all regrets."

"That's up for debate. Some other time though." Our food arrives and Sean raises his orange juice. "Cheers?"

"To no mistakes," I say raising my glass, scanning my eyes across the pancakes and eggs on our plates just as we'd ordered.

"And to staying in Belmont." Our glasses clink.

TWENTY-TWO

Kallie's eyes are blazing with excitement as we settle into our desks for Norderick's class. "My parents never go out of town. Ever. They're already gone and won't be back until Sunday. You guys can sleep over and I'm calling in sick to work, too. We're most definitely having a party."

My stomach high dives as I turn my smile to Sean.

"Sweet. What should *I* bring?" Justin asks.

"Beer. And maybe some snacks. But not messy ones."

"Wait. I can really come?"

I'm not surprised. Kallie's been extra sweet to everyone these past few weeks. Who knows, with all the extra socializing, she might actually have a chance at Prom Queen.

"Yeah, why not?" Kallie shrugs.

"Can I bring a date?" Justin asks.

Sean leans in. "As long as it's not your Prom Date."

Kallie turns to Justin. "I still cannot believe you're going with her. You've officially hit rock bottom."

"She's right," I say. "I would've rather gone to 'Prom: Parties of One' than with Jane Hulmes." I open my mouth to say something else, but catch a glimpse of the empty chair that Maisey always sat in. No one's been in it since she's been gone. I grab a lip balm from my bag, swiping it across my lips to stop them from saying anything else mean about Jane.

"Whatever," Justin says and leans back in his chair. "If you talk to her on the phone, she's not that bad. Plus, she's hot. My Prom pictures are gonna be fly as hell."

Kallie tells Justin to bring anyone but Jane. When the bell rings, Kallie says she'll see us all tonight and sprints out the door to meet up with Todd.

****

"It's pretty crazy that she gets to have a party," I say to Sean as I ring Kallie's doorbell. "She's been waiting since we were like thirteen for her parents to leave her alone. I'm serious. It's the perfect party house. There are no neighbors close by, so it shouldn't get busted. Knock on wood." I knock on the door twice, then twist the handle, but it's locked.

"You're right," says Sean. "It's great for a party. It's also great for a horror movie where the dead guy rises out of the lake or the ax murderer comes creeping out of the woods."

"I know. Good thing you're here. He can eat you first while I run."

Kallie swings the door open. "Breeeeeee!" She smiles and shakes me by the shoulders. "Finally. Get in here." She locks the door behind us. "Take your shoes off and help me by making sure this door stays locked. This is definitely invite only. I can't have a bunch of dirt rats coming in and trashing my house. But it shouldn't get crazy, I only invited like fifteen people."

Brian Wang appears from around a corner, saluting us with a clear plastic cup of something.

"Whaaaaaat's up Prom Court bitches!" He disappears back into Kallie's kitchen.

"Brian's here? Whoa." Sean shakes his head.

"I know," says Kallie. "Brian never has time for our parties. Ever since he got a boyfriend, he got boring."

"Wonder if his college boyfriend will make a cameo?" I ask.

"Doubt it," says Sean. "This is a *high school* party."

154

"Everyone's out back getting ready for beer pong, I think," says Kallie.

"Sounds fun," I say, adjusting the extra weight in the bag slung over my shoulder. I can almost hear the faint sloshing of the bottle of wine I snatched from the fridge in our basement. My plan's pretty tight: Don't get trashed. Don't shotgun beers after doing shots like I did with Kallie, Sam, and Kendall last summer. Keep it simple and chill. Be smart, be cool. Drink slow. Don't puke.

"You guys need to try the punch I made," Kallie says. "My mom would be impressed. It's clear, so no mess. Just in case anyone spills. You know my mom would shit."

"I better check it out before Bree does. You know, to make sure it's not poison."

"Hey, I thought you didn't drink?" I ask.

"Well, I don't usually drink but when I do, I drink . . . white punch. At slumber parties."

Kallie laughs and tells Sean to check it out and keep an eye on everyone out back while we rush upstairs to drop off our bags.

TWENTY-THREE

11:11. *Make a wish.* I glare at my cell phone for the umpteenth time. *I wish Kyle would leave so I can get the hell out of this stinky closet.* It's been about fifteen minutes already. I'm in the lavender and moth-ball infused walk-in closet of the Vate guest room, scrunched up behind a wall of puffy coats with my backpack and phone. *Kallie's party was fun while it lasted.*

No one figured Kallie's older brother would drive over to check up on her. Me and Kallie should know better. How did we *not* plan on this happening? Kyle only lives twenty minutes away and there's no way her parents would've left town without some sort of backup. Her brother's pretty cool, but not that cool.

During our smoking phase he was the one who bought us the cigarettes, but when he turned twenty-one he made it clear that if Kal wanted to drink illegally, he wouldn't be making any beer runs.

I don't even know where Sean is. Once the doorbell rang and Kallie peeked through the window, she mazed back through the house like a rabid rat. She ran to the back porch with the loudest whispered scream I'd ever heard.

"Everyone get outta here! My brother's here! GO GO GOOOOOO!" Then she rushed back to unlock the front door, whispering for me to run upstairs and hide.

Buzzzz. My phone blinks with a text: KALLIE VATE.

OMG Kyle is pissed & making sure everybody is gone! SORRY!!!! Where RU guys?

I text back. **I'm hiding in a closet!!!! WTF!? When is he leaving??!!** My phone goes *Shwoop* after I hit Send.

Buzzzz.

As soon as he clears the house. At least he's going back home! LOL U OK?

Again: KALLIE VATE.

AAAAHHHH He just dumped our white drink!! NO!!!! ☺ I'll let U know when he leaves

I text back: **I'm ok! Oh no! I didn't even get to try it. Waaaah! ☺**

Shwoop.

I hit the screen again to text Sean.

Hey! Where R U?

Shwoop.

Buzzzz. SEAN MILLS.

In Kals closet Can I come out yet?

I type back: **NO!!!! Her bro is still here!**

Shwoop.

Buzzzz. SEAN again.

Where RU?

I text back: **I'm upstairs too. In guest rm closet! HA! Great minds think alike ☺**

Shwoop.

Buzzzz. SEAN.

Not alike enough. Ur so close but so far away. I'll find you

I text back: **OMG PLZ DON'T GET CAUGHT!**

Shwoop.

My heart picks up the pace and I fan myself with the neckline of my collar. After five minutes or so I hear loud footsteps and the closet door jerks open.

"Anyone in here?" It's Kyle's voice. I stop breathing and moving. The door closes and the footsteps fade away. About two minutes later, the door swooshes open again and then a whisper.

"Breeze?"

"Sean?" I whisper back.

"No, it's Brian. I think you're hot for a high schooler and came to play seven minutes in heaven."

I stifle a giggle.

"I'm back here," I whisper, "around the corner behind the coats."

"Scoot over smalls," Sean whispers, his hand gliding down my bare arm. "Nice hiding spot."

"You were so close to getting caught. Kyle was here like two seconds ago."

"Yeah, I know. I heard him coming and literally dove under the bed. Dude, this closet smells like my grandma's house—sad thing is, it's also about the same size as her *entire* house."

"So, about that seven minutes in heaven?" I tap my wrist although I'm not wearing a watch and it's pitch-black in here.

Sean's hand travels up my arm, over to my sides. His fingers graze my face and then his lips are on mine. The scent of him—sandalwood and faintly, Kallie's punch, dizzies me. I kiss him back until my breathing starts to get *maybe* too loud for the closet. Exhaling, I lean away and reach into my bag for the wine.

"Look what I got." I hold up the bottle.

"I can't see. What is it?"

"Wine. Want some?" I ask.

"You brought wine?" His phone clicks and he holds the screen, shining a faint light onto the bottle. "Nice label. 'Black Heart, Red Ruby Wine.' Scandalous. I thought *you* didn't drink."

"Touché. I don't usually drink. But when I do, I drink wine. In closets." I twist the cork but it doesn't budge.

"Hold up the light on your phone," I tell Sean. He clicks the light on and I give the cork a twist and hard pull until it finally pops out with a *plunk*. I take a swig. It's cool, then warm going down my throat into my stomach. "Whew. That's kinda strong. But not terrible. Want some?"

"Sure," says Sean, putting his hand over mine, then taking the bottle. Are we going to play a drinking game?"

"Well, since watching people play beer pong all night did get a little boring, I might be up for it."

"Mostly boring," says Sean. "But how funny was it when Justin and Molly lost and had to jump in the lake?"

"Almost as funny as watching Kallie going hard core PDA with Todd whenever Molly was within four feet. Even though Molly doesn't seem to care anymore. I'm so glad Jane didn't show up. That would've made for an even more awkward addition to the Todd love triangle. Or square or whatever shape it is these days."

Sean passes the bottle back and I swallow another sip of wine. "Tastes like bitter grapes and tree bark." My lips pucker. "It's not that bad, really."

"You're not that bad." Sean says and kisses me again.

"You're not either," I murmur into his mouth.

His lips slide over mine, then he runs his tongue over my lips. "Mm. This is the best seven minutes in heaven slash drinking game ever."

"Let's play a real game," I say, taking another sip. "Tell me something about you I don't know. Like a secret, a weird hobby, or a funny story and I'll do the same."

"I'm interested," says Sean. "But where's the game—the challenge?"

"That's all I got. You're the football game guy. You make up the rules."

"No problem. I got this. So, you give me the number one, two, or three, and that's how many points—how many drinks the story or secret is worth. If I tell you, you'll take that many drinks. If I don't, I have to drink and then it's your turn."

"You're on. But you're going down Mills, you're going down." I stifle a giggle and a joke that's more appropriate for me and Kallie. "Okay, I'll go first." I hand him the bottle. "How many?"

"One." Sean says.

"One point, one drink? That's all?" I ask.

"Didn't you say you got sick last time you drank? We can't have you hurling in a closet. Who knows how long we'll be stuck in here."

"Good call. I won't have to drink anyway, a one pointer is easy. Let's see. Oh yeah, I stole makeup from the grocery store when I was in sixth grade." I hear Sean swallow a drink and he passes me the bottle.

"Wow, you're a wild one. Can't believe I'm hanging out with a criminal."

I smack his knee next to my leg and then rest my hand on it. "Middle school was full of bad choices. But enough about me. Your turn. Two points. C'mon, 'fess up."

"Two? No problem." Sean says. "I've liked you since the beginning of the semester. I'd watch you walk into class every day and hate that you'd sit behind me because I couldn't see you unless I turned around to talk to Conner."

"Really?" My stomach flutters and I'm relieved he can't see how huge my smile is. "That's really cute. That was a good one." It feels like my veins are getting tingly. I take two sips.

"Two back at you, Hughes."

"Weeeeell, *I* have had a crush on *you* since the beginning of the semester. And the reason I sit behind you is so I can look at you without you watching me." I take a deep breath and exhale the rest of my sentence in a rush. "Your ears drive me crazy. Drink up." I pass him the bottle.

"Hey, that was easy. You can't steal my secrets." I hear the wine slosh. "Tastes like victory."

"Hey, it's not if you win or lose, it's, it's . . ." I giggle. "Sssshhhh. Don't make me laugh. Trust me, if Kyle finds me in the closet, with booze and a boy . . . "

"Yeah, we better keep it down. When's he gonna leave?"

Buzzzz. KALLIE VATE.

I raise my phone so we can read Kallie's text: **OMG. I think he's leaving soon. I'm getting WORLD'S LONGEST LECTURE are you still OK?**

I turn my phone so I can text her back: **Yes Seans here so I'm cool ☺ Hopefully I wont hv to pee anytime soon**

Shwoop.

"Three points," I say. "I want a three point secret. Give me the goods or drink up."

"Okay, I guess halftime's over, game on. Hmmmm." Sean pauses. "I don't know."

"You're gonna have to drink, then."

"No, wait. I got one," he says. He passes the bottle back and I rest it in my lap. "Last night I called my aunt's house to talk to my dad. That's it. Three drinks for you."

"God, really? Um, that's heavy." I take one sip. "I'm only taking one drink until you tell me what happened."

"I almost called you after but didn't want to be a buzzkill."

"Sean, please. I want to know what's going on with you, good or bad. I wish you would've called. What'd he say?"

Sean takes the bottle, gulps, and hands it back. This time I don't sip; I take two big gulps that swim hot fire down my throat.

"He didn't say much. He sounded high. Or maybe not, who knows? Either way, it was 6:30 p.m. and he said he was taking a nap. Who takes a nap at night? Said he hopes to have his car fixed in time for graduation. It was . . . I don't know. I don't know what I was expecting. I told him I had another call and then hung up."

"Oh you hung up, huh?" I hmph. "Not to change the subject but here's a secret of mine. Probably a one point five pointer drink. I hate when you just hang up. You never say good-bye."

"To you?" Sean asks. "What? Really?"

"Yeah, to me. I say bye or it's time to get off the phone and you just hang up. Like click, no good-bye, no see ya later, no adios."

"Oh, weird. Sorry. I'll work on that."

"Yeah, you should." I hand him the bottle. "I'm really sorry about your dad. You really could've called me. That sucks."

"Oh well. Like my dad used to say, life sucks and then you die."

Maisey's face flashes into my head. I blink a few times until she disappears, then say, "Or life sucks, *so* you die. Like Maisey Morgan."

"Geez Breeze, way to make a depressing conversation even more depressing. Let's both take a drink for Maisey. I'd pour a little onto the carpet but Kallie's mom would shit, right?"

"She really would," I say, muffling the laugh trying to escape my mouth. Lifting the bottle to my lips, I swallow the laugh and take another sip of wine. I snort and alcohol burns my nostrils. Once the laugh escapes, I can't stop. I wipe my mouth on a cushy down coat then bury my face in Sean's shirt. He's laughing too.

"Mmmm. You smell so good." Our laughter fades and I raise my chin until Sean's nose brushes the side of my cheek. "I can't get that stuff out of my head, you know."

"What stuff? My smell?"

"No, the Maisey stuff."

"Why? That's creepy, the ghost of Maisey Morgan." He exhales a soft, but drawn-out sigh. "Suicide is such a . . ."

"Cop out, a sin, a loser move?" I ask.

"No," Sean answers. "I was going to say something like an enigma. I don't get it, I guess. It's hard to understand. When it gets that bad, so bad you want to die, that's your crunch time, that's when you're supposed to look that shit in the eye, and just take it. You wait it out or run. You wait because it'll get better at some point, it always does. Or, you can run ahead and find ways to make it not so bad. But you don't bail. Suicide's not supposed to be an option."

"Yeah but listen, when shit gets bad, it's probably easier to handle if you're the hottest quarterback in Belmont. What happens when you're Maisey Morgan and shit is bad? What if things at home are bad and then you go to school and it's just as bad."

"I guess it'd be worse. A lot worse. I feel like an asshole about how bad we treated her. I know what you're saying, Breeze." He grabs my hand. "But hey, try not to let that stuff get you down. It's not your fault. You barely knew her."

I take a deep breath and tell him I did kind of know her. And how she felt like she knew me. Like, enough to write me a letter. I tell him about elementary school, the bathroom, going to her house, meeting her parents and seeing her pictures and the urn. I don't tell him *everything* the letter says, and I don't tell him about Jane at the wake.

"Now that's heavy, I can't believe you've been dealing with this." Sean pulls me into a hug, his arms wrapping me tight. His words are muffled against my shoulder. "What are you going to do?"

Sighing, I pull away. "I don't know. I'll figure it out. I just need to, I don't know, get over it, I guess." I shrug and let another sip of wine warm my throat.

"Or figure out a way to make sense of it and learn from it."

I giggle again. "Thanks, Mom. How did this game get so fucking depressing? We're so lame."

"Speak for yourself," Sean laughs. "I've just been proclaimed the hottest quarterback in Belmont."

"I wouldn't let the title go to your head. There are only two quarterbacks to choose from."

"Still. I'll drink to that." He pulls the bottle from my hand.

I reach for him, feeling my way to the waistband of his jeans. I hook my finger into one of his belt loops, then run my other hand to the back of his neck, pulling him in. I press my lips to his ear.

Suddenly, the sound of the guest room door swinging open is followed by a slam that rattles the closet door. Sean and I squeeze tight into the corner, while I perform a silent rearrange of the coats. Sean grasps and squeezes my hand.

"WHAT THE HELL'S GOIN' ON IN HERE?" A loud male voice bellows as the closet door swings open.

"Olly Olly oxen freeeeeee!" Kallie yells from outside the room. Todd laughs. From the closet doorway.

Sean jumps up and runs out of the closet, tackling Todd onto the bed.

"You bastard. Dude, you scared the shit out of us!"

"Omigod you guys are crazy." I run my hand over my hair as I make my way out of the closet.

"I am so sorry, you guys. I can't believe my brother. What an ass. Everyone's gone now except us, Molly, and Justin. They hid in the woods. And get this. *In their underwear.* They were swimming when my brother got here and I'm pretty sure they hooked up."

"Which is total bullshit if it's true," says Todd. "I went out with her for a year and didn't get past second, so—"

"Um, really?" Kallie slaps Todd on the side of the head. "I think you're all set now."

"Yes, babes, I am. I was just sayin'."

"Know what I'm just sayin'? I'm jus' sayin' that I gotta pee so bad." I run into the bathroom.

"Is she drunk?" Kallie asks.

"We just had a little wine. Doubt it."

"I can hear you, ya know," I shout through the closed door. I did feel a little light when I got out of the closet but now I feel fine. Quite fine. I pee for like three minutes. I check the mirror and my cheeks are flushed and hair is a little messy. *Sexy messy.* Tonight just might be *the* night.

I throw my backpack onto the bed. "We're calling this room tonight."

TWENTY-FOUR

Kallie sequesters us to the rec area in the basement, just in case Kyle returns, or anyone else trying to crash. "I'm over parties. Too much stress. I should've just invited you guys."

"Whoever heard of a bar with no alcohol?" asks Justin as he tours the area.

"Sorry, my parents don't drink, it's the devil's something or other."

"The devil's brew. That's what my parents say." Molly winks. "Drinking isn't that bad, though. I don't know what I was afraid of all these years."

"Maybe you were afraid of getting sick and puking on my shoes," I say.

"I know something else you were afraid of and maybe now you think is fun," Todd says.

"So who wants to play pool?" asks Kallie, snatching a pool stick off the wall and shooting Todd a death stare.

"I want to play *Call of Duty* on this big ass movie screen." Justin runs to the media console. "Please tell me your parents don't think video games are the Devil's playthings?"

"Check the media cabinet. Xbox is already hooked up." Kallie grabs a remote, clicks a button, and two doors slide open. "There you go. My dad and brother play all the time."

"Sweet," says Sean. He looks at me, "Care if I play for a while?"

"Yeah sure, it's cool." I shrug and turn to Kallie who's dropped the pool stick and has Todd pinned against the wall. His hands are all over her ass.

"Get a room guys." Sean launches a pillow over at Todd's head.

"Good idea. We're going upstairs." Grabbing Todd's hands, Kallie pulls him toward the bottom of the stairs. "Make yourselves at home. But don't go bananas, okay?"

"Oh trust me, I'm gonna go bananas," I say.

"I'm going bananas too," Molly says and throws her hand up for a high five.

"Oh yeah," I say as she misses my hand.

Molly and I hover in-between the pool table and watch the guys groping video controllers to shoot a bunch of soldier zombies. Molly's phone rings and she talks for a minute then hangs up. "Everybody, Jane says 'hi.' Well, sorta. She said to tell Justin and Sean hi."

"What's she up to?" asks Justin.

"Being sad and mopey. She would've come but she thinks everyone hates her."

"I can't picture Jane as sad or mopey," Justin says.

Maybe mad and bitchy is at the tip of my tongue but my stomach twinges with guilt. "I don't think Kallie invited her anyway. It's probably for the best but that's all we need to say about that." I slam the eight ball with my pool cue and it swishes into the right corner pocket. "Molly, wanna come upstairs with me to get the wine I brought? There's not much left but hey, it's something."

"Every since the night you held my hair I knew we were gonna be great friends." Molly wraps her arms around me.

"Seriously Molly, it's probably like three sips each."

"I don't care Brittany Bree—le'sgo!"

We head up the stairs and shush each other as we pass Kallie's room giggling. I cannot even explain the noises coming from her room except to say that it sounds, well, inappropriate for us to hear, but probably pretty fun for them.

"That's a lotta hot drama right there," Molly says. "I'm so over him but I definitely didn't need to hear that."

"Ugh," I groan. "If I never have to hear Todd having sex again it'll be too soon. Kallie too, for that matter." I grab the bottle of wine from my backpack.

"What else you got in there?" Molly reaches toward my bag.

"Nothing, why? Just the wine." I cover the bag's opening with my hand.

"Why're you so defensive then, eh?" Molly raises her eyebrows and smirks.

It feels like I have writing on my forehead. I swipe my palm over my brow just in case. Just in case it says *I bought a three pack of condoms at Walgreens after school today.*

"You're totally blushing. You do!" Molly's grin widens and she grabs my bag and rummages inside. She pulls out the little box. "Whoa, I was expecting cigarettes or an extra can of beer, but I won't say anything if you have one for me too."

"Are you serious?" I snatch the box out of her hand. She reaches for the wine bottle and gives it a shake.

"Geez, it is a pretty skimpy bottle. And yeah, I'm serious. I like Justin. He's cute. And he's fun. And we almost—promise you won't say anything?"

"What? Don't tell me, you guys had sex in the woods?"

"No. But we almost did. We were so close. But Justin didn't have anything. I'm glad we waited." Molly's face is dead serious.

I laugh. "You waited? Do you mean you're glad you waited a couple hours, so your relationship could reach the next level? That's hilarious."

"No, I mean waited because we didn't have *protection.*" Molly whispers the word *protection.*

"I don't get it. Why would you go out with Todd for a year and *not* do it but then hang out with Justin Conner for a couple hours . . . yeah I guess he's nice, but for your first time?"

"Justin wouldn't be my first. I didn't sleep with Todd because, well . . ."

"Spit it out Molls. If you expect me to give you one of these, I need to know that you're of sound mind and you won't regret it."

"It's not going to make sense to you, but I'm okay with sex for fun, but when I care about someone, it becomes a bigger deal. I didn't have sex with Todd because I loved him and I wanted to wait until we're married."

"Marrying Todd. That's sad." I hand her a condom like it's a piece of gum. "There you go. Fornicate in peace."

"It's not sad. It's reality. As far as Justin goes, if you look at someone with lust in your heart, you've already committed that sin. Like, you've already done it, so I might as well, right? So, let's have fun." She leans over and flips my hair off my shoulder, then tucks the condom in her pocket. Molly's smile is big and bright white. As late as it is, she still looks fresh off the page of *Cosmo* selling lip gloss.

"Yeah, sorry. Let's have fun." I smile big, like my face could be on the page after Molly's. *Maybe selling tampons*. I laugh and slide one of the condoms into my pocket too.

"Woo hoo!" She raises her hand to give me a high five.

"Woo hoo!" We miss, then take turns emptying the last few sips out of the wine bottle.

****

"What took you so long up there—what's going on upstairs?" Sean asks.

"Lemme put it this way," I say. "If you look up 'TMI' in the dictionary, you're not gonna see a picture. You'll hear a highly inappropriate sound bite. And that, my friend, is what's going on upstairs." I start laughing like crazy. Molly grips my shoulder before dropping to the floor in giggles.

"And lemme tell you," Molly adds. "It wasn't pretty. Not that I saw anything because hey, maybe . . ." Molly tries to stop laughing, "Maybe, ha—maybe, they, maybe they were just exercising."

"Cross-fit or yoga is my guess," Justin says, putting down the game controller.

"Want to take a walk?" Sean asks me.

"I could watch you guys play video games all night long but sure, I can walk."

Justin jumps up. "Holy shit! I just realized I have a six-pack of Hot-Shotz in my car. Hell yes."

"Let's go get it," says Molly. She winks at me. "We'll meet you guys back here later."

Sean and I step outside of the basement's sliding glass doors. We tread up the small hill to where the dock and main level of the house is.

"Looks like Kyle made Kallie pick up all traces of alcohol." We survey the patio. All signs of the beer can and clear plastic cup debris from earlier have been erased. "Big change," says Sean. Just a few hours ago and this place looked like a bomb went off."

"I know, right? I'm kind of glad Kyle came. It was getting . . ."

"Bananas?" We exchange a smile, then he says, "I'm glad Kyle came and we got to hang out in that closet. And I'm glad we didn't get caught, so we can hang out more. Ya know?"

"Yeah."

We sit on the dock for a while, laughing about the party. How funny it was to see Brian outside of school, Molly too. I tell Sean I'm surprised; everyone's pretty nice and fun. I'm about to joke how drinking might actually be a good thing for Molly when we hear her and Justin traipsing and laughing their way back from getting the alcohol. We turn around and Justin's arm is wrapped around her shoulder. Molly stumbles over something—probably her own foot—and then she's literally rolling down the hill. Like a hot dog in jeans and a pink sweater on a conveyor belt. I'm not going to lie: It's one of the funniest things I've seen in a long time.

"Is somebody gonna catch her? *She's rolling.*" Sean laughs.

"Like a hot dog." I laugh.

Justin does a running skid down the hill and the second he reaches her, she pukes.

"I'm not on puke patrol tonight. Let's go," I whisper to Sean, grabbing his wrist. We run into the woods, laughing in whispers and squeezing each other's hands. I lead him through the edge of the woods and onto a path.

"Where are you taking me?" he asks.

"The Point. It's where the Vates' land ends and Lake Crystal Woods meets Lake Belmont. It's been me and Kal's spot since we were twelve. It's the place where all the magic happens," I say. "You know, swimming, tanning, maybe doing stuff we don't want Kallie's parents to know about." *Smoking, practicing kissing, sharing her brother's Red Bulls because Kallie's mom wouldn't let her have caffeine.*

"I didn't bring swim trunks," Sean says. "But it sounds like a plan." We walk along the dirt path, branches and leaves extending from the trees. The smell of lake and mossy spring heat is so heavy it feels like summer. We reach the end of the path and head down the sandy hill that meets the lake. We kick off our shoes and peel our socks off, rolling our jeans to sit in the sand with our ankles and feet dipped in the water.

I break the silence. "This is nice."

"I like that we can just sit here and not say anything," Sean says.

I want to tell him that I have a lot of things to say, but I'm scared. I tuck my foot under his, feeling the sand and water glide between my toes. All of this feels so good and almost perfect. How he had me give him a ride home from Java Joint instead of Jane. The way his eyes and voice warm up when he calls me Breeze or Breezy. How he wrote the haiku and Prom song, and showed me his old house and played the guitar. How I got soincrediblyclose to losing my virginity the night after the drive-in. Telling him about Maisey in the closet. Hearing about his dad. Sharing wine.

We lace our fingers together and they sink into the sand.

"I wonder if this is what falling in love feels like," I finally say out loud.

"I wouldn't know," Sean says. My heart does a quick dip into my gut.

"Right, yeah." I roll my pants up a little more as if it's a very important task.

"I wouldn't know because falling sounds like it takes a while. But a real fall is so quick that it only lasts a few seconds. If it's not that big of a jump, you don't have time to feel it." His fingers trace over the top of my hand, then locks his fingers back in mine.

"You lost me at jump. What?"

"What I'm saying is that I don't think you're the kind of person I could've spent a long time falling in love with. It was too easy. Just a short jump. Like one second I had a crush on you and the next second I was already in love with you, there was no time to fall."

"Oh, wow. That's . . . *thank you.*"

Sean leans in and says, "I love you, Bree. Bree *Hughes.*"

"I love *you.*" I say it straight into his eyes and the words warm up my whole body.

We lean in and our lips meet. We kiss, just kiss, for what feels like forever. My toes dig into the sand as my ankles graze and rub into his. The same kind of fire that I felt last weekend ignites. Like the first crackles of a bonfire, it's a slow burn with hot ashes prickling my skin. It feels hot and then sometimes it flies away leaving its mark, the tingles burning into my pores. I want to do everything to make this feeling go away and everything to make him want me even more. The slightly cool air turns tepid. The sand beneath my back molds to my body. And then we're hands all over, under and in, bodies moving, seams brushing, gripping, jeans unsnapping.

"Do you want to?" I say on a heavy exhale.

Sean looks down at me, leans to his side, and rests on his elbow and hip. "I do, but, um . . . I don't have anything—a condom." His breath is heavy, his eyes burn. "I have one in my wallet in the house. We can run back."

I finish pulling off my jeans and reach into my front pocket. Then, I hold up the little plastic square, feeling a pang of nervousness, embarrassment, and empowerment—somehow all at once.

"Are you sure?" he says, closing his hand over mine.

I close my eyes, inhaling the moon's reflection on the lake. "Yes, *I'm sure.*"

TWENTY-FIVE

Breeeeeeakfast in ten minutes, courtesy of Molly!" Kallie pounds on the bedroom door. I hop up, rushing into the bathroom, leaving Sean rubbing his eyes. Sean and I. Me and Sean. My reflection stares back from the streak-free mirror of the Vates' guest bathroom. *So this is what non-virgins look like, huh?* I feel a little different. Maybe vulnerable, awkward and for sure a little sore, but my face looks the same. My mouth tastes terrible so I brush my teeth and do a double rinse with mouthwash. Just because he said "I love you" last night doesn't mean I'm going to chill in bed with morning breath like they do in the movies. I rake my hair into a loose ponytail and wipe the mascara smear from under my right eye.

"I'll be downstairs." I kiss Sean on the corner of his mouth, then back out of the door as he smiles and pulls the covers over his head.

"We'll be down in a minute," yells Kallie as I head downstairs toward the sound and smell of sizzling bacon.

"Good morning Sunshine!" Molly says with her pink glossy smile and a spatula. Not a trace of puke in her hair or the corners of her mouth.

I smile back. "How is it that the last time you got sick, I'm the one who woke up looking and smelling like puke? Last night you drink, throw up, and all of a sudden you're downstairs making breakfast looking like a hot Martha Stewart Barbie. It's just wrong."

"You're so funny. And please, look at you. You look great and you don't even have to try. I had to take a shower, blow-dry my hair, and put

172

on makeup. You waltz down here in your sweats and a ponytail looking like—like hot morning-after Barbie. Soooooo?" Molly turns off the
burner, and leans over the breakfast bar at me. "Spill the beans. Did you
or didn't you?"

"Oh please," I say. "I'm boring. I want to hear about you. What happened with Justin?"

Molly scans the empty kitchen, then leans in and whispers, "We
didn't. Can you believe that? We ended up talking too much. He thinks
I'm still hung up on Todd. The more we talked, the more I realized that
he's actually the kind of guy I'd want to date. So, now I'm confused."

"Justin Conner. Who knew?"

"I know, right? Do you think he likes me?"

"Molly. Who wouldn't?"

"Okay, here's an even bigger question? Do you think Jane would kill
me if I asked her to switch Prom dates? I'd rather go with Justin."

"Oh, wow."

"I know." Molly's face crumples like paper. "She's extra edgy lately.
You never know with her."

"She's tricky, that's for sure. But what about Brian, he'd care, wouldn't
he?"

"Oh please. He's just going to take pictures, see if he gets Prom King,
and he'll be out. Dances aren't his thing."

"Well, if you really like Justin, it's worth a shot. Ask him and maybe
he can break the news to Jane."

"Jane's my best friend. It has to come from me. We tell each other
everything."

Yeah, sure, everything. Ask Todd or Maisey about that one.

"Well," I shrug. "Let me know how it goes."

"So, back to you, Brittany-Bree. Do you think you'll wait until Prom
night to finally do it? He really likes you, you know." Molly brings her
voice back to a whisper. "I think you should go for it. I can tell he's so
into you because when him and Jane had sex they never even hung out
or anything after that . . ."

Molly's voice keeps chirping but I can't hear her. My heart is lodged in my throat. And I want to throw up. Throw up all over everything she just said. But I don't. I swallow really fucking hard and try to push it all down, down, down.

"Bree? Hello?" Molly waves her hand in front of my face.

"Oh yeah," I say hoping the quaver in my voice doesn't give me away. "Well, yeah I don't think he thought it was that serious, ya know."

"Yeah, for sure." Molly nods and starts popping toast in and out of the toaster.

"So," I say, grabbing the orange juice and some cups. "When did they do it?"

"Oh gosh, I don't know, it was . . ." Molly turns around real slow, her face falling into a frown as she stares me down. "Oh my *gosh*, it was way before you. Like the beginning of March." Her eyes widen. "You didn't know?"

I line up the glasses real straight and focus on pouring juice.

"Shoot. I figured you knew and that's why you hate her so much."

"Nope. I didn't know. Oh well. It's not a big deal." I count the glasses over and over. "There's six of us right?"

"Yeah, Bree. Six." Molly grabs the container from me. "Hey, you can't say anything to anyone. Please? I mean it. Jane made me swear not to say anything. She didn't want anyone to know."

"Jane didn't want anyone to know what?" Kallie asks as she and Todd come into the kitchen.

"Breakfast. Cool! You should be the one makin' me breakfast Kallie." Todd laughs.

"Yeah, well, I was up early, so . . ." Molly looks at me.

"Don't even try it," Kallie says. "Finish what you were saying. What is it about Jane you're not supposed to tell us?" Kallie grabs a piece of bacon and takes a bite, glaring. Her eyes dart from me to Todd. "I'm pretty tired of everyone knowing but me."

Molly shakes her head at me, wide-eyed and biting her lip.

"Don't worry guys," I say. "It's not what you think."

Justin steps into the room and so does Sean. Everyone stands still. I'm not sure if they're not moving because the air's so thick or they don't want to be the first to grab a plate. Sean walks toward me but I step back.

"What's not what we think?" Justin asks. "The bacon? Please don't tell me it's turkey bacon."

"Oh well, nothing *serious*," I say looking right into Sean's eyes. "We were just talking about forks. Yeah, forks. And how Jane and Sean had sex. No big deal."

Justin snatches a plate from the counter. "Well, alrighty then. I guess it's real bacon."

Kallie exhales. Todd clenches his fists but his mouth looks clamped shut. Molly studies the floor.

Sean steps forward again, his arm reaching toward my waist. "Bree, that was before you and I even . . . it was . . ."

"It was what? Just something you didn't tell me during a whole conversation we had about sex or something you might have mentioned in one of the million conversations where I'm telling you everything about me? So, it was what? Something you forgot? A mistake right? Just like last night. A big fucking *mistake*." I sprint out of the kitchen and upstairs. I grab my things and run back down, passing Sean on the way.

"Breeze, c'mon, just talk to me for a second."

I can't hear him because I am running. Out the door. To my car. Out of here.

On the way home, Sean's sweatshirt stares me down from the passenger seat. I roll my window down to throw it out, but the car in my rearview stops me. I grab it and toss it in the back.

****

Once I'm home, I drag myself into the shower and put my pajamas on. I lay in bed, like a butterfly trying to wrap itself back into a cocoon. Everything is awkward, crooked, heavy, bent, and broken. All the feelings from last night. The magic, the lake, the moon, the heat, the loveliness of it all, the high of it, is dissipated. Washed away in a hard, cold, face-slapping morning. My phone vibrates off and on throughout the day beneath my damp pillow. Every buzz is a needle that drags along my skin, jagged, sharp, in and out.

The doorbell rings around two and then again an hour or two later. Both times I tell Mom I'm sick. I'm not talking to anyone.

"Just please leave me alone, please," I tell her from under my blankets, a fresh parade of tears springing to my eyes. I cradle my pillows, my stuffed dog Pippa, and an ache that feels like winter.

TWENTY-SIX

Sunday morning after the doorbell rings, Kallie marches into my room. "This is crazy. C'mon. Get up. You can't let this get you down."

"How'd you get in here?" I pull myself up and wrap my comforter around me like a cape.

"Your mom. Duh. I told her it was about a boy and the only panacea was your BFF and this." She tosses me a white paper bag.

I open the bag, "Mmm donuts." Powdered jelly. I take a bite and the tears fall out of my eyes and onto my donut.

"Omigod, this is so sad." Kallie hops on my bed and wraps me in a hug. She starts crying too.

"It's pathetic." I pass her the bag. "You're gonna need one of these." We sit on my bed, eating donuts and wiping powdered sugary mouths and tears with paper napkins.

"So what're we doing? Prom: Parties of One?" Kallie smiles.

"What're you talking about?"

"Don't make me say it. The scene after you left. Oh shit, it was a mess."

"Really? Oops." My shoulders slump as I sigh. "I'm sorry. I'm really sorry. I hope my drama didn't ruin everyone's breakfast."

"It wasn't you. Trust me, it wasn't. It was the can of worm crap that hit the fan after you left. Poor Justin." Kallie laughs through her tears. "He just sat there. You know it's bad when Justin Conner runs out of jokes."

"What happened?"

Kallie sighs. "Well, Todd asked Sean when him and Jane hooked up, like *demanded* to know when exactly this happened. And I'm standing there, pissed. So I'm asking Todd why. Why does he care—what's it matter to him, right? Even though I know why, *you know I know*. Then Sean's like, 'Dude, not that it's your business but it was the beginning of March, the night of that basketball game against Anoka. The one where Monroe kept missing those three pointers.' So Todd says that's fucked up and he couldn't believe it. He was so pissed. And Molly was so clueless, telling Todd to chill, saying that Sean wasn't with you yet so it's okay. As if Todd was mad because he cared about your feelings. He looked like he wanted to fight Sean. So, Sean steps up and looks Todd right in the eye and says, 'Yeah, well I didn't know you were screwing Jane at the same time too so it looks like I'm the only one in the clear here, right bro?' Todd stood there like an idiot, Justin didn't say anything, and Molly started crying.

I told Todd to grab his shit from my room and get the hell outta my house."

"Oh. My. God. That's craaaaaazy. I'm so sorry. I mean this in the nicest way, *I tried* to tell you so."

"Yeah, I know." She grabs my wrist. "*Thanks.* I'm sorry I acted like such an idiot. I believed you but I didn't, if that makes sense. I really didn't want to know. I think a big reason why is because of this Prom stuff. This stupid Prom stuff. I just wanted to keep being Todd's girlfriend so bad and then I wanted to be on court, and once I got it, it felt like I actually had a chance to be Queen. Lame. At least the sex was good."

"Can we stop force feeding me images of naked Todd? I'm trying to enjoy these donuts."

"My bad." Kallie grins. "You know who I actually felt sorry for? Molly. She couldn't stop crying. She was more upset about Jane betraying her than Todd. After Todd left, Molly and Justin took off and then I drove Sean home."

My mouth goes dry as I try to swallow an ounce of my pride. "Sean. What'd he say?"

"All the right things." Kallie looks into my eyes with her half smile half frown. "You're lucky, like really lucky. He's so into you, Bree. I mean, he slept with her before you guys even went on a date—or anything. It's not like he cheated on you."

"Here's the thing," I say. "Jane is such a—" Maisey's letter worms its way into my head. I clamp my mouth before "bitch" pops out. "She's a mess. She was awful to Maisey and look what happened to her. She didn't have to be like that. She should've . . ." I try to fight the battle against another barrage of tears. "Jane's got issues. I mean, I'm sure she does. But she's been a dick to me since day one. Sean *knows* that. I thought it was because of Prom and because she didn't like you. But Sean knew why. Sean and I've talked about a lot of stuff. Like, *everything*. He should've told me. Especially since we . . ."

"Since you what?" Kallie smirks and raises her left eyebrow.

"You know what I'm talking about."

"No, I don't know what you're talking about. Because if it's what I think you're talking about you would've told me, right after, since we're best friends."

"Well, it *is* like right after. It happened Friday."

Kallie shakes me by the shoulders and jumps up on the bed. She pretends to hold up a microphone. "Bree Ella Hughes. You've just lost your V card, what're you gonna do next?"

"Well, by the looks of it, I'll never find out if sex actually does get better, and worst of all, I'm going to Prom as a party of one."

"Absolutely not. And ya know what? Neither am I. You're gonna work this out with him. You have to. You guys are too cute together. Yes, he should have told you, but let him explain. Let him apologize. Like you said, Jane's a mess. Look at her track record. No one wants to admit to sleeping with her. Can you blame him?"

TWENTY-SEVEN

"Too bulky. Let's try something a little more classic, maybe?" My Aunt Jen hands me a string of pearls as Mom adjusts the antique full-length mirror.

"So glad we have your help and expertise today. I'm not sure Bree always trusts my judgment."

"That's not entirely true, Mom. We also needed more jewelry to pick from."

"Very funny," says Aunt Jen. "I didn't even go to my Senior Prom, not that I cared at the time. But still, how exciting. Oh Bren, this is happening too fast. Our little Bree is a lady."

As I string the pearls around my neck, I push away the memory of Sean's fingers grazing my skin after playing the guitar, and the way his breath always sped up when I touched him. Especially at the lake. "Can you unhook this necklace Mom, it's too old ladyish and it's suffocating me."

Aunt Jen nudges my shoulder. "I hear you've been busy lately. Spending a lot of time with your new little friend."

"Funny you should mention that. Bree came home around two a couple weekends ago," says Mom.

I narrow my eyes. "Really, Mom?"

"So it's getting serious, huh?" Aunt Jen asks. "Then let's not beat around the bush. Are you still on birth control?"

My cheeks redden. "Omigod I can't believe we're talking about this."

"Believe it, girl. Otherwise the next thing you know you could be knocked up and living in a van down by the river."

"Jen, don't joke. We're serious about this, Bree."

"How can I focus on the right accessories with you two butting into my sex life." I push through Aunt Jen's jewelry box frowning at an aquamarine the same shade as Sean's eyes.

"Your sex life? Good Lord." My mom falls back onto her bed. Aunt Jen laughs, fanning Mom's face.

"Yes, my sex life. I'm seventeen, and only a few short months away from legal adulthood. But since you're just dying to know, I don't have an actual sex life per se." *Not anymore anyway.* "But no one knows the future. I know all about STDs and thanks to MTV reality TV, I'm not trying to have a baby until I'm like a hundred years old. I've been taking my pill every single day for the last year and a half, and I also might even have a condom in the bottom of one of my purses."

"Well, okay, I guess you told us." Mom swats me on the butt.

Aunt Jen laughs. "Who knew your own daughter would be more of a lady than you were, huh Bren?"

"Don't you dare," Mom swings the string of pearls toward her. "This one. Wow. This might be the one, Bree." She holds up another necklace.

"That was Mom's. It's a sapphire and probably perfect." Aunt Jen throws my hair into a high bun as Mom clasps the necklace.

"Oh hon, it looks great on you. It *is* perfect. It would look good with a crown as well."

I shake my head. "Well, if Kallie manages to win over Molly, I'll let her wear the necklace for the crowning."

As Mom and Aunt Jen lecture me on believing in myself and other things that have no relevance over Prom politics, I can't help but wonder what Maisey would have worn. If she would have gone at all. I let my hair fall back down over my shoulders and try to picture her in my dress. I can't. I can't picture her in anything but the faded army green cargo pants and old gray sweatshirt she hid in every day.

If Maisey would've been at Prom, Jane and everyone would've been taunting her about declining the nomination. Kids would've been singing snippets of the Maisey song and throwing stuff at her. And I probably would've stayed silent. I grasp the sapphire between my fingers, the edges smooth, then sharp at the corners. At first I wasn't sure if I'd be able to do anything else with Maisey's letter—or how I could make it right. But as I soak in the realities of my reflection, a girl, almost a woman looks back at me, alive, looking like she has everything. Even without Sean, for once it almost feels like I do. Almost. And for that, I decide that I don't really have a choice. If I deny Maisey's last request, I know I'll never forgive myself.

"Hey don't look so bummed," my Aunt Jen says. "Don't listen to us, we're old!"

"Yeah, yeah, I know. I do believe in myself okay? And I definitely don't need a crown on Prom night to validate me. I also won't need it to put some of those other kids in check."

"That's what I'm talking about." My mom smiles and Aunt Jen wraps me in a hug.

TWENTY-EIGHT

School and home are a blur the next week. Everything moves fast but me. Teachers hand back stacks of old assignments, surprising us with last-minute review quizzes, and assigning busy work. I move through it like a zombie. Dead, cold, and hungry. Everyone has checked out. And everyone is talking about Prom.

"So, let me get this straight," Kendall asks over a tray of pizza and wilted salad. "It's gonna be you and Sean, but you're not even speaking to him; Chris and Laura since they're back on again, Brian and Jane, Molly with Justin, and Kallie's still going with Todd?"

"Yep," I say with a mouthful of pizza, "that's about right."

Sam leans in. "You're starring in a reality TV episode with too many stars and too many side plots. It doesn't make sense. First off, why are you and Sean in a fight?"

"Just like I told you on Monday, Tuesday, and yesterday. It's not a big deal and I'm not getting into it."

"Okay. It was worth a try. So, second most important question: Why is Molly going with Justin now?"

"I don't know Sam, maybe she likes him. Why am I the one being interrogated here?"

"Because," says Kendall, "You're the mole. Friends with *them* and friends with *us*. You're a double agent so give us the goods."

"Yeah, spill it." Sam whispers, "You know what people are saying, right?"

"No." I shift my gaze to the left and right, then pretend to pull out a notepad and pen. "What are the people saying?"

"Well," says Sam, "they're saying Todd cheated on Kallie but they're still pretending to be a couple for Prom."

"Yeah, they don't want to mess up their chances at King and Queen." Kendall stares me up and down. "Is it true?"

"I can neither confirm nor deny any allegations directed toward my best friend."

"They almost had this whole thing in the bag."

"Exactly." Sam nods. "We're sick of Molly and Jane winning everything. Kallie is friends with everyone, and Todd's super hot, for a *guy*."

"Who knows," says Kendall. "With these rumors going around, maybe you actually have a chance."

I pop a mushy carrot stick in my mouth. "Gee thanks."

"No I mean it. It's too bad you and Sean are so low-key. People barely even know you guys are a thing."

"Yeah." Sam adds, "You guys need to hang out in public more or do something scandalous."

"Like what?" I ask. "Stage a pregnancy scare or check into rehab?"

"I know," says Sam, her eyes lighting up. "You could throw a big party like Kallie did, but invite everyone. And have a theme. It'll give you more visibility."

All I can do is laugh and try not to spit out my carrot in the process. "You guys are out of control. It's not a presidential election."

"You're damn right it's not," Kendall says. "This is Prom. It's important."

****

In last period, Justin passes me a note from my regular seat. I've forced Justin to trade spots with me every day since Monday. Opening the note for even a split second is painful. Sean's handwriting stares right back at me. "I don't want this," I whisper and turn to give it back.

Mr. Norderick clears his throat. "Let's stay focused guys."

Reading. Writing. As if I can concentrate. We're supposed to be reading Emily Barrett Browning and working on a remake of her "How Do I Love Thee" poem. It's due tomorrow but I can't concentrate worth crap. Love shmuvv. I crush Sean's note into the pocket of my jeans. My book sits open while I try to ignore the loud pattering of my heart by doodling words and pictures into my notebook.

Like clockwork, the bell rings, everyone rushes out and the new routine we've been doing since Monday starts. Molly meets Justin outside of the door. They walk behind us, in their own world. Todd still waits for Kallie and they walk together as usual, holding hands, but nothing more. Kallie and I make small talk so the boys can't get a word in.

Sean glides up next to me, "Did you get my note?"

I turn to Kallie. "So, Kallie, did you watch the new episode of *The B Crew* last night? It was so boring."

Kallie shakes her head. "No, but you know what movie I watched? *The Grudge*. It was old and it wasn't very nice."

I roll my eyes. "Humph. I bet."

Justin yells from behind us, "Know what movie I saw? *Weekend at Bernie's Two*. A classic."

****

Kallie calls me right after school. "Prom is next weekend. That's like nine days. You have to talk to Sean. Laura said Jane supposedly asked him if he wanted to trade dates."

"Trade dates? What the hell? How come everyone thinks they can pass their dates around like a bad case of chlamydia?"

"Exactly. Jane would be going with Sean. As his date, Bree. You can't let that happen." "What if you go with Sean, and Jane goes with Todd and I go with Brian?"

"Nice try. Jane would love that. She asked Todd after school today. *Right in front of my face*. She walked up to us in the parking lot and asked

185

him what he was doing about Prom. Todd actually laughed. In his world, Jane cheated on him. Tell me that's not twisted? He said he's not even talking to her anymore. I don't think anyone's speaking to her right now. You can't let her go with Sean."

"I don't care if he actually goes with her." I press my phone onto speaker then pummel my fists into my mattress. "I don't care."

"Listen to yourself. Yes, you do. Sean's going to give up eventually, and you'll miss out on a guy that loves you. And, you're gonna have a shit Prom."

"Oh really Kal, like yours is gonna be such a blast. I can't believe you're still letting Todd take you."

"I don't really have a choice. I thought about it and I'm not going alone. Aside from the depresso factor, it wouldn't look good. I'm on the Court, my parents will be at the pep rally, and Todd's parents are coming over for pictures at our house when he picks me up. My parents are more excited than I was. Who wants a bunch of Prom pictures of their daughter . . . by herself?"

"I guess I know what you mean." I sigh.

"Exactly. You better figure it out, before it gets figured out for you. Or you might end up going alone."

I hang up with Kallie and slump into the seat of my desk. Out the window, the tops of the trees wave silently, leaves glistening with flickers of the soon-to-be setting sun.

Even with all the bad shit Jane's dealt with, she has no problem juggling dates and going after what she wants. Kallie has no problem sweeping Todd's crap under the rug just to save face. Maybe I should just do what everyone else would do.

A small robin flies past the trees, landing on my window's ledge. Maisey's words echo in my ear. *Enjoy hanging out with all those assholes, seems like you'll fit in just fine.*

TWENTY-NINE

How do I love thee? Let me count the ways.
I can't. The fear overrides.
If I love you as much as I do,
the pain will be greater, the loss more vast.
If I love you now, who's to say it'll last?
I'm not sure I'm enough to make you stay,
I love you as far as I can run
As deep as an ocean of words I just can't say.

I wake up in yesterday's clothes, slumped over a furry blue pillow, my poem still on my lap. My alarm beeps from beneath my hip.

7:12 a.m. Damn it. It's been going off for over an hour. I switch shirts, brush my teeth, swipe on deodorant, and rush out the door.

The first warning bell rings as I'm running into the school. I throw my hair up and race to my locker with one untied shoe. The whole time, I'm running through things in my head to say to Sean.

Let me count the ways to tell him I can't do this one more day.
Pretending I don't see you, hear you, miss you is exhausting.
Who you were with before me means nothing.
Maybe I should be sorry too.

Maybe I just got so mad because I was scared. Scared of loving someone and them loving me back and everything that means.

Maybe being with you is almost too comfortable. Things haven't been easy lately but us being together made it better. That even when things were awkward, or we had uncomfortable things to say, scary things to talk about, things we were embarrassed about, we were able to just say it.

And I love that about you, and I love that about me. That talking to you and being with you has been so freeing and so scary at the same time.

I meant everything I said and did. I wouldn't take back a second of it. The sex wasn't a mistake. We're not a mistake, us being together has been the only thing that's felt right to me in a long time.

And I miss you like crazy.

I go over all of these things in my head. A hundred times during every class. Over and over in the hallways.

At the beginning of Nord's class, Sean doesn't try to say hi for the first time this week. It throws me off a little and my heart feels like it's attacking me from the inside so I decide it's best to wait and tell him everything after the final bell rings.

Once my breathing gets back to normal, I pass Kal a note.

I'm going to talk to Sean after class, so go ahead without me. EEEEEEK. Wish me luck!

She passes one back that says:

FINALLY!!!!

Nord has some of us read our poems during class. Thankfully, he doesn't call on me. I'm not in the mood to give the class more insights into my love life than they probably already heard in the hallways. Sean doesn't get called on either. This leaves us at the mercy of such works as Shandy's poem about the majesty of sunbeams and four-leaf clovers and Justin's scribed love for old movies and hockey.

The bell rings and Kallie grins and nudges me before making her way out the door. Sean steps out behind her without turning around. He doesn't try to make eye contact the way he's been doing all week. But as he turns the corner, I take a deep breath and clear my throat.

"Hey Sean."

He spins around. "Oh, uh, hey." Our eyes finally meet. But it's not the way I planned. There's no *I've never stopped loving you* eye talk. It's just him with an expression that's mopey and confused.

I feel a pinch in my heart. "Can I talk to you for a sec?"

He nods, squinting his eyes, "Sure . . . I, um, yeah."

We make our way down the hall, an air of thick tension between us.

"Can we talk in the parking lot? Is that okay?" I pretend to straighten my folders and notebook in my arm. Someone walks in-between us, almost elbowing me out of the way. I drop my folder and quickly pick it back up. "Excuse me, you just—"

"Sorry." Ugh. It's Jane. Her eyes meet mine for a beat before she turns to Sean, handing him a shiny red cloth. "I brought a swatch of my dress so you can match it with the corsage. But listen, make it minimal. I don't want too much red. Tell them to use white as the *main* and the red as the *accent*."

"Yeah, sure no problem," Sean says, tucking the cloth into the back pocket of his jeans.

Jane says, "Cool, I'll call you tonight so we can go over other stuff." She touches my shoulder and smiles, "Sorry about nudging you. It really was an accident." There's an actual sincerity on her face that I want to smack off. "Later guys." She turns and heads the other way.

The pace of my walk triples, but Sean keeps up. "Yeah, the parking lot is fine."

My eyes glaze over. I walk with steady long steps, eyes straight ahead. "Actually that's okay. I, um . . . I thought I had your sweatshirt in my car, that's all. But I just realized I don't. I don't have it. I'm sorry."

"All right, well if you still—"

And once again I'm running. Running away from Sean. Pushing through bodies, backpacks, armies of friends, lovers, frenemies, planning tonight, planning tomorrow, laughing, hopes high, shoulder to shoulder. I keep running even though everything gets more and more blurry. I just need to make it to my car.

C'mon Bree, keep it together, don't cry don't cry don't cry.

I can't let anyone see me like this. Before I get to the front doors, Jane and Laura are coming from the opposite way. Kallie, Todd, Molly, and Justin are right in front of me. I hold my folder and notebook up like a face shield. A single tear falls. A thin straight line down my cheek. I make a sharp right turn into the girl's bathroom.

Opening the door of the last stall, I heave a breath of the air that's been trapped in my lungs. Sitting down on the edge of the toilet seat, my tears burn trails down my face. I wrap my hands in toilet paper and bury my face into them, convulsing into sobs.

Who was I to think he would wait? After coming by the house at least five times, numerous unanswered calls, and voicemails I haven't even heard. Kallie was right. If I wait too long, I'm going to lose him. Apparently time is of the essence when Prom's one week away and Jane is waiting in the wings. My whole body shakes, feeling lighter and lighter as I sob the last of my tears. I just want to go home.

Before I leave the bathroom, I check the mirror. Even my eyebrows and the divot above my lip are red and puffy like my eyes. I grab my sunglasses from my bag and as I'm wiping the lenses with my T-shirt another glimpse of myself in the mirror taunts me. Something feels familiar.

Maisey. Her face practically stares back at me in the mirror. She's just like when I saw her in this same spot two months ago. Crying, wiping her eyes. Pitiful, humiliated, lonely, defeated. *Like me.*

****

The parking lot is nearly emptied. Brian is leaning against his car, parked right next to mine.

"Hey Brian, what's up?" I ask, adding a fake dash of pep to my voice.

"Geez, what took you so long? I was beginning to think you were kidnapped by Janitor Bob."

I adjust my sunglasses. "I wish. Were you waiting to talk about Prom?"

"Yeah. No offense, but this is exasperating. Everyone's turned Prom into a joke. As immature as it is, Prom King is a nice title to have. I'm a writer and it'd be kind of quirky to have "Former Prom King" as part of my bio. But the vote usually goes to a couple. A stable, beloved, amiable couple. We'll never win. Not that anyone else has a chance either, with everyone cheating and sleeping with each other. It's like a bad episode of . . . something. Help me out here. I don't watch TV."

"Anything on Wednesday nights. Yeah, I thought the same thing. Sorry you got stuck with me," I shrug. "We can still have fun though."

Brian raises an eyebrow.

"But I mean, if you don't want to, we don't have to go together. If you have someone else in mind." I tap the dirt off the foot of my Converse.

"Like Molly or Jane? Or my boyfriend who says he wouldn't be caught dead at a high school Prom?"

"Ouch. Sorry."

"It doesn't matter. I'm not even out yet to my parents. Oh well, at least you're on the Court. That means something. You'll have to be my date because I don't have a choice."

I stare at him for a second and then click my car door unlocked. "But you know what Brian? I *do* have a choice. You'll have to figure something out. I'm going alone." I jump into my car and slam the door. As I drive away, Brian throws down his backpack and kicks his car. Brian Wang, Class Valedictorian, Homecoming King, Class President, Most Likely to Succeed at Everything. Last week he was getting drunk, this week he's throwing a temper tantrum. I turn up the radio and laugh for the first time since last week.

****

When I get home, something crinkles in the pocket of my jeans. Sean's note. From yesterday. Instead of ignoring it, like I've been doing all week, I open it.

Bree,
I've figured out some lyrics for that song I'd been working on. It's a work in progress but I hope you'll let me know what you think:

You're not answering the door
The phone
Of course not the texts
I don't want to keep waiting to apologize
For something that was nothing
Compared to you
For something that was only
there
before there was you
For something that
(I admit) you might've wanted to know
Something that could've changed our course
Changed where we went and how you felt
If that's the case, then I'm not sorry
If that's the case, I'll take what I can get
The long conversations
Your hand in mine
The night by the lake
dirt in our fingernails
Moon in your hair
Love felt infinite
How can you just run away?
Turn your eyes
From what we felt just yesterday
I know you love
I know you care
Because I felt it when I held you
I was there
—Sean Mills

P.S.

Breeze,

Please let me know if you still want to go to Prom with me. If you don't call tonight, I'll stop bothering you. I don't want you to think of me as another stalker ex-boyfriend.

Please call.
Love,
Sean

THIRTY

The weekend hours slither by without a word from Sean. Kallie doesn't even call. Probably making appearances at parties and the diner with Todd. I spend my time going over all the things I wanted to say to Sean, but instead of me waiting until Friday like I did, in my mind, I tell him on Monday or Tuesday. I also replay every conversation we had about Jane, and how I could've asked about her. I'm not sure if he's right that it would've been a deal breaker for me had I known. I don't know. Maybe in the very beginning. But not later, not now. I wish he knew that.

Late Saturday night I spend an hour almost-calling Sean. Today I do the same. Finally, I give up and go to my car to get his Bengals football sweatshirt that's been balled up on my backseat. I bring it into my bed, crawl under the covers, the faint smell of sandalwood taunting me until I fall asleep wrapped in his sleeves.

Molly calls Sunday, leaving a message to say "hi" and see what I'm up to. I don't call her back. It won't be long until people find out that I'm going to Prom alone. And since Sam and Kendall's group is already set, I'm going *totally* alone. I thought I'd moved past using my "fake it 'til you make it" mantra but I'm bringing it back. There's no way I can go to Prom by myself without stepping up my game. I'm going to look and feel like I belong and I don't care what anyone thinks.

It doesn't take long for word to get out about my solo status. By Tuesday I've had three guys, one girl, and even a junior ask to take me.

Sam slams her orange juice carton on the table. "Damn it. I had no idea Jess was into girls too. Theatre girls usually aren't my type, but still. Could've been a game changer."

"I'm sure there are a lot more bi girls in our school than you think." Kendall shrugs then meets my eyes with an extreme look of pity. "I still can't believe you're going alone," She pushes the suspiciously bright green broccoli around on her plate. "I feel really bad that we don't have any room."

"It's eight of us total, but you can definitely hang out with us once we get to the dance," Sam says.

"Sure. Don't worry about it. It's not like I expected you to hold a limo and dinner reservation just in case Sean decided to go with Jane. Of course it would've been nice."

"Yeah we should've known. Those guys think they can do whatever they want no matter who gets dicked over."

"Well, just for the record, I screwed up with Sean. And I'm the one who told Brian I'd rather go alone than with him." I finally tell my side of the story and we laugh, comparing it to the versions Kendall and Sam have been hearing since yesterday.

"Oh shit," Sam says. "If you would've just read the damn letter on the day he gave it to you. You must be kicking yourself."

"So aside from being totally hot and super popular, Sean Mills writes love letters and is madly in love with you. He sounds amazing. But he's going with Jane? I can't believe you're giving up, just like that."

"Are you guys trying to make me jump off a bridge tonight or what? Jesus."

Kendall's eyes look past me as the sound of footsteps approach.

"Don't jump Bree, don't do it. I won't have anyone to bother in Language Arts."

"Hi Justin," I say without turning around.

"Molly told me to ask if you wanted to come with us to Prom?" He sits down next to me. "Hello ladies."

Kendall and Sam say hi and smile like jack-o'-lanterns with blinking eyelashes. Kendall practically drools into her chocolate milk carton. Sure he's walking around with a little more confidence lately and toned it down half a notch with the jokes, but hanging with Molly Chapman has turned him into like, the eighth hottest guy in the school.

"I think I'm fine," I say. "It's not that big of a deal. Thanks though."

"Don't say I didn't offer. Really don't say that. I promised Molly I'd ask. She said you haven't called or texted her back. She thinks you're mad at her for everything." He quickly glances at Sam and Kendall. "You know, for everything that came out about well, you know. Everybody."

"Justin, everybody seems to know everything about everybody these days, so it's not a secret." I shake my head. "I'm not mad at Molly. I've been busy. I don't feel like talking to anyone about this stuff. I'm over it."

"Got it. See you in class." Justin salutes us and takes off.

Kendall watches him walk away and slides her hand down her hair. "I never noticed this before, but there's actually something hot about him. I mean, I've always had a thing for funny guys."

"Yeah, like there's something sexy about him." Sam nods. "I think it's his cologne. It's really feminine."

"Definitely his cologne." I say. *Eau de Molly Chapman.*

****

In Language Arts, I have to keep reminding myself to stop staring at the back of Sean's head from behind Justin. It's too depressing. I know he watched me make my way into class. Instead of feeling good about it, I feel sad. The girls at lunch were right, so was Kallie. I totally let him get away.

Mr. N. gives us busy work and I write absentminded words and doodles in my notebook. My full name, a horrible sketch of my Prom dress, pictures of eyes and flowers, question marks that look like penises. I stare at my paper and feel alone as hell. I feel even lonelier than I did before Sean and I started hanging out.

****

196

Over a plate of scrambled eggs and salsa, I tell Mom I'm going to Prom alone. I don't tell her the salsa tastes more like ketchup and onions than Dad's recipe.

"Oh, honey. By yourself? Really?" My mom leaves her mouth hanging open. Literally. I reach across the kitchen table and gently push her chin up to close her mouth.

"Mom, don't be so dramatic. It's Senior Prom, not my wedding day."

"Well, I don't know, babe. Why did you wait so long to tell me?"

"Because I didn't want to suffer more than a day with you looking at me like I'm a dying puppy."

"Oh no, I don't feel sorry for you, I feel—oh Bree Ella, I just wanted this to be perfect for you."

"Yeah well, it's perfectly fitting. That's for sure."

"What about the pep rally today? Do you have to sit up there by yourself? I wish you could've patched things up with Sean. I really thought he was a sweet guy."

"Mom. It's fine. All the girls are on one side and the guys sit on the other. It's not that serious." Mom's face falls farther. "It's just a pep rally. As for the dance, I have a ton of friends to hang out with there. It's probably better this way. Now you don't have to worry about me not being home by curfew or coming home pregnant." I smile to reassure her.

"Oh please, I was your age once, I know there's no curfew on Prom night."

"Well now ya tell me. Maybe I can find a date online."

"I did take the day off, so I have a few hours before the pep rally. Don't tempt me. Maybe I'll Google you a nice young man."

We finish breakfast, and then Mom helps me hang my dress and accessory bag in my car. She sends me off with a hug and a wave. I spend the whole drive trying to shake the dying puppy vibe.

I make my way into the girl's locker room, the roar of the gymnasium at my back. Molly gleams from a row of mirrors in a white and gold beaded gown.

"Hey girl, you better hustle. Everyone is already in their dresses."

Laura walks in, glistening in a turquoise mini dress. Kallie's right behind in a fire engine fire-starting red dress. It's tight, strapless, and flares out from a mid-thigh slit, sending her legs into infinity.

I whistle. "Looking good ladies, looking good."

"Hurry up, your hotness," says Kallie giving me a high five. "Dance team is out there. As soon as they're done, there's a speech and then we're on."

Butterflies clink in my stomach like a pocketful of pennies. I run into the locker area to change.

Jane peeks her head from behind a row of lockers sliding her legs into a tight red lacey thing, "Can you be a darling and hook me up?"

Like I hooked you up with my boyfriend? "Sure," I say as she adjusts the straps. "So, how are things lately? Are you okay?"

She looks over her shoulder with a slight frown. "I'm fine as long as I won't have my underwear line or any seams showing."

I take the hint. "Um, okay. Is this your dress? It's pretty revealing." I hook a short row of clasps.

"Thanks. Actually this is a slip."

"Yeah I knew that. I was joking."

"Oh." She ducks behind the other lockers.

Tough crowd.

"C'mon Bree, we need to get some makeup on you!" Kallie yells. I rush to the mirrors along with the other girls for a quick douse of makeup.

As Kallie swipes frosty blue onto my eyelids, Molly gives me a hundred and one reasons why three would be company at Prom.

"It's not like we've been together forever, ya know? We're gonna be laid back and fun—not making out at dinner or anything."

"Yeah, I don't know. If you guys are dying for a third wheel how about Brian?" I laugh.

Kallie holds up her hand. "He's going with Jane and Sean now. Word is that Jane gave him—" Kallie's eyes pop and her mouth drops open. I follow her gaze expecting to see a cockroach or giant tarantula.

"Oh. My. God." Molly and Laura say in unison.

Jane. Wearing the same dress as Kallie. Not one in a similar style or another red dress, but the *same exact dress*. Up until now, whenever the "same dress" scenario has come up in a conversation, movie, or something, I didn't really get why it was such a big deal. *Now* I get it.

Jane crosses her arms. Her eyes travel up and down Kallie's entirety as her nostrils flare, "This is not going to happen." Jane sneers. "You're not wearing my dress."

Kallie steps forward, squaring off with Jane. "*This* is my dress. I ordered it months ago. I have no idea how this happened. If this is another way for you to steal something that's mine, it's not happening. Not today. And not for Prom tomorrow night. Feel free to wear it Sunday. You can wear it all summer long for all I care." Kallie takes another step up, practically *into* Jane's nose.

Molly, Laura, and I stand there waiting. I'm not sure whether we're hoping it does or doesn't come to blows. It's that close and that heated.

"You don't scare me Kallie." Jane takes a step back. "I'm wearing the dress."

"Fine. I can't rip it off you. But I promise you; I will not back down. *Wear it.* If you're up for a game of 'Who Wore It Best,' I'm in. You look presentable, *Jane*," Kallie narrows her eyes with a syrupy evil smile. "But next to me, in the same dress, you're a joke. A plastic, trashy, lonely, and desperate knockoff."

A pit forms in my stomach. Maybe Jane did this on purpose but she doesn't deserve this. "Hey," I say. "Maybe if you guys sit on opposite ends of the stage it'll be okay?"

Jane does a quick spin out of Kallie's glare, tears springing to her eyes.

"Fuck you. All of you." She grabs her bag and runs out of the locker room door.

"Don't let it hit ya," laughs Molly.

"That was so mean." Laura shakes her head. "And so awesome."

"I've never seen her back down like that," Molly says.

"Do you think she's coming back?" I ask.

Kallie snorts, "I don't give a shit."

Shandy peeks her head in the door waving a clipboard. "Prom Queens! Five minutes to showtime! I'll be back to line you up, alphabetically escorted by the Kings."

"Damn," I say. "That girl's such a type A freak about everything. Kal, does my hair look okay?"

"You're fierce. Sean's gonna faint. But what about your shoes? You can't go barefoot."

"She's right," laughs Molly. "Hillbilly chic is so last year."

I run over to grab my heels but they're not there. "Shit. Shit. *Shit*!" I yell, ripping through my dress and accessory bags. "They're not here. Has anyone seen my silver heels?"

Everyone scours the room. The benches, the unlocked lockers, the stalls, everywhere. Jane rushes back in with an enormous garment bag, a hoop, and a tight smile. She disappears behind the lockers, then emerging, like superman, in a new candy pink dress. A loud, shiny strapless ball gown leading to layers upon layers of ruffles. Supported at the bottom with a hoop.

Jane spins and rests her hand on her hip. "You guys have nothing on me. You were right, Kallie. That red dress was cheap. I've won two titles in this dress and I plan to win another. Thanks for setting me straight."

"Give it a rest, Jane. You look like a quinceañera cake topper. Where the hell are Bree's shoes?" Kallie asks.

I stride over and snatch Jane's bags, swiping a pile of her clothes from the bench onto the floor.

"I swear to god if you took my shoes . . ." Huffing through my nostrils, I rifle through her bags and piles of clothes scouring every crevice for my silver heels. "She took my shoes, she took my freaking shoes."

"Let's go girls! Get out here! Time to line up!" Shandy's voice echoes into the locker room.

Jane looks at me, "I didn't touch your shoes. This isn't a teen movie. Get over yourself."

Molly offers me Belmont's tiniest pair of green flats. "This is the most dressy pair we have between us. C'mon, we gotta go."

I run over to my stuff one last time, fighting angry tears. I double-check my bags. Still no shoes. I look down at the shoes I'd purposely mismatched this morning. One yellow and one purple Converse is all I've got.

We rush outside, following Shandy to the double doors of the gymnasium. The boys, like a raft of penguins, stare in awe.

"Ohhhh pretty shiny things," says Justin, wriggling his fingers.

"Hi-yo." Todd grabs toward Kallie's waist.

Kallie swerves from him. "Don't even think about it."

Chris kisses Laura on the cheek and says she looks nice while Sean stands, shuffling his hands in and out of his pockets, looking down at his feet.

Jane mumbles something to Sean about her dress.

Shandy eyes her clipboard and says, "Okay, Molly. You're with Justin . . ."

I mentally alphabetize. *Chapman, Conner all the way to H . . . I'll come before Jane and then . . . Mills before Monroe. Mills. I'm with Sean.* I take a deep breath.

"Bree's next to Sean, Jane with Chris, Laura and Brian, Kallie and Todd. C'mon, c'mon, let's go." Shandy herds us into a line, two by two.

I put my hand over my heart, as if it will slow it down or make it beat softer. Sean grabs my hand and places it in the crook of his elbow.

"Hi." My fingers tremble on his arm.

He smiles, slightly. "Hey," he whispers, staring at my fingers. "Relax Breeze–*Bree*, it's just a pep rally."

While we wait for Principal Finley's cue, Molly tries to sweet talk Shandy into letting her help with the Prom decorations. "Well, I just thought maybe you'd need some help. I mean, with all the gloom and doom colors and the weird cutouts, maybe you just need another set of eyes? I'm going to college for interior design, you know."

Shandy smiles with a swift nod of her head. "No. Everything's perfect; I've been planning this theme—I mean the whole committee has since last year. But thanks, that's really sweet of you."

Brian steps forward. "You're aware that cardboard werewolves and vampires are more kid's birthday party than Prom, right?"

"Yeah," says Molly. "It's not a Bat Mitzvah.

"They're right," says Jane. "It's so two thousand and late, and it's going to ruin a lot of photo ops having that shit in the background."

The rest of us give Shandy our two cents about Prom decor while she grips her clipboard as if it's someone's neck. "Seriously guys, this is *my* thing."

Just as Justin starts to make another joke, Finley announces the Court.

As I sit onstage, applause slowly dying, Mom and Dad wave from the audience behind a small roped off area. They're in the front row next to Kallie's parents and Beth, Sean's mom. Jane's mom is there too, but without her dad. For Jane's sake, I'm glad. I try to guess which parent goes to which kid but get interrupted by Shandy tapping and saying something about us stepping up to the microphone.

"Each nominee will introduce themselves as a member of the senior class Prom Court. And tell us why they'd best represent Belmont High School as Prom Queen or King."

Wait. What? I didn't sign up for this. There was nothing about public speaking on the Prom Guide. Kallie meets my eyes with a smile, then shrugs.

Molly stands up and is flawless. She tells everyone how she's truly been blessed by this experience, and would be honored to represent her class as Prom Queen. It all happens so fast that I don't even have time to run though what to say before she passes me the mic.

I rise, grateful that my dress is long enough to cover my violently shaking knees. I wait for the applause, two random boos, and "Go Molly's" to subside.

"Is this thing on? Um, just kidding. Okay . . . hi. Hi Mom, hi Dad." I wave. "Um, I'm Bree Hughes and I'm . . . um, I'm really sorry that I don't have anything really poised or cool to say right now. To be honest, I'm probably not the best candidate to represent BHS. I mean, um, not like in a way that, um . . ." *Totally choking here. My voice is shaking, my armpits are sweating, and everyone's staring at me. Breathe, just fucking breathe.* I dip the microphone from my mouth to my hip, take a deep breath and bring it back to continue, "Okay what I'm trying to say is that I may not be the best choice. I couldn't even find my shoes today." I lift my dress and point my foot, turning the toe of my sneaker on the stage. "So, yeah, this is really cool to be here, but I'm definitely not a Prom Queen."

Dropping back into my seat with a thud, I smile. My heavy exhale is drowned out by the roar of applause. There are more kids yelling my name than I've ever even spoken to in the past four years here.

I pass the mic to Jane and maybe it's the sweat of my palms or just the nerves, but I let go before she grips it. It hits the stage with an amplified thud. The woo-hoos ring out as half the class cheers as Jane bends down, trying to reach over all her ruffles in order to pick up the mic. Her Barbie pink ruffles are so big and awkward with that stiff, giant hoop in it, that she's swinging her hips to the side to move the dress out of her way. Instead of making space to pick up the mic, Jane falls. Right on her ass. For the briefest moment, Jane's perfectly coifed updo and wide-eyed horror is obstructed by the flipped-up hoop. I catch a glimpse of an equally ruffly pair of pink underwear.

As best as I can in my dress, I leap over, grab the mic and her shoulder, yanking her up. "Are you okay?" I whisper.

Half the class jumps out of their seats, laughing. My mom's hands shade her eyes, and it looks like Dad's laughing into his hand.

Jane snatches the mic as I mouth the words "I'm so sorry." Still, she brands me with the evilest stink eye ever. My smile widens and all I'm thinking as I slide back into my seat is *fake it.*

I've gotta give Jane credit. If she wasn't breathing venom right now, her speech is an A plus for effort in her attempt at damage control. This is not her first rodeo. Her lips purse, her shoulders come back, and her chin tips up. "Things happen that change you. Life happens. Other people happen. But we have choices. You can become someone bigger and better than the evil you've been running from. In the face of adversity, we can become giants. We cannot only survive, but overcome. I've worked my ass off to be me. To exceed when jealousy and monsters with claws are within seconds of bringing me down. But I'm always quick on my feet and ahead of the game. We are fighters, Belmont. I am always fighting." Her voice is a knife dipped in honey butter. Sharp and sweet. "A vote for me is a vote for strength and poise."

The only problem is that someone keeps bellowing "Booooo" every few seconds. Jane dips into a curtsy and passes the mic to Laura. Shandy runs over asking that everyone *please* refrain from any lewd or negative comments while the court candidates are speaking, *thank you so much*.

Someone yells, "Shandy, you suck."

Laura frowns. "No she doesn't. Shandy is a really good person." For some reason that gets another big laugh from the audience.

Everyone else's intros drone on, the class becoming more restless with each candidate. I run through things to say to Sean when we walk out. I don't get much more detailed than "hello" and a daydream that he'll be the one with all the things to say. Things like "I never stopped loving you" and "I can't go another minute without you." Before I know it, we're herded back into couples by Shandy.

As we file off stage, Principal Finley thanks everyone for their school spirit and gives a few rules about Prom tomorrow night. Basically: don't come drunk or high and don't punch anyone in the face.

Sean says, "Nice shoes."

I glance down as if I haven't seen them yet. "Thanks."

The guys and girls part in a red sea fashion as the double doors of the gym close behind us. I turn to say something to Sean. *Something, anything.*

Instead Jane steps in front of me, pinning me up against the girl's locker room door with her ruffles. "You have some nerve, really. Un-be-fuckin-lievable. First I'm bullied into wearing a different dress, accused of stealing your shoes, and then you humiliate me onstage. Who the hell do you think you are? You're nobody. You think your reverse psychology speech up there is going to get votes? You're wrong. Nobody cares about you *Brittney*. You don't even have a date. You're all alone. You are right about one thing though. You're not a Prom Queen. You are a Prom loser."

The principal walks out of the doors and Jane spins around.

"Oh hey, Mr. Finley. Great pep rally, right?" Jane smiles, not a drop of venom in sight.

THIRTY-ONE

As soon as I sit up to stretch on Saturday morning, my heart is ticking in my chest like an amped up version of my cat clock. TickTickTickTick. Tiny heartbeats, super close together. If I wasn't starting to get used to these faster and harder hitting palpitations, I'd think I was having a heart attack. Lying in the fetal position, I repeat over and over for it to *go away go away go away*. Finally after about five minutes of me talking myself out of dying of nothing, my breathing becomes less shallow and I can move again.

Kicking off my sheets, I release a frustrated growl. *What is wrong with me?*

Once I pull on a pair of sweat shorts, I pad over to mom's room. "Mom, you up?"

"Come in," she answers as I'm already pushing her door open. She rakes her hand through her short spiky hair and closes her e-reader. "You're up early."

"I know. I was wondering about going to that appointment you made for today. Did you actually cancel it?"

"Nope," she quirks her eyebrows. "It's still on. I was going to make one last-ditch effort to convince you and maybe throw in a bribe. I was pretty sure I'd be taking the appointment for myself instead."

Swishing my foot through the carpet a few times, I try to fight back tears. "I feel like I'm always crying."

Her arms are out so I jump on her bed and let her pull me in. A few tears trickle down my cheek as I wish there were more words to explain what I'm feeling. She smooths her hand over my hair and says she'll drive me to meet with the therapist at 9:30.

****

The office behind the waiting room is a little smaller than my bedroom. The walls are a muted gray and the two paintings hung on opposite sides are abstract swishes and swooshes of rich yellows and cool blues.

A short, pale-skinned woman with a bronze-streaked bob extends her hand. "Hi Bree. I'm Donna Jarron. You can call me Donna if you'd like. Please, have a seat."

I grip her hand for a second and scan the seating options. A floral print loveseat is flush against the wall and a burgundy chair hugs a corner. I hold back a joke about the window being my best bet.

"Thanks," I say and plant myself on the chair. "I thought couches were just a cliché. I didn't know shrinks or therapists actually use them." I keep my tone light as I wipe my damp palms on my jeans.

"Maybe so, but it's comfortable so I keep it around." Her smile is brief and I'm worried she's analyzing me for making jokes already.

There's a short break of silence as she flips open a small black notebook on the table next to her. She lifts a pen and says, "I'll be taking notes occasionally during our session, do you mind?"

"No, it's fine." I take a small sip from the half-empty water bottle I'd brought in.

"But don't worry, I'm listening. I'm usually not much of a note taker except for first sessions."

I say, "it's fine" again.

As I'm wondering when we're going to get on with it, she asks why I'm here.

"My mom brought me, so I guess that's why." My leather bag that I'd shoved in-between my thigh and the edge of the seat crowds me. I wedge it out and drop it to the floor.

207

Her smile is genuine. "You might not have wanted to but I'm glad you're here. Jumping into the unknown is brave. What made you decide to come?"

I dig my palm into my knee to stop it from bobbing up and down. I don't want her thinking I'm crazy. "Something bad happened a few weeks ago and all of a sudden I couldn't breathe. I thought I was going to pass out but instead I just hyperventilated for a while and then I cried and it was over. My mom said it was a panic attack. She said maybe I have some things I should deal with."

Donna nods her head. "Was this the first time you experienced a panic attack?"

"I guess I get panic-y about stuff. But I'm not really sure what you mean by a panic attack. I thought that was just a word for like, *freaking out*."

Donna gives me another one of her soft smiles. She reaches for her notebook and paper, and says, "Tell me what happens when you're feeling anxious or nervous."

"Sure," I say. I take another couple sips of water and wish I'd brought a full bottle. Apparently counseling makes me thirsty. "I get little stomachaches when I'm worried about something. And my heart races. Like, a lot. My hands get sweaty and sometimes it feels like I won't be able to breathe. It can feel like something is clogging my throat and my lungs are having to do triple the work to, I don't know, keep me breathing. When I'm really anxious, it's like I'm seconds away from suffocating." My eyes tear up. "I guess I'm just kind of a freak about some things, you know."

She jots down a note or two, and then raises her head again. "What types of situations are you in when you get this anxiety?"

The view of the parking lot from the window up here is pretty clear and I wonder if anyone can see me. I slump farther in my seat. "All kinds of situations, I guess. Like going to parties or being at a party. Sometimes just walking into the cafeteria even when I know I already have friends to sit by. I feel like I'm overthinking every little thing, even when good things are happening. Sometimes it's little things but then sometimes it's not." I rub my finger against the ridges of the water bottle. "I don't know. This is kind of embarrassing."

She tilts her head. "What do you mean by embarrassing?"

"Telling you about how I overreact to things. Some of these things shouldn't bother me." I frown and give the water bottle one last sip of air. I shake the empty bottle and drop it into my bag.

"It sounds like you're an introvert and sometimes lots of people can be overwhelming. Why do you feel you shouldn't be bothered by these things?"

"It just doesn't feel normal. So many things stress me out. Usually it's the stuff I told you about, but today I woke up and wasn't even thinking about anything yet. My heart started beating really, really fast. It felt like I was having a heart attack or something. It was scary."

"How did you know you weren't?"

"It happened so fast that I didn't have much time to think. I just had time to tell myself to stop freaking out. Then, as my breath started coming back to me, I realized that the whole thing felt a lot like the other times. Except this time I wasn't even stressing about anything. No one was fighting, no one had just died, I just woke up." I sigh and make eye contact before staring back to the floor and the scuffs on my old red Converse. "What's wrong with me? Is this something crazy or do I have heart problems?"

"Well," Donna smiles. "I'm not one for the word *crazy*, but either way, no. You're having some physical reactions to your anxiety and you've probably experienced a panic attack or two. But it's nothing you can't handle."

I narrow my eyes with a slight smile. "Can you just prescribe me a pill so I can chill out? You know, a chill pill?"

She returns my smile. "You'd need a psychiatrist for that. But I can definitely work with you on some ways to deal with your anxiety. So far, you talked a bit about little things bothering you. But you did mention something about fighting and dying. Are those things you worry about?"

"Yeah," I say as the muscles in my back tighten. I hunch over, folding my arms tightly across my lap. "Those are a couple of the things I've been dealing with lately. My parents fought a lot. *A lot.* It was a lot of screaming and yelling. Then they divorced. And one of my classmates, someone I knew, died. I didn't help her and she died. It's like everything is broken and since I can't fix anything, so am I."

My breaths quicken and my knee bounces again as I wait for this lady to tell me how much of a mess I am.

Donna's eyes meet mine. She doesn't frown or look like she feels sorry for me. Her face is certain and sure. She nods. "This makes sense, Bree. You were alone in a house with two adults, fighting and yelling. But those were their problems. Let the adults be the adults. There was nothing you could do to stop it. And now you've lost someone? These are life-changing events. It sounds like you're holding on to a lot of guilt for choices you didn't make. All of these things would be stressful for anyone in your situation. It's not out of the ordinary to feel the way you've been feeling. Even without the 'big things' as you called them, anything and everything you're dealing with is real. You get worried about things, places, people. Other situations that are unknown to you, things you might not be able to control. Your mind gets put on 'alert' and your body responds to that as well. That is your reality. It's how you've dealt with things in order to survive. There's nothing wrong with you."

The second I realize she's telling me it's okay to feel the way I've been feeling, I lose it. My shoulders shake as a sob falls from my mouth. A huge, giant wave comes over me and a million sighs of relief pour down my face disguised as teardrops.

Donna steps over to me and for a second I'm worried she's going to hug me but she doesn't. She reaches for the tissues on the table next to me and sets the box in my palm. As she sits back down, I probably use a hundred tissues to blow my nose and wipe my face.

Once I finish crying, Donna leans back in her chair and asks, "Crying can be really cathartic. How does it feel to release those emotions?"

"It's a little awkward, I guess. Not in a bad way, but just because I'm surprised it was easy to talk to you." I sniff and wipe my nose again. "It feels like someone saw everything I'm dealing with and finally heard me. And you still said I'm okay."

Donna then talks a little about learning some coping skills to "add tools to my tool belt." It's hard not to actually imagine her wearing a bulky leather belt and passing me a hammer as she gives me tips on breathing. She says that trying to fight the anxiety by telling it to go away is usually going to make it worse. "Don't just tell yourself to calm down and breathe. Try not to put so much energy into pushing away the fears and anxieties. Acknowledge them and allow yourself a moment or however long you need with those feelings. Do your best to take longer, slower breaths. Keep breathing, and keep going."

I want to tell Donna everything about Maisey, and maybe even about Sean, but our time is up. When I told Mom I wanted to do this appointment today, I thought I'd just come in here and this lady would tell me what to do about feeling so mad at myself about Maisey. I thought she might tell me what to do about going to Prom without Sean, but I didn't even have time for that.

When Donna says she'd like to see me again next week, I say, "All right, sure." As if that was my plan all along.

Stepping out of her office, I feel lighter and at the same time, a little heavier. Maybe it's because I realize I have a lot more shit to deal with than I thought. Or maybe it's because this appointment helped and now dealing with things might be a little easier. It's as if now I'm wearing some armor and if things get bad, I won't always have to run away. I guess I'll find out.

****

After relaying some of my therapy session with Mom over brunch, the day feels like it should already be over. But it's not. It's still Prom Day. Too-much-crap-in-my-head-today day.

Once I'm finally back at home and kicking back in my bed, I set my alarm for one hour so I can take a nap.

First thought when I wake up is about Maisey. My heart twinges a little. Reaching into the drawer of my bedside table, I grab her letter. Sean's, which was on top of it, falls to the floor. I reread them both. I don't cry this time. For me or either of them. I have some ideas. Sure they probably won't have me coming out on top, but it's Prom night. There's only a week left of school. Not much left to lose. And face it, Jane was right, I'm alone.

Around five, I head over to Kallie's so we can do our hair and makeup together.

Kallie groans. "Are you sure you don't want to come to dinner with me and Todd? I don't think I can sit through a whole meal with him, alone."

I laugh. "You made that bed, you're gonna lie in it. By yourself. But make sure you order the most expensive meal."

"Of course. I'll probably order two. But what if we pick you up on the way to the dance? That way you can arrive with us?"

"Kal, really, I'm fine. I'm gonna go home, eat pizza with my mom, and go to the dance around eight. I'll see you there."

Kallie's mom and dad take a few pictures of us. Me smiling, still in jeans with my hair up and makeup done, and Kallie is even more stunning in her dress than she was yesterday.

"I can't believe it's finally here. The night we've been waiting forever for. Sucks that these guys had to mess everything up, right?" Kallie shakes her head.

"When it comes down to it, I'm not sure if it was the guys that messed everything up. I think we kind of led ourselves here, to this point."

"You might be onto something, Dr. Hughes, but no way am I admitting to it. Hells no. I'm blaming Todd all night long." She checks her phone for the time. "Speaking of snakes, he should be here any minute."

"That's my cue to leave. Tell your parents I'm taking a walk to the point before I head home." I hug her and head down the trail that Sean and I walked, holding hands, only weeks ago.

At the bottom of the hill, I sit facing the water, raking my hands across the sand. I watch the water moving beneath the setting sun and wonder if Sean is reading my letter. The letter I left at his door after standing there motionless for at least five minutes this afternoon.

When I finally forced my finger to push his doorbell, I slipped the letter in the door, and jumped back into my car. A little more cowardly than I'd planned but at least I'd gone through with it.

> *Hey Sean Mills*
> *I miss you.*
> *If you can spare it,*
> *please save the last dance for me.*
> *Love,*
> *Bree Hughes*

****

I drive to the school around 8:45, taking my time. I feel good. My mom hugged me before I left, and I'm pretty sure her eyes were proud this time instead of pitying. My Aunt Jen, pair of emergency silver heels in tow, told me I've never looked more beautiful. I check my sun visor mirror and believe her. Grinning, I pump Maroon 5's latest song the whole way to the dance, feeling like a rock star.

Pulling into the school parking lot, there are a few scattered cars and limos pulling up to the door. Apparently I'm not the only one fashionably late. Stepping out of my car, I reach into the backseat for the clutch purse Mom gave me. As I reach for it, something shines from the floor. My silver shoes. The ones I thought Jane stole. *Oops.*

I slam my door and head toward the main doors.

"Bree!"

Sitting on the hood of his dad's fancy red BMW convertible is Chip. He's smoking a cigarette and sharing a beer with my drop-dead pretty neighbor Langley Stone. Langley was last year's Prom Queen and is this year's head waitress at Crystal Wood Cabins, the restaurant slash souvenir shop known for their sexy-tacky bar-maid slash lumberjack uniforms.

"Hey Bree," Chip nods.

Instead of fighting heart palpitations and fear, this time I look him straight in the eye. "Hi Chip."

"Nice speech at the pep rally. You got my vote."

"Thanks," I say, fighting an impulse to roll my eyes. "Hey Langley. What're you up to?"

"Just hangin' with Chip. Guess I'm his date. Plus I gotta crown the new Queen, passing on my torch, ya know. Good luck." She smiles, flicking ash onto the gravel.

Making my way through the back parking lot, I tiptoe to keep my heels from sinking into the gravel. Once I hit pavement, I click short strides to the stairway leading to the double doors. I take one at a time instead of my usual two. I push a stray curl from my face and slide my hands over my dress, smoothing the silver shimmers hugging my body.

An army of sophomore girls and Judy, the school secretary, guard the door. All in red and black.

"Just one?" asks a sophomore girl looking over my shoulder.

"Absolutely one," I say. I tell her my name.

"I know who you are," she smiles. "Here you go." She hands me a slip of paper and says the ballot box is near the gymnasium doors. I scrunch the paper into my grandma's beaded clutch bag, unsure of whether I'll vote or not. The thump of bass leads me to the gym while the lyrics command me to "get on the floor."

The gym looks like any other Prom I've seen in the movies. Kids dancing, school faculty scattered around the edges. Punch and snack table, DJ at the front, giant speakers. And there's a shitload of streamers and balloons in red, black, and silver. A little morbid, but overall, it looks pretty sharp. A lot cooler than I'd expected. Good news is there aren't any werewolf or vampire cutouts in sight. I shrug and scan the crowd.

"Bree! Over here!" Sam and Kendall wave their hands from their Parties of One group by the DJ booth. I hang with them for a while and then Kallie finds me and drags me onto the dance floor. I stare over her shoulder at Sean, Todd, and Jane standing over some tables in a corner. Sean's eyes meet mine and I smile just as a hand grips my bicep.

"Do you guys know what happened to all of our cutouts?" Shandy yells in my ear.

"No," I yell, pulling my arm away. "Why?"

"Someone stole them. Our committee spent a lot of money on those, you know. *A lot.*"

"I have no idea. I'll let you know if I hear anything."

She stalks away, looking back twice to glare over her shoulder at us.

"Shit. She's onto us." Kallie laughs.

"Wait, do you know where they are?" I ask.

"No, but it's the thought that counts. Justin said he brought tacky underwear to tape on them but when he got here, they were already gone. Someone beat us to it. Still would've been funnier to see a vampire in valentine boxer briefs."

"Or a werewolf in a tight purple thong?" I laugh. "Shandy's pissed. I've never seen her this mad before."

"I know! It's awesome." Kallie spins me around and we dance until a slow song comes on.

Molly and Justin glide to the middle of the dance floor while Jane pulls Sean up from the table. He tugs his hand from hers but still follows her onto the floor. I hang with the Parties of One group, eating black cupcakes, trying to sip blood red punch without staining my teeth. I open my clutch to check my phone for imaginary missed calls and texts every five minutes while everyone goes all fashion police on everyone's formals.

Just when I think I can't stand faking it any longer, Shandy makes an announcement for Prom Court members to make their way to the stage. Sam and Kendall tell me "good luck" and push me out of their circle.

Principal Finley makes an introduction and thanks everyone as we file into position.

I tap Jane's shoulder. Leaning over, I whisper near her ear, "Hey, I'm sorry for giving you shit about my shoes yesterday, I found them in my car."

Jane twists a thin gold chain on her arm. "It's okay." She shakes her head. "No one ever believes me." Her mouth drops into a slight frown before she quirks her lips back into a smile. She drops into her seat and fans the ruffles of her dress out.

Shandy waves a red envelope as Langley makes her way to center stage gripping two glittery, shiny, golden crowns.

"Ahem." Shandy clears her throat loudly into the microphone. "Listen everyone. I'm asking you guys for some serious cooperation here. We're missing some major decorations for tonight. Please see me ASAP if you know anything about any life-size werewolf or vampire figures." Everyone laughs as soon as she says werewolves and vampires. I'm pretty sure they think she's joking.

My nerves kick in with the whole thing again about looking happy and gracious when I don't win. The only consolation I have is knowing that once this king and queen stuff is over, I'm marching over to the DJ booth, requesting a song, and giving a short dedication in honor of Maisey.

Even though Kallie's my best friend, my money's on Justin and Molly. Kallie's probably thinking the same thing. Her deep burgundy lips are frozen into the kind of smile you might have before throwing up. Laura takes extra interest in straightening her dress, Molly crosses and uncrosses her legs. I'm doing all of the above.

Jane sits tall, shoulders back; most likely holding her big white smile with the same Vaseline she'd applied to her gums at the pep rally yesterday. She looks so sure of herself that I almost feel bad.

"And for Prom King, Juuuuustin Conner." Justin hops off his chair and bows. Langley places the king's crown on his head and kisses him on the cheek. Everyone is yelling and cheering, "Speech, Speech."

Justin takes the mic from Shandy. "This means the world to me. The world. I've been dreaming about this day since I was a baby. Literally.

This one time, when I was a baby, in my crib, I had this dream. I was right here. Right now. Telling you about a dream I had. Seriously folks, thanks." Shandy yanks the microphone from Justin's hands. Then she grabs his shoulder to keep him next to her on stage.

"And now the masses have spoken. Belmont High's Senior Prom Queen is . . ." She looks back at us. "Breeeeee Hughes!"

Molly leans over Jane and pats my shoulder, smiling. Kallie jumps up and hugs me.

"We did it, girl!"

The roar of the audience clapping and Jane sucking her teeth sound like echoes. I'm not sure but I think they just called my name. Molly stands up, walks behind Jane, and pushes me up out of my seat.

"What?" I say to Kallie.

"Oh please, give us a break with the theatrics. You fucking won," Jane hisses in my ear.

My heart is a goddamned drum in my chest. "I know, I heard. So, um, okay." I squeeze Kallie's hand before stepping next to Justin, Langley, and Shandy. I am center stage.

"Welcome to the club," Langley says, placing the crown on my head.

"Congrats," says Shandy, handing me the mic. She whispers in my ear, "I voted for you."

"Thanks," I say into the mic, looking back at her. Beyond the edge of the stage, there are faces, smiling, cheering, and looking directly at me. My face warms up and my dress shimmers beneath the lights beaming onto the stage.

A group of kids in the back yell, "Boooooooo."

"Can't please everyone," I say, my face getting hotter. Then I picture Maisey. I think of how asking the DJ to let me do a personal song dedication is nothing compared to this platform. It's even better than I hoped.

I inhale, lock my knees, and a wave of composure comes over me. "This is weird. Senior Prom. Crazy, right? Thanks for your votes, really. I'm not going to pretend it doesn't feel good. Gosh, you probably think we're all jerks. Just like I thought of these guys last year. Or maybe you think some of us are better than you. Or you're jealous, like I've been. Maybe you think some of us have it all. But, you need to know that's not even close. No one up here is perfect. We're bitches, cheaters, bullies, backstabbers, and totally insecure. We have parents that don't give a shit or parents that care so much it suffocates us. Some of us might even have a parent with a criminal record." I look over my shoulder to the girls.

Molly and Laura beam. Kallie gives me a thumbs up. Jane's pageant smile and luminous eyes are washed over with something I'd call *poised panic*.

I turn back to the crowd. "Don't worry, I'm not going to shout anyone out. Let's just say that some of us try so hard pretending we're someone we're not, that we become evil bitches stepping over people struggling to get through the day. And *some* people end up dying feeling like they're less than human, because we didn't care. So don't think any one up here is better than you. We act like we've got our shit together, but we don't. We're faking it. Just like you guys. You're liars and losers like us.

"Most importantly, I think we're even bigger losers if we don't acknowledge who should really be up here wearing this crown."

I switch my focus to a line of black and silver balloons along the back wall. "Listen you guys, if things had gone according to plan, someone else would be up here right now." I picture Maisey hunched over, tears falling onto her good-bye letters. How tired she must've been, pissed off, resentful, and broken. How that walk out of the office to decline the Prom Queen nomination must've felt like one more giant kick in the face. "Yeah, I'm talking about Maisey Morgan. Most of us would be laughing right now. Or just watching from the sidelines, glad it wasn't us. I'd like to think that she wouldn't have gotten my vote. But that doesn't matter. I wouldn't have stood up for her. I didn't. Year after year and I never did. I wish I would have. I'm sure some of you do too. She was messed up. And *we* messed up."

Shandy reaches her hand out for the mic, but I walk to the other side of the stage and continue. "You know, I've been hanging out with these guys for the past couple months and it didn't take a genius to figure out that we're all fucked up in some way or another."

Sean meets my eyes with a small nod and a smile.

"School shouldn't make things worse" I say. "We're supposed to make things better for each other. High school is supposed to be like a getaway from everything else. Ask any 'grown-up.' It should be like a break from the real world—the one at home and the one we'll have to deal with next year. I'm not saying what happened to Maisey is because of us, but I'm not saying that it's not. What I'm saying is that it could've been pre-vented—here. Inside our school. Maybe we could've made a difference. I don't know. And I hate not knowing. Because it's too late. She's dead. I never stood up for her. I laughed. I made jokes. I was glad it wasn't me. And I was never *really* sorry until it was too late. I actually tried to apol-ogize to her once. You know what I did though? I made sure no one else was around. She didn't care. And I didn't care enough either.

"Anyway, Maisey wrote good-bye letters to her family and friends. I wasn't her friend, but I guess since I'm the only jerk who made a half-ass attempt to apologize, she figured I might be interested in knowing who she really was, and just maybe I'd pass along the message."

I pull the letter out of my bag. Shandy's wiping her nose with her wrist corsage. Everyone is silent, even Mr. Finley and the group of teach-ers along the wall. A male teacher nods and winks. I glance down at Maisey's letter, then back at the teacher. It's Mr. N. in a tux. I smile as one of the tears I'd been holding back falls. Right onto my paper, next to one of the splotches of faded ink from Maisey's tears.

I clear my throat, "I'm not going to tell you everything she said. But the people that hurt her the most, you know who you are. And you know why it hurt her so bad." I grip the letter and read: "You are all a bunch of bitches. Wherever I am right now, you can bet that I'm no longer worried about feeling like shit and going to school and feeling even shittier. I hope everyone has a great time at the Prom. It won't be at my expense. To any-one that has ever felt like a loser: sad, damaged, shitty, ugly, small, invisible or lonely, I'm sorry. It was really bad for me but just because I didn't fight anymore doesn't mean you shouldn't. I hope you dance tonight. Dance like no one is watching. I'm going to be okay now. I'm dancing too, and this time no one is laughing." I fold the paper back up and wipe my eyes.

Someone yells "Wooo-hooo!" and some people begin to clap. Shandy lets loose a high-pitched, horror movie scream.

Justin yells "Duck!"

I throw myself to the ground as my crown is knocked violently off my head, shattering into a thousand pieces. Everything happens in a matter of five seconds. I raise my head, expecting Maisey's ghost or pig's blood dripping onto the stage. Instead my attacker is a cardboard vampire cutout, now lying on the floor next to me, among the crown pieces. And what looks like a dozen more, swooping down like flying monkeys, on strings hung from the rafters.

We are being attacked by cardboard vampire and werewolf cutouts.

Jane is knocked out of her chair while everyone else jumps and dives, scattering onto the stage, sprawled out like dead bodies. Langley is rolling all over the stage, cry-laughing like a madwoman. The laughter and squeals of fear from the kids in the crowd are deafening. Sean army crawls toward me but is stopped, in the nose, by a low flying werewolf. Kallie's taken cover under Todd, and Laura's on the ground, sobbing into Chris's arms. He guards her while his whole body shakes with laughter. Brian lays flat, belly to the floor, with his hands covering his head. Jane lays next to him, the cage of her dress bent; pink satin ruffles and white tulle hiked up, exposing a matching pair of bloomers.

Molly screams, "There's blood, there's blood!"

"Chill out Molly, it's my nose," says Sean. "You okay, Bree?"

"Who did this? Who freaking did this?" Shandy screeches, clawing over the stage to us.

Todd lifts his head and laughs. "It sure as hell wasn't us. I don't think any of us are willing to lose an eye for a prank."

"Yeah, not even me," says Justin.

Shandy glares. "I knew it was you jerks." She slides to the end of the stage and climbs the stairs backward, as if they're a ladder.

"I'm fine. Are *you okay*?" I ask Sean. "It's a lot of blood."

He smiles and winces. "I've felt worse."

"Holy shit, dude." Justin yanks his tie from his neck and passes it to Sean.

Sean reaches into Justin's breast pocket, and pulls out a gold handkerchief. "I'll use this instead. Thanks, man."

"Shit, I was saving that."

"Now it'll have my blood stains on it. Makes for a better story." Sean wipes his nose and stands, pulling me up with his other hand. "Coast is clear guys, we can get up."

"Oh, snap. Look at all these." Justin props up a vampire and a werewolf. "It looks like there's one for each of us." He holds the werewolf next to him and smiles. JUSTIN CONNER: PROM IDIOT. He passes the vampire to Chris.

CHRIS MONROE: PROM JOCKSTRAP. We get up examining the others. I pick up the one that was lying next to me. The one that almost took my head off.

BREE HUGHES: PROM POSER.

Sean sees it and laughs. "Could be worse." He holds up a vampire. SEAN MILLS: PROM ONE-HIT LOSER.

Laura cries even harder when she sees hers. LAURA ROSE: WHO CARES?

"Oh really, you're going to cry? Look at mine," Kallie says holding hers up. KALLIE VATE: PROM STAR FUCKER.

Todd holds up his. "Pffft." TODD WHITE: PROM GONARHEA. "What the hell? Is that even spelled right?"

Brian says, "I found mine!" He lifts it like a trophy. BRIAN WANG: PROM QUEEN. "This is hilarious, I'm keeping it."

"Well, I guess I know what everyone thinks of me," says Molly. She holds up a sexy vampire cutout. MOLLY CHAPMAN: PROM FAKE FUCK.

"Oh don't forget this one. Here's yours, Jane," I say walking to the back of the stage, grabbing the werewolf that knocked her over. "Honestly though, I hope things get better for you." I drop the cutout onto her lap. JANE HULMES: PROM BITCH.

Principal Finley walks onto the stage looking over his shoulder and up to the rafters. Shandy follows. They stare up to the ceiling. Shandy pulls Finley over to a corner, her mouth moves a mile a minute as she points back and forth to us, the decorations, the cutouts, the stage, and back to us. Finley nods and marches over to us with Shandy, his eyes blazing, hers glaring.

"I don't see any more up there. I think it's over Mr. F," Justin says.

"You bet it is." Mr. Finley yanks Justin's arm and walks him over to a corner of the stage. Shandy tells the crowd to party on and that we're all safe and everything is under control. The DJ puts on "Dancing Queen." Fate. I'd almost say everything had gone better than I'd planned. Except for the flying cutouts and Sean's bloody nose.

And maybe if it wasn't for the look of death on Mr. Finley's face. "All of you. Right here. Right now," Mr. Finley says.

"Even me?" asks Brian.

"I said *all of you.*"

We drop the cutouts, half of them still attached by their strings to the rafters. Sean leads the way as we straighten our dresses and tuxedos and slink over to him and Justin.

"We had nothing to do with this, if that's what you're thinking," Laura says to Mr. Finley.

"Yeah," says Justin. "That was nuts."

"Well, I've been given many reasons to believe some or all of you were involved. Not to mention two anonymous tips. I hate to do this, but I hate even more for my faculty and students to have been disrespected the way we just were. It's deplorable. In lieu of any disciplinary action, contacting of your parents, suspension, marks on your school records or whatnot, I'd like you to voluntarily leave. If you have any questions or protests, we can discuss it *in my office*, with your counselor and parents on Monday morning."

"Are you serious?" Justin asks.

"Leaving Prom early is me cutting you a break. I'm as serious as a heart attack. Don't test me. Who's got another question or comment?"

None of us say a word. Molly and Laura are crying. Kallie and Jane are pissed. So are the guys. Even Brian. Shandy gives a sad smile to Mr. Finley, shaking her head at us, then waltzes off the stage.

"Ladies, you can make your way out the door and wait for your dates outside. Gentlemen, you can pick up and untie these monster pictures and follow me to the dumpster out back." Mr. Finley looks at me and Justin. "This should've been a magical night for you both. I hope it ended the way you had hoped."

I walk away, back to the spot where I'd fallen, kneel to the floor, and gather as many of my crown pieces as I can. I sweep them into my clutch bag. *Actually Finley, this night hasn't been all that bad. Maybe not exactly what I'd hoped for, but definitely magical.* I see Maisey's face again. This time she's the one laughing.

THIRTY-TWO

I dodge into the bathroom on my way out. I don't pee or check the mirror. I lean against the wall, the cold tiles against my bare shoulders. My heart's racing and my breath is heavy again. I run my fingers slowly across the beads on my purse, taking care to talk my breath into slowing down. *You did it. It was scary, but you said everything you wanted to say. It's over. Now, breathe. Slow and steady on the ins and outs.*

My phone buzzes. KALLIE VATE.

Hey PROM QUEEN, We're going to Chris's after-party! See you there! CONGRATS!!!! LOVE YOU! XOXO.

As I leave the bathroom, soft muffled laughs and fast footsteps echo behind me. I turn and tiptoe back toward the bathroom door. I push it open a sliver and see Maisey's friends, Tera and Anne. Tera's barefoot in a tuxedo suit as she zips Anne into a toile and floral mini dress. A shopping bag overstuffed with black clothes sits next to their feet.

I push the door open wider and they freeze. Anne's eyes get baseball size and Tera sucks in a deep breath.

"Holy shit. You scared me," says Tera, her voice shaking. She pushes the bag with her foot.

Anne steps in front of the bag. "So, congratulations on getting Prom Queen."

"I saw the bag. I know what you guys did."

224

Tera snatches the bag and shoves the black clothes farther down. "We didn't do any—"

"And I don't care," I say. "It was a good one. I think she would've laughed." Tera cracks a small smile.

"You're really not going to say anything?" Anne asks.

"No. It's the least I could do. I'm really sorry about her—for your loss. I . . ." Tears spring to my eyes again.

"Don't do that." Tera slides her feet into a pair of black and white wing-tipped dress shoes. "We said we were only going to laugh tonight. It was supposed to be just for her. It's what she . . ." Her gaze falls as she tugs the tail of her tuxedo jacket. "It's what she wanted."

"Yeah," whispers Anne. "Only dancing and laughing and no tears. Of course you did kind of mess that up because I got teary-eyed during your speech. But, I think Maisey would've been okay with that."

A teacher in a tacky orange formal walks in and waltzes up to a mirror to adjust her poufy updo. Anne turns into a scared rabbit statue again and Tera stares at the bag. I grab it and stuff it under my arm.

I whisper "No worries, I'll hold on to this and give it back to you guys on Monday." I smile. "Have fun, dance. You deserve it."

I walk out the school's doors the same way I'd come in. Just me. There's a figure waiting by my car. I squint under the bright lights of the parking lot. *Sean.* I squeeze the bag tighter under my arm, lift my dress slightly and pick up my pace. My clutch purse smacks my hip with each stride. And then I don't care anymore so I run. At least this time I'm not running away.

Sean's lips curve into a smile. "Hey, Prom Queen."

"Hey," I say trying to catch my breath.

"So, I know it's last minute and everything but I was hoping you'd have room in your car. Maybe I could get a ride?"

"Yeah, sure," I say. I try to hold back a grin as I click the doors unlocked.

Sean lifts the keys from my hand. "Can you wait a second?"

"Okay," I say as he leans into the driver's side and starts my car.

Armies of butterfly wings flutter in my chest as he turns the volume up on my radio. A song I've never heard hits the air and even though I don't know the words, they're beautiful, romantic, and absolutely perfect.

Sean grabs Anne and Tera's shopping bag and my purse, tosses them into the car and pulls me into his arms. "Got your note. I missed you too."

"I know," I whisper. "I'm sorry." I reach up and wipe a smudge of blood from his cheek.

"Me too." He looks me in the eyes and there's a silver blur of myself shimmering in his.

I feel myself drowning deeper into his eyes more than I ever have before. My chest swells with relief, and a million tiny shards of emotion I can't name. The fabric of his tux brushing against me and the smell of sandalwood from his collar raise the hairs on my arms. I shiver myself closer into his chest.

Sean's hand brushes over my hair and across my jawline, cupping my chin. His lips part. "I love you like crazy."

"I love you like crazy too." I push my lips onto his and I'm warm, enveloped in him, in us, and in the feeling that everything is right.

Our kiss deepens and lasts until his lips move from my mouth to my ear.

He whispers, "How about that last dance?"

EPILOGUE

With the early morning sun lighting my way, I step through a maze of tombstones and markers to find her gravesite. I kneel, laying my purse down and arranging the yellow roses above the inscription on the grave marker. My finger traces the grooves in the cement that spell out her name. May Louise Morgan. I close my eyes.

It's too late but now I know you—better than you did. Because you thought you couldn't make it. I say you could have. You would've made it. You made it through so much already. You were a survivor. You were surviving. That means something. You only had a couple months to get out of here. You could've moved far away. You would've gone to college or not gone, you could've done whatever you wanted to do, Maisey. Become some great teacher or writer or lawyer. Anything. Met someone who didn't know you from Belmont High, someone who'd never believe that once upon a high school, people used to treat you like shit. And maybe some day you would've told your story to girls like you, like Jane, and girls like me. And not everyone would've listened. But some would've. You would've made a difference.

I'm sorry.

My eyes open and tears fall onto her grave marker. I see her face again. This time her eyes don't look so empty. I open my purse and spill its contents onto the stone. I unfold her letter and place it next to the flowers. Chunks and specks of gold crown, broken red and purple gemstone glisten over the stone beneath my knees. I brush and wave my hand over the shimmery pieces, scattering them across her name. The sun's rays heat my scalp and shine off the crown pieces.

Maisey's not here to tell her story, but that's where I come in. I won't forget her. I have to remember her story. So maybe someday it will reach someone. And it will be enough.

Maisey's Letter to Bree

Bree Hughes,

You're probably wondering what I'm doing writing you this letter. You're reading this because I'm gone. No longer here. Passed Away. Offed. Dead. Suicided.

Before I decided to do this, I wondered what everyone would think. I ran through everyone. People that cared, or tried to care about me, and people that cared about making me feel like a piece of shit every day I went to school. None of you know me. At all. You only know what I am on the outside. Too quiet, too skinny, too clumsy. Too ugly. A loser. I thought about all the people who never let me forget any of those things. What will they do now? Then, because of what happened last week in the bathroom and the library, I thought about you, where you fit into that. I don't owe you an apology, but I think it's only fair to give you an explanation. Two reasons. One is that I'm not a total bitch. I'm not trying to leave certain people thinking it was all their fault. The other reason is pride. School has been hard for me and everyone sucks. But still, I'd hate for people to think that they were the number one reason for me ditching life. Here's the deal: I'm sorry if I didn't accept your apology but at that point, my decision had already been made. I didn't want anyone or anything messing with my head.

There's one person at school who knows how shitty things are and never once tried to make it better. She went out of her way to make sure I'd never forget what a loser I am for ruining her fake perfect life. I'm sure you don't know this, but Jane is my cousin. We were best friends until we were six. That's when everything went to shit. Her dad is a monster and I can only imagine how different my life would've been without him ruining me,

228

erasing me with his hands, and asking me to keep his secrets. After a while I did tell someone. I told Jane but she said we couldn't tell anyone or we'd all be in trouble. She told me to wait and we'd run away. But after another year of just plans, I couldn't wait anymore, I told my parents that he'd been sexually abusing me and he got locked up. I never saw Jane again except in school. She made it clear where she stood. She blamed and hated me. She didn't even need to threaten me not to tell anyone else about what her dad did. I haven't said a word about it since the day I told my parents and an officer at the police station. But last month, her dad got out of prison. I can barely breathe knowing he's not locked away anymore. I'm tired of feeling cold, and damaged, and invisible. It's not going away and knowing that he gets to walk free and start a new life has chipped away at whatever was left of me. He gets to walk around living his life like he didn't ruin mine. He's trying to apologize to me and my family and we don't want anything to do with him. I can't talk to anyone about this. I don't talk to my parents. My friends don't even know yet. When you saw me and Jane at the library, she had asked if I was going to be okay. Bullshit. I told her to tell her dad to leave my family alone. It's too late to apologize. She doesn't care about me, she only cares about people finding out. I hate our school and I hate all the people in it. I don't know if Jane or anyone will feel bad once I'm gone, but they won't have me to bully anymore.

You're the only one in our class who ever apologized. I was really mad at the time, but I'm glad you said something. I wish you would've a long time ago. The day you apologized I wished I could be like you, because you're different and people still care about you. I was nominated as a joke. As much as I wanted to daydream about Prom being this big deal and me being able to feel special, it's impossible. Because of everything. How they think of me, and how I feel about myself. As long as I'm here, no one's going to change their mind about me. No way. And I can't either. Please don't forget about me on Prom Night. Prom Queen stuff is kind of a joke, but if it means anything, I hope you win. If it has to be someone, I hope it's you. They're all bitches. If you get the chance, please make sure you tell them. You owe me that much.

Tell them I said this: they're all a bunch of assholes. Wherever I am right now, you can bet that I am no longer worried about feeling like shit and going to school and feeling even shittier. I hope everyone has a great time at the Prom but it won't be at my expense. To anyone that has ever felt like a loser: sad, damaged, shitty, ugly, small, invisible, or lonely, I'm sorry. It was really bad for me but just because I didn't fight anymore doesn't mean you shouldn't. I hope you dance tonight. Dance like no one is watching. I'm going to be okay now. I'm dancing too, and this time no one is laughing.

Forever,
Maisey

THE END

AUTHOR'S NOTE

I am a survivor of childhood sexual abuse. The scars left behind do not define me. If you've been a victim of sexual abuse, sexual assault, rape, or any type of sexual trauma, tell someone. It is never too late. Telling someone was the most freeing thing I've done in my life. The next most important step is reaching out or accepting help in order to heal and manage the feelings that abuse leaves behind. You are not damaged. The abuse does not define you. You are worth so much more than the pain you've endured.

Depression and thoughts of self-harm are serious. The best thing to do when you feel like there's no way out, is to reach out. Asking for help doesn't make you weak or a burden, it makes you stronger because there is strength in numbers.

To get help for you or someone you care about, here are some wonderful resources:

1-800-273-TALK (8255) OR
1-800-SUICIDE (1800-784-2433)

National Alliance on Mental Illness (NAMI)
www.NAMI.org
800-950-NAMI

RAINN (Rape, Abuse & Incest National Network)
www.RAINN.org
National Sexual Assault Hotline 800-656-HOPE (4673)

A life of happiness and light is possible. You are worth it. You've got this.

—Ami Allen-Vath

ACKNOWLEDGMENTS

This book, this dream, has made it through with the support of my husband. Justin, you're an anchor, and I'm grateful to have you in my life and as my partner. Many more books shall be written on our anniversary vacations. Hello, I love you! Thank you!

Victoria Lowes, my agent and friend. Your encouragement and hard work fills me with more gratitude than I can express. Thanks for believing in me and in my books.

Kristin Kulsavage. Your support for my book and the trust you've shown in me as a writer means so much. And it really does take a village to get a book out into the wild, so kudos to Team Sky Pony, especially Julie Matysik, Kylie Brien, Joshua Barnaby, and Cheryl Lew. Another huge thanks to Sarah Brody for the awesome cover. Thank you all so much.

Laura Stearns and Jen Young who've been there since page one for the book formerly known as *Prom Bitch*. You two read and waited for more chapters and expressed your support from first draft to agent to book deal and every single "cool fun thing" along the way. LoLo, you've been there from my YA years to my YA writing years. Infinite gratitude for all the back and forth poem sharing, sleepovers, and phone calls back when we used real phones. CCMCBF. Jen, oh jeeeez. Your leveled-up best-friendship is so special to me. Thanks for reading my words and sharing yours. Also, a final thanks for not letting me write the "Bree sleeping with the guitar scene." I heart you, TLP.

Much gratitude and glittery crowns to these kings and queens: Jadzia Brandli, the first person to read and CP who wasn't already my friend. Brent Taylor, for your critique, help, and being right about this baby book growing up and making it to shelves. Sarah Glenn Marsh. Your friendship, writerly support, and CPing is a life vest. Where would I be without your red pen and all our commiserating? Glenn, the guitarist from Mr. Flood's Party, thanks for the music 411. Teresa Yea, you freaking rule. You're a CP rock star and extra special thanks for zipping through this book with notes of wisdom and greatly appreciated inappropriateness. Christina June, thanks so much for the sensitive and professional eye. And Tera Waalen Gilmore, my "cool" friend since eighth grade, thanks for your magic—wink, wink.

If I formed a band, I'd call it Super Fem-tastic and insist the following ladies join: Natalie Blitt, Natasha Sinel, Rachel Simon, Christa Desir, Marci Lyn Curtis, and Dahlia Adler. Thanks for the reads, insightful notes, emails, and/or general coming through in times of "OHMYGOD-WHATAMIDOING?!" CAN YOU READ THIS?" and/or "HELP!" XOXO

To Seth Marquette and Melissa Bechthold. Aw, man. You guys listened to my angsting and read my query when we barely knew what the hell I was doing! *cranks up *Golden Girls* theme song and forces you into awkward group hug*

And for the love of Adam Levine, how the hell would I've made it without the writing community? To my writer friends, bloggers, and readers who've been on this journey with me. Your kindness humbles me and has been that extra ray of sunshine on bright and rainy days. #LOVEandTHANKS

Last, but never least, an ocean of thank-yous to my family. To my children, my sun and star, M&M. Thanks for sharing me. I love you both the most. The Roths, Jaakolas, and Vaths. Your support and cheering has been wonderful and I'm lucky to have you on my side. For my mom and dad: your support in me pursuing my dreams has never faltered. I'm so grateful. To my sisters, Holly, Crystal, and yes, you too, Sierra. Thanks for the unconditional love for me and a book you haven't read. Roth sisters forever.